The Escape Artist

friendships while nursing a problematic relationship with the idea of 'home'.

In a deeper sense, this novel kicks off a project which Sanchez has refined in his later work: the fleshing out of a necessarily critical glance at Gibraltar, its society and its governing mores; all those hidden assumptions that provide the background to life on the Rock. The main achievement of Sanchez's oeuvre, to me, is this making explicit of a host of truths that we've all tacitly believed, or sensed with increasing discomfort, for a generation.

In this vein, *The Fetishist's* (2021) exposure of the risible but profound extent of military fandom and *Marlboro Man's* (2022) brave analysis of machismo find their seeds in this novel's unflinching look at local bourgeois values.

Although all the ingredients of the campus novel are also here – the homesickness, the pints, the terror of exams, the romantic encounters and the whole catalogue of eccentric and sexually alluring students – the novel's real interest lies in how Sanchez paints the predicament of the thinking Llanito abroad, a 'thinking Llanito' standing for a new generation of university-educated, articulate and self-aware men and women who are overturning lazy assumptions (both domestic and international in origin) about the validity and sophistication of local culture.

For example, the main character, Brian Manrique, a student at Cambridge, holds an ambivalent attitude towards the Rock – a keenly felt nostalgia complicated and tempered by critical distance.

At one point he says: “Strange that, wouldn’t you agree? That you can miss a place without missing anyone in it? But it does happen.”

Where Manrique is reflective and shy, the most potent impression by way of contrast is left by the character of Henry Portas – the intellectually confident seducer from a monied and well-connected family. He’s the first in a line of beguiling Sanchez alter egos who stalk the pages of his later novels and he emerges as a bewitching, sinister presence even when he enacts his own ‘escape’ in a novel that probes the many senses in which the human condition can be regarded as one of permanent escape: escape from obligation, from home (whatever that means) and from oneself.

The novel is also particularly valuable as an interrogation of Gibraltarian identity. In particular, the work lays bare Manrique’s Britishness and how this is perceived, misunderstood and mocked by our purported compatriots in the UK, a concern which receives a more extended treatment in *Gooseman* (2020).

In its non-university sections, *The Escape Artist* also serves as a portrait of the closed border years and the claustrophobia of a city whose links with the outside world were suddenly severed. Manrique’s humdrum work and amorous exploits in a closed frontier Gibraltar emerge as a stale account of a life lived in the doldrums.

Political and historical accounts of this period have inevitably missed out on the precise lived and felt aspects of these years. A read of these pages will convince you that to discount fiction of this kind – local, visceral, unafraid of the ugly and the mundane – is to cling to an impoverished view of the world.

That Sanchez returns to the same themes, in book after book, is not a limitation. Writers are obsessive creatures who often become fixated on a restricted number of interests and locations. If Sanchez's characters enact long, flâneur-like walks through familiar streets day after day, it is both to forget their troubles and to let every fine detail of drain cover, lamp post and smell to permeate their being. Their walks are like the activity of their creator who finds himself returning to the same crucial matters, unable to shake off their intoxicating allure.

Gibraltar, 22-7-2023

The Escape Artist

1.

The first time I saw Henry Portas I was walking along the South Gallery in Cambridge University Library. My books were back in the main reading room and I was out on one of my *escapatorias*, short strolls that I did every few hours within the building to stretch my legs and clear my head. It was the twenty-third of October 1971 and I was feeling low and demoralised. I had been in Cambridge for five weeks now and was still very homesick, constantly thinking about Gibraltar and the life I had left behind on the Rock. As I passed by one of the South Gallery's arched windows, I saw a tall and athletic guy crossing the square in front of the library. Something about him seemed familiar to me, recognisable. I watched him for a moment, trying to place where I had seen that tousled mop of blond hair before, then it hit me that I was looking at a fellow Gibraltarian. This is what happens when you come from a micro-territory like Gibraltar. Once you see a face a few times in the street, it strikes roots in your head; it becomes a part of your mental architecture. We Gibraltarians even have an expression for it: *'nos conocemos todos de vista'* (we know each other 'by sight'). That is why, when I saw that kid striding out of the library that day, I didn't have the slightest doubt: he had to be Gibraltarian. 'And if he is a *llanito*,' I thought, filled with excitement, 'well, that makes two of us in Cambridge! Better go and catch him before he disappears from sight!'

I left the window and jogged down the stairs into the foyer. By the time I went through the main doors, however, Portas was on the other side of the

A-levels were actually difficult exams to pass instead of the meaningless travesty they have become nowadays, ensured that only three or four students from Gibraltar Grammar School and Loreto High School (the local girls' school) made the grade each year. It also meant that those who won the scholarships were feted and granted all kinds of accolades — like having their picture appear in the centre pages of the *Gibraltar Chronicle*.

'I'm a little confused,' I said, slightly irritated by Portas's continuing smile. 'You're obviously studying here at Cambridge. And you speak Spanish with a Gibraltarian accent. Yet you don't sound Gibraltarian when you speak in English and I know for a fact you weren't on the list of government scholarship holders either this year or during the last couple of years. Are you Gibraltarian, or aren't you?'

'I *am* Gibraltarian,' he said in a tone which made it clear he was no longer kidding. 'This ridiculously posh accent is what happens when your snobby bastard parents insist on sending you away to prep and public school in the UK.' He extended a hand towards me. 'The name's Portas. Henry Portas.'

'Portas?' I asked, shaking his hand. 'As in Portas and Sons, Gibraltar's largest tobacco and spirits importer?'

'Yes, that's us,' he said, looking a shade embarrassed. 'Dutifully supplying Gibraltar's alcohol and tobacco needs for the last six generations. What's your name?'

'Brian. Brian Manrique.'

'You're not related to Adolfo Manrique, the owner of Manny's Electrical Services, by any chance, are you?'

'No, I'm afraid not.'

'Anyway, that doesn't matter.... What are you studying, Brian?'

I told him I had just started a Modern Languages degree at Fitzroy College. He replied that he was a fresher too — only he was studying Law at Trinity, the hardest of all the Cambridge colleges to get into. Impressed, I asked him what A-level grades he had got to be admitted to such a hallowed establishment.

'Two Cs and a B,' he said in the same tone he had used when letting me know about his family business.

'You got accepted into Trinity with two Cs and a B?'

'My family have been studying at Trinity for nearly one hundred years. I suppose you could say we have strong connections with the place.'

Our conversation began to flag after this revelation. For the next few minutes we talked a little about Gibraltar — about its beaches and the things one can do there during the summer — but our dialogue now was unnatural and strained and consisted largely of me asking him different questions and Portas supplying increasingly curt replies until he announced that he had to go, saying that it was nice to have met me and that he hoped to chat with me some other time. As we shook hands, I couldn't help feeling that I had messed things up by asking him about his A-level grades. That had been insensitive on my part, hadn't it? Trust me to bugger things up like this, I thought. I spend over a month wishing I'd come across another Gibraltarian here in Cambridge and then, when I finally meet one, I go and offend him in all of five minutes!

'Well, Henry,' I said, clumsily retracting my hand, 'thanks for talking to me. I really enjoyed it and it's nice to know there's at least one other *llanito* in town. Hope I see you again.'

I turned around and scurried away in the direction of the library. I was a bit annoyed that I had sounded so soppy (especially when it was obvious that Portas just wanted to get rid of me!), but I rapidly got over it. 'So what if this Portas guy thinks I'm a dweeb?' I thought, clenching my fists in my pockets. 'It's not as if we have a lot in common, is it? More chance of me liking this awful English weather than of us becoming friends.' At that moment, however, I suddenly heard Henry's voice behind me:

'Hey, Brian. Wait a minute!'

'Yes?' I replied.

'I was just thinking. I'm organising a party at my place this Friday. Do you want to come?'

'Sure, why not?'

'It starts at nine o'clock. I'm expecting quite a few people, so it's going to be a real cracker. The thing is, I don't actually live in Trinity. I live in Trumpington, which is kind of like a *villagey* suburb of the city. My family pulled a few strings to allow me to live outside the college and in a house of my own. It's way too big for a single bloke like me — but, as always, I had no say in the matter. You can catch the number 93, 97 or 101 bus from Queen's Road and you'll be there in fifteen minutes.'

'Don't worry. I'll walk there. I know where Trumpington is.'

'You've been to Trumpington before?' he asked.

'Yes,' I replied, already feeling less self-conscious. 'I like to go for long walks when I don't have much to do, and I've already walked through Trumpington a few times. It's about two and a half miles south-east from here, I believe.'

'I suppose it is…. Anyway, my address is 10 Acacia Lane. When you enter Trumpington, you will see a pub called the Tally Ho. Acacia Lane is the third street after it on your left. Here,' he said, reaching into his coat pocket and bringing out a small business card, 'I'll give you one of these in case you forget my address. Come any time between nine and ten. I'll be expecting you.'

2.

Let's get this straight before I continue: I have never liked big parties. I always get irritated by the lights and the music. I also become incredibly awkward in front of people I don't know. Why, then, did I tell Portas that I'd attend his party? Mainly it was because I felt guilty for having offended him by asking about his A-level grades, but I also didn't want him to assume that I was just a lonely homesick geek who never did anything interesting. Anyway, I wasn't planning on going. I had decided that much even before I got back to the library. In all likelihood the party would be full of toffs like him, all of them brandishing their expensive Rolexes and listening to bossa nova records and talking about girls and cars and rugby and getting drunk with their mates and other stuff like that. I tobacco-like smell lingered in the air. Cannabis, I assumed. Clutching the bottle of Black Tower to my chest, I made my way through the throng, anxiously looking for a corkscrew. I hoped that someone would come over and talk to me, but so far everybody was keeping their distance. After a while I spotted a corkscrew lying on a windowsill next to a line of empty beer cans and a packet of Rizla rolling papers. I picked it up, opened the bottle and took a couple of swigs. I then plunged back into the crowd and tried to chat to people. One or two students did exchange pleasantries with me, but they couldn't have been terribly impressed with my conversational skills — seeing that they kept excusing themselves and leaving. This inability of mine to sustain a conversation depressed me, made me turn more and more to my bottle of Liebfraumilch. Soon I had finished the entire bottle and moved on to a bowl of rum punch lying unattended in a corner. For someone who until that same evening had barely touched alcohol, this wasn't a good idea. Actually, it was *an utterly, utterly idiotic idea.* While I was slowly decimating my powers of reasoning in this way, this dude popped up beside me. Little Asian guy. Wire-framed spectacles. Type 3 on the Hamilton-Norwood scale. I knew a bit about this kid: his name was Rajit and his room was on the far side of the corridor, about ten doors away from mine. He was from Luton and I think he was studying Astrophysics. He was always on his own and he seemed like a quiet and reasonably pleasant chap. Under normal circumstances we might have hit it off and perhaps become friends. But unfortunately we got off to the worst possible start:

'Ah, so you're the Spanish guy studying Modern Languages, aren't you?'

I know that Rajit was only trying to be friendly, but I was always going to take offence at his words. In the last seven days, after all, this sort of thing had been constantly happening to me. The moment I mentioned I came from Gibraltar, folk would assume that I was as Spanish as paella or flamenco dancing. Every time it happened, I'd bristle up and try to set the record straight. Overcoming my natural shyness, I'd start telling these people everything that separates us on the Rock from our Spanish neighbours: that our schooling is conducted in English; that in the street we speak *llanito*, a kind of 'Spanglish' that both Spaniards and Englishmen find almost impossible to understand; that many Gibraltarian families have lived under British rule since the days of the Peninsular War; that we love Cornish pasties and Yorkshire pudding, as well as *jamón ibérico* and *gambas al pil pil;* that we support English football teams like Arsenal or Liverpool in addition to Spanish teams like Barcelona or Real Madrid. I'd even tell them about our incredibly hybrid ancestral origins. 'Look at me,' I'd say, nodding animatedly, 'my surname is Manrique, which of course is Spanish. But my mother's maiden name is Smith, which is as English as fish and chips, and, if you go back even further to my two grandmothers, you will find that their maiden names were Farrugia and Baglietto. Maltese and Genoese names, respectively. And don't think I'm atypical in this way either. Most Gibraltarians have similarly mixed bloodlines. This is because most of us are the sons of immigrants who came to Gibraltar from other parts of the

Mediterranean from the mid-1750s onwards. In fact, in the nineteenth century everybody used to call us "mongrels" because we were neither Spanish nor British, but a strange composite of the two with a bit of Genoese, Maltese, Irish, Portuguese and Jewish thrown into the melting pot as well.'

However, *all that* was when I was sober. At present I was drunk and struggling to stand up straight. I also despised myself for my poor social skills. My natural reaction, therefore, was to blurt out the crassest, most insulting words I could think of:

'No, I'm not Spanish. I'm from Gibraltar, mate. A British dependent territory attached to the end of the Iberian Peninsula. You must be the Paki from the other side of the corridor, right?'

I know that I was out of order and that I should have never said that horribly degrading word. But I couldn't help myself: I was sick and tired of having my Gibraltarian status undermined and I was also annoyed that nobody appeared interested in talking to me. Rajit's response, meanwhile, was to turn around and walk away. He looked hurt and fed-up, his balding crown reflecting some of the tealights and candles scattered along the room's perimeter. I stared at him with a mixture of pity and devious relish, already wondering if I had gone too far, then returned to the punch bowl and helped myself to more of the beverage. One glass, two glasses, three glasses, four glasses. Before long, I was totally hammered and spouting the most cringeworthy rubbish (mainly about how loyal Gibraltarians are to the UK, and how we all love the Queen, the Union Jack and the Royal Family). It didn't matter that nobody was listening to me and that people were starting to avoid me; I was too smashed to notice *any of that.* Midway through my drunken monologue, Angelle Price came into the room. Shoving bodies aside, I stumbled towards her and told her that I loved her and longed to kiss her. 'Just go to your room and sleep it off, Brian,' she said, masking her unease with a smile. 'You'll feel a lot better in the morning if you go now, trust me.' Drunk as I was, though, I wasn't going to take no for an answer. So I persisted with the sweet talk. Tried to explain to her how much I loved and adored her. This excruciating to-ing and fro-ing continued for a few minutes until a rugby-playing brute called 'Bazza' Stannard stepped in between us and, without warning, without even bothering to explain to me that I was acting like a drunken fool, socked me in the jaw and sent me sprawling arse-first to the floor. Dizziness. Confusion. A strong urge to vomit. A constellation of squiggly floaters dancing in front of my eyes. As I lay slumped on the carpet, I reached for my mouth and felt a sticky wetness. I then looked up and saw that Angelle and Stannard were arguing — the Welshwoman saying that the square-jawed brute should have never hit such a harmless little patsy, and the brute responding that the dirty greaseball had had it coming. *Oh God, oh God, oh God,* was all I could think, lying on the floor and suddenly feeling remarkably sober. *What have I done?*

3.

The Stannard knockdown turned me into an even greater recluse. Whereas before I had acted more or less like any other shy foreign student, now I began to predictability, the fact that, at any given point in time, regardless of where I was or what I was doing, I knew what to expect from those around me. That is what Gibraltar is like. Everything's safe. Everything's familiar. Everything's categorised and compartmentalised. Even the layout of the town contributes in some ways to this feeling of security and dependability. You have two and a half square miles. And maybe a hundred or two hundred streets. Apart from one or two of the more remote Upper Town ramps, you walk through most of these streets on a daily basis. You walk through them *again and again,* absorbing every last detail, internalising the urban landscape. Without being aware of it, for instance, you know that the first lamp post outside the Trafalgar Cemetery gates buzzes slightly differently from the other lamp posts nearby. That the crack on the second flagstone on your right as you come out of the Catholic cathedral looks remarkably similar to the Christian 'Chi Rho' sign. That halfway up Hospital Steps there is a two- or three-yard stretch of wall which, for God knows what reason, *always* smells of dog's urine. These details cannot be summoned up at will. They are not like telephone numbers, say, or anniversary dates — things you can retrieve at any given moment with the help of memory. But they are embedded in your subconscious nonetheless. Growing up in a small, hemmed-in territory like Gibraltar does that kind of thing to you: you develop a hyperaesthetic awareness of your surroundings, you become almost umbilically linked to everything around you — the sights, the sounds, the smells, the quality of the light, the various cloud formations, the different blues of the sea. Ultimately, that's why so many of us struggle when we engage with the big bad world out there, why nearly every expatriate Gibraltarian returns to the Rock sooner or later. Where else, after all, could you live surrounded by your family and friends? *En qué otro sitio se vive tan bien?*

4.

By the time I met Henry Portas outside the library, I had been walking around Cambridge for over a month. Much had changed in this period. From the centre of town I had gradually taken my walks out into the Cambridge suburbs. Some — like Trumpington and Grantchester — were wonderful places that lived up to the hedged and thatched stereotype of English village life drummed into me during my colonial upbringing. But others — like Teversham and Romsey — were real enclaves of deprivation and the sorts of areas where it was best not to let anyone know you were a student (and a foreign one to boot)! One thing that remained fairly constant, though, was the staring that greeted me wherever I went. In the posh neighbourhoods, the perpetrators tended to be middle-aged ladies in cardigans or Barbour-jacketed older men with something of a military air about them. Suave middle-class types. They'd be buffing their cars or mowing their lawns or maybe walking back from the shops with the *Sunday Times* and a pint of milk. It never took long — just a second, perhaps half a second. But in that compressed period of time you sensed they were analysing you, scrutinising you, trying to fathom out the dark-skinned, badly dressed interloper who had materialised before them….

In the rougher areas things were somewhat different. You didn't get stared at as much, but when you did it was full-on glaring, with none of that namby-pamby dissimulation practised by the genteel classes. You'd be about to climb the steps of a pedestrian overpass, and — bang! — there they'd be in front of you: a gang of feral kids staring at you straight in the eye. Or else you'd be strolling past a pub with an outside terrace and all the regulars' heads would turn towards you, eyes oozing hostility. Once, as I was climbing the red-brick footbridge linking Newmarket Road to Coldham Common, I was confronted by two youths with a huge bullmastiff. They had been hiding in a recessed niche within one of the bridge abutments and abruptly jumped out as I went past their secret lair. Sixteen or seventeen years old. Spittle-moistened lips, ruffled hair, close-set eyes. They asked me where I came from and if I knew that I had ventured into Ghetto Boys' territory. I replied that I had no idea that this was Ghetto Boys' territory and that I was only making my way to the city centre. I then swallowed hard and tightened my stomach muscles, convinced that I was about to be clobbered to an insentient heap. But to my surprise the youths didn't hit me. Instead they moved aside, let me go through and, once I was about fifteen yards further up the bridge, shouted 'Fuck off and never come back round here again, if you know what's good for you, you shitty little foreign fuck!'

Another thing that I discovered during those four or five weeks was the dubious pleasure of walking through Cambridge at night. Although the city centre was packed every day with shoppers and tourists, after five o'clock the place became practically deserted, with alleyways like Trinity Lane or All Saint's Passage acquiring a Jack-the-Ripperesque quality in the evening gloom. Sometimes you felt as if you'd accidentally wandered into the set of a Hammer horror movie — what with the wispy bands of fog, the lamp posts that hardly gave off light and the echo of footsteps bouncing off medieval stone. Now and again, too, you'd come across angry drunks or quarrelling couples, most of whom wasted no time in letting you know what they thought about you being there. *'Ere, what you looking at? Go fook off before I fookin' lamp you one, you fookin' ugly turd!* Episodes like these always frightened me and made my heart pound like a drum. Nevertheless, my melancholy was so strong and so all-consuming that, as soon as I had left my antagonists behind, I'd quickly forget about their drunken threats and once again concentrate on my own unhappy predicament as a Gibraltarian far from home.

There is one last thing I should mention about those long and lonely walks through the city of Cambridge. It has nothing to do with the surrounding landscape or the people I encountered during my journeys, but all to do with a change in my own perception. I will try to keep it brief. In the days before I came to the UK, I, like most Gibraltarians my age, had always taken it for granted that I was a *British Gibraltarian*. This idea had been driven into us at school, branded on our hearts. We Gibraltarians were as British as Big Ben or Earl Grey Tea, as Marmite or Mary Poppins. If any outsiders questioned the legitimacy of this belief, we'd point them in the direction of our 1967 referendum (in which 12,138

5.

This, then, was the situation when I met Henry Portas outside Cambridge University Library. I was still unhappy and unsettled, unable to concentrate on anything other than my own problems. As if that wasn't enough, I felt really confused about my British Gibraltarian identity and intensely suspicious of humanity in general. Moreover, this discontent was reflected in my essay and project work grades, which were among the worst of my supervision group. With all this going on, the last thing I wanted was to attend the party of some toffee-nosed kid who claimed to be Gibraltarian but had probably never spent longer than the odd summer holiday on the Rock. But then something happened that made me change my mind about Henry Portas and his do. Returning to my block one evening after a walk that had taken me out as far as Great Shelford, I saw a handwritten sign sellotaped to our common room door. The sign, which was covered in star-shaped silver stickers and written in an intentionally childlike hand, invited everyone in D block to attend Angelle's twentieth birthday party that Friday in our communal lounge. As soon as I saw its message, my heart sank. Angelle Price, having a party this very Friday? How crap was that! First, the party was being held on a Friday night, which meant that the revellers would stay up until three or four in the morning (and, what was even worse, that I couldn't just go out for a long walk to avoid the event). Second, no less importantly, it was Angelle's party, which ensured that I'd not only have to stay grounded in my room all night; I'd have to stew in my juices knowing that the odious Stannard and others would be sniffing around her skirts. In the light of all this, Portas's party — also taking place that Friday — no longer appeared such an unattractive proposition. Indeed, the more I thought about it, the more it seemed to provide me with an escape route. Sure, I'd have to walk all the way back from Trumpington at three or four in the morning and, yes, there was no guarantee that Portas's friends weren't just as bad as 'Bazza' Stannard and his cronies. On the other hand, I was used to walking at night and, even if things came to the worst and I once more made a drunken fool of myself, I'd be doing so in the company of complete strangers whom I'd never have to engage with again. So the matter was settled: I'd go to Portas's party, after all.

6.

I arrived at 10 Acacia Lane in Trumpington at nine-thirty that Friday evening. For once I had taken a bus to reach a destination in Cambridge, having figured that it wouldn't be a good idea to turn up at a party stinking of sweat and car fumes. Portas's house was an enormous four- or five-bedroom semi-detached property separated from the road by a large enclosed garden and a twenty- or thirty-yard drive. It was just like the other houses on his street, only slightly bigger and slightly grander. From the cacophony of music and voices coming from the inside, it was clear that the party was already in full swing. Timidly, I knocked on the door and took a step back. When thirty or forty seconds had gone by without anybody appearing to greet me, I reached out and opened the door myself. Right away a blast of Thin Lizzy or Led Zeppelin hit me in the face. Vibrating wooden floorboards.

Darkness laced with flashing lights. The same pungent, herbal smell that had been in the air the night 'Bazza' Stannard attacked me. However, none of that bothered me or concerned me. What *did* concern me was that there were ten or twelve students, both girls and boys, sitting on the floor on each side of the entrance corridor, merrily chatting away with their legs extended before them. Muttering my apologies, I threaded my way past this lattice of legs and turned left into the living room. Here I got an even bigger shock. Although the room was almost the size of a five-a-side football pitch, it was *entirely packed* with revellers. They were spread out across the room in clusters of seven or eight. Each of the clusters, moreover, seemed to have a 'character' of its own: for example, one was composed of serious-looking young men engaged in a fiery academic debate, another by nine or ten girls dancing with their hands above their heads, another by a group of men and women sharing a joke. I stood for a few minutes on the periphery of the room, trying to spot Portas among the different cliques. I then moved near the circle of debating guys and, somewhat to my disappointment, realised that they were talking about tomorrow's football fixtures — and not quantum physics as I had naively imagined. Unsure how I could contribute to the present discussion, I inched away from the football fans and walked through a connecting hallway into the kitchen. Here I came across three couples involved in three different forms of activity: the first arguing about the boy's ex-girlfriend, the second kissing passionately, and the third discussing (of all things) whether General Franco was really ill or whether he had already died and the military junta were covering up his death. Feeling acutely self-conscious (although none of the three couples had so much as glanced at me), I backed out of the kitchen and cut across the living room to the entrance corridor. Leaning back against a wall, I deliberated what to do next. Should I make my way again through the obstacle course of interlocked legs and leave the party? Or should I climb the staircase to my left and try to find Portas upstairs? After contemplating the matter for all of five seconds, I plumped for the latter. I told myself it was the least I could do, seeing that I had come all the way to Trumpington from bloody Fitzroy College. Find the bugger, let him know you've come to his party, and then *get the hell out of here!*

Upstairs there were five doors centred around a large landing. There were still quite a few people about, though not as many as on the ground floor. Because of this lower density of bodies, I was suddenly conscious of the decor, which was sober and bourgeois, with lots of thick carpeting and clunky wooden furniture. Pictures of clippers and steamships adorned most of the walls; a howitzer shell casing stood propped up against the newel post at the top of the stairs. Fancy living in a place like this, I thought. Involuntarily, I found myself thinking about *The Forsyte Saga*, that television programme that my mother used to watch back in Gib. Wiping the sweat from my forehead, I took a deep breath and decided to try the different rooms. In the first bedroom, there was no one. In the second, three long-haired guys sitting around a glass water bong. In the third, a lit fish tank without any tropical fish. Finally, in the fourth room I looked into,

I found Portas holding a girl in his arms. He was whispering in her ear and kissing her on the neck; she was laughing and shaking her head. Not wanting to rain on the guy's parade, I began backing out of the room … but Portas spotted me and stopped me.

'But look who's here!' he cried. 'If it's not my fellow *llanito* in Cambridge!'

I smiled uneasily by the door and shifted my weight from one foot to the other. Sensing my discomfort, Portas disengaged from the girl's embrace and came towards me.

'Good to see you, *amigacho*,' he said, warmly grasping my hand. 'Glad you could make it. Come and meet my friend Mary Ellen.'

He led me away from the door and introduced me to Mary Ellen, a curvy, flat-nosed blonde with a tight-fitting pink T-shirt. As he spoke, Mary Ellen chewed gum and scratched her neck with her scarlet-painted fingernails, a look of irritation in her eye. Realising that my presence was seriously pissing her off, I told them I needed to go downstairs to grab a drink … but Portas was having none of it. 'What do you mean?' he rebuked me with a laugh. 'You need to grab a beer? What sort of over-formal talk is this? Come, we'll go down together and I'll introduce you to some of my friends. Mary Ellen doesn't mind, do you, Mary Ellen?'

Mary Ellen smiled a smile which suggested that she minded *a hell of a lot* and then sauntered disgustedly through the door. Portas laughed and patted me on the back.

'Come on, Mr Gibraltar Scholarship Holder, let's go downstairs,' he said. 'My friends have somehow got it into their heads that there's only myself and two or three monkeys resident in Gibraltar. They'll totally flip out when I tell them there's another Gibraltarian in the house!'

We went downstairs into the living room and plunged into the crowd, pausing every few yards so that my guide could introduce me to different people. I was very nervous at first — unused as I was to meeting complete strangers — but with Portas at my side I soon relaxed and began to enjoy the experience. Over the next half hour I was introduced to what had to be the most disparate collection of individuals ever gathered together. A handsome well-built Greek who was doing a PhD in Linguistics and whose nickname (for obvious reasons) was 'the harpoon'. A Welshman who had worked as a roadie for the Rolling Stones and was now studying Archaeology at Corpus Christi. A German Law tutor whose stepfather was supposed to be a big-shot member of the Baader-Meinhof Gang. A Ugandan medical student who supplemented his meagre government scholarship by selling encyclopaedias and reading Tarot cards. A London cabbie who had come to Cambridge to attend a conference on the history of lead toy soldiers. A Frenchwoman who wore an eyepatch and claimed to be the niece of the artist Yves Klein. A Senegalese author who worked as a part-time postman with Cambridgeshire County Council. And then, of course, there were the girls. Tonnes and tonnes of girls. East Anglian girls. Essex girls. Welsh girls. Scottish girls. London girls. American girls. French girls. Scandinavian girls. Truly, the place was packed with them! And Portas sure knew how to butter them up!

With a mischievous grin on his lips, he'd flatter them, he'd tease them, he'd mimic their words and gestures, he'd hug them to his chest and then suddenly pull back, he'd pretend to forget what they were studying and then, just when they were starting to get annoyed, tell them not only what they were studying, but everything they had previously told him about their courses. For someone like me, who had been educated in a single-sex Catholic school, and never had much confidence with women anyway, it was a real revelation! By the time we had made our way to the far end of the room and stopped next to the bay window for a smoke, I no longer had any doubts about it — this guy Portas was not just a stinking rich Gibbo with a posh accent, he was *a bloody frigging genius!*

'Wow!' I cried above the din. 'That was some performance!'

'What do you mean, Brian?'

'You and those girls,' I replied, bringing out my packet of cigarettes. 'Man, you do know how to charm them!'

'Well,' Portas said, shrugging his shoulders, 'you know what it's like with women…. Anyway, listen, do you fancy a drink? I'm getting a bit thirsty myself. Why don't you stay here and I'll nip into the kitchen and grab us some beers? Better for one of us to go on his own than for both of us to struggle through the swarm, *no crees, amigo?*'

I wanted to tell him that I was happy to accompany him to the kitchen (anything so as not to be left alone in the middle of that throng!), but it was too late: he had already swivelled around and was pushing his way through the crowd. For some moments I stood next to the window, scanning the multitude while puffing at my cigarette. I calculated there were fifty, maybe sixty people in the room. I wondered if they were all friends of Portas, or if they were a combination of friends and *friends of friends.* Definitely had to be the latter, I thought. One could not have such a huge number of friends, surely. Meanwhile, I couldn't help dwelling on an amusing irony: having been so reluctant to attend those small-scale common room parties back at Fitzroy, here I was now at a party with five or six times as many people. Ha ha ha, yes. That had to be one for the books. *El Manrique* coming to a party like this. *El Miliki* (like they mockingly called me back at the Gibraltar Grammar School) hobnobbing it with all these interesting individuals. Ha ha ha. If only my old classmates could see me, I thought, taking a self-satisfied puff of my cigarette. If only Angelle and Stannard and the others in my block knew that I was here! That would have shut them all up, wouldn't it? That would have taught them *what's what.* Not that I felt entirely comfortable in that large and crowded room. In fact, as the minutes passed and there was no sign of Portas, I began to feel increasingly isolated and self-conscious, constantly surrendering to the paranoid thought that everyone in the room was now looking at me. *Jesus Christ, how long can it take to grab a couple of drinks?* At last, just as I was about to lose my nerve altogether and scamper out of the living room, Portas suddenly emerged from the crowd with five bottles of beer clasped between his hands.

'It was such a struggle getting to the kitchen,' he said, noticing the look of surprise on my face. 'So I thought I'd bring some extra supplies for us. Here,' — he handed over two of the bottles — 'I hope they're cold enough for you.'

I smiled and took a small sip of beer. As I brought the bottle down, Portas leaned over towards me and said, 'I'm sure that bird fancies you.'

'You what?'

'Melanie, one of the girls I introduced to you earlier. The one with the red hair who's studying at Girton and whose cousin is living in Montmartre. She wasn't half giving you the eye as I was coming back with the beers!'

'You've got to be kidding!'

'No, I'm not kidding! Didn't you notice the way she was looking at you earlier?'

'Oh, come on, Henry,' I said, defensively folding my arms across my chest with a beer in each hand. 'I know I'm no Latino charm merchant like yourself — but there is no need to take the mickey, is there?'

'I'm serious, man,' Portas insisted. 'She couldn't take her eyes off you. If I were you, I'd go and get in there straight away.'

I raised one of the bottles to my lips and held it there for a few seconds. Was all this some kind of joke? Had Little Lord Fauntleroy here decided to have a laugh at my expense? Or did he really believe that the ginger lass with the saucer eyes truly had the hots for me? My instinct — that is to say, the part of me that was convinced that no reasonably attractive girl could be interested in me — told me that he HAD to be taking the mickey. But, then again, the way that Portas just stood there, looking so earnest and so serious … well … it was all very confusing.

'Anyway,' I said, bringing my beer down, 'even if you're right and for some reason she does like me a bit, I'm not going to go over there to her. That's not my style of doing things.'

'Oh, really, Mr I-got-my-picture-in-the-*Chronicle* Gibraltarian. So what's your style, then?'

'I just like to play it cool.'

'Cool?'

'Yes, cool.'

'You mean you stand around like a dumb ass hoping that she'll defy the natural order of things and *come up to you?*'

'Err … well … I-'

'Listen, mate, I know that in Gib we got this funny Mediterranean Catholic thing going on when it comes to courtship and dating, but, take it from me, old boy, that Melanie's a cracking bird and some other bugger's going to steal her from you if you don't get your act together.'

'Nah, I'm fine, man,' I said, feeling extremely uncomfortable. 'Honestly, I am. I just want to take it easy tonight.'

'So you want to take it easy?'

'Yeah, you know, chill out and all that. Feel quite tired, as a matter of fact.'

'Oh, do you?'

I nodded tensely. 'Yeah, must be all the walking I've been doing lately. Really been pounding those roads, you know.'

'Okay,' Portas grinned, 'you know what they say, "If Mahomet don't want to go to the mountain, well, the mountain will have to come to Mahomet, won't it?" '

With these words, Portas put his beers down on the windowsill and started walking towards the red-haired Melanie. From my place by the window, I could only stare at him in horror. *No, no, no — what are you doing? — come back! — come back, will you? — I said come back here right now!...* Too late, though. Suddenly Portas and the girl are at my side. He is talking incessantly and she keeps nodding, her pupils contracting and dilating in the hazy half-light. From up close she is even more beautiful than I first thought. About five foot five and eight and a half stone. Dainty, elegantly dressed. Extraordinarily blue-eyed. Embarrassingly, I find myself staring at her breasts, so I quickly look in another direction and start on my second beer. Meanwhile, Portas is telling her that I am an old friend of his and that he has known me since primary school. 'This guy here's the business, Mels,' he says, giving me a manly pat on the back. 'The real deal. Do you know that when we were ten years old he came and rescued me after I got stuck on a rocky ledge trying to climb a cliff? You should have seen the bugger, scampering up the Rock just to help his pal. Was up there quick as a flash. The guy's a legend, Mels. Wouldn't know where I'd be in this world without him.' Things continue in this vein for the next ten or fifteen minutes, with Portas singing my praises and Melanie hanging on to his every word. Most of the stuff he is coming up with is fairly conventional — that I was the best football player of our year; that I was always top of the class; that all the school bullies feared me because of my 'untouchable integrity'. But every now and then he throws a couple of curveballs into the mix as well — that I had a pet iguana called Max who died after he drank some weed killer which Portas accidentally spilled in my parents' backyard; that Portas and I used to smear seagull droppings on our willies because his cousin Joe had said that the alkali in them made your willy grow bigger; that we had once kidnapped a baby macaque from the ape's den which we named Danny and kept in Portas's Dad's tool shed for three days (feeding him chocolates and tinned Ideal Milk) before our exploit, alas, was sadly discovered. It is pretty impressive stuff. Dizzyingly original. All I can do in the meantime is nod and modestly concur, wondering where on earth the guy gets his powers of invention from. Every so often, Portas leaves us for five or ten minutes to grab more drinks. Each time this happens, Melanie and I exchange a few awkward words. She tells me she is studying Theology, but wants to switch over to History and Politics; I reply I'm doing French and Italian. She says she'd love to visit Gibraltar; I answer that it's nice, but there's not much to do there. As if by magic, whenever our conversation begins to falter, Portas reappears by our side with three beers nestled in his arms. 'Come on, folks,' he says, handing us a bottle each. 'Time to finish your old drinks and start new ones. I haven't imperilled body and soul to reach the kitchen so that you guys can continue with your slow-coach drinking!' By the third or fourth time this has happened, my powers of concentration are failing and the music and party-goers around me are merging into a slow-moving blur. I am also slurring my words and cannot stop staring at Melanie's breasts. And then, all of a sudden, I find myself alone with

Melanie in the corridor. The music sounds really distant and I am kissing her on the mouth. As I nuzzle into her perfume-scented neck, I vaguely recollect Portas saying something about Melanie to me in the living room, but I am too preoccupied with what I am doing to give the thought much attention. Ripples of sensation pulse through my body. Shivers run down my spine. Time and again the thought creeps into my head that this cannot be me, that all this is a dream, that Brian Manrique cannot possibly be doing something like this. *El Miliki snogging a hot bird? Nah, you gotta be kidding. That can't be right.* And then, just as abruptly as it all began, the music stops and the lights in the corridor are switched on and Melanie is pulling away from me, saying that she has to go home. I drunkenly try to convince her to stay a bit longer, but she mumbles something about choir practice in the morning and trots off down the hallway. 'Goodbye,' she says. 'It was nice talking to you. I hope I'll see you around some other time.' After this I try to make my way back into the living room — a problematic task, seeing that I am having to push against the departing crowd. When I at last manage to enter the room, it is empty except for a girl and a lad clearing away bottles and paper plates. Something about their manner makes me think they are postgrads. I ask them if they have seen Portas. The girl says no, but the guy tells me he saw him leave the house earlier with 'some bird.' Thanking him, I turn around and follow the other partygoers out of the property.

When I finally reached Fitzroy, Angelle's party had finished and everybody in my block had gone to bed. Following an impulse, I walked into the deserted common room and spent a few moments surveying the mess. Ashtrays overflowing with cigarette butts. Half-melted candles on the windowsill. Shards of brown glass glinting on the carpeted floor. On any other occasion these sights would have repelled me, but during those five or six minutes I could only regard everything with an amused smile. The simple truth was that I was happy. I was buzzing with joy. Portas's incredible generosity towards me, the experience of meeting all those people in his living room, the knowledge that for once I had attended a party without making a fool of myself: it all had the effect of a heady tonic, liberating me from the usual doubts and defeatism. Above all else, it was those moments with Melanie in the corridor that had really inspired me. Those precious moments, drenched as they were in the aroma of rubbed-off lipstick and cheap perfume, had regenerated me, they had given me a new lease of energy, they had made me feel that perhaps, you know what, despite what Angelle and 'Bazza' Stannard and all those other assholes in my block believed, I was not such a loser and a 'lost case'. Actually, I was so happy that I almost lamented the fact that everybody had gone to bed and there was no one there with whom I could share my amazing news. *Listen to this, I snogged a girl tonight! Can you believe that? Can you really believe it? Her name was Melanie! And she was really attractive and intelligent too! Yes, me! Me! Brian Manrique! The weird little guy from room 23! Can you, honestly, hand on heart, believe it? Tell me, can you?*

7.

My 'high', however, did not last long. Although for the next few days I was in a good mood and once or twice even said hello to my flatmates, by the end of the week my enthusiasm fizzled out and I was again seized by the same old mixture of homesickness and despondency. Actually, that is not quite true: things were not the same as before because, unlike some days ago, my homesickness now came interwoven with a pathetic romantic yearning. Yes, that's right: I was lovesick. Couldn't stop thinking about Melanie and those moments I had spent in her arms. In vain did I tell myself that Melanie had been drunk at the time, that the poor thing would probably run a mile if she saw me advancing towards her in the cold light of day. As daft as it sounds, I had got it into my head that Melanie and I were destined to become one of those '*grand amours*' so often spoken about by Flaubert and Stendhal and the other great French writers I was studying back then. One day, out of sheer desperation, I even forgot about my lessons and spent part of the morning and afternoon camped outside the Faculty of Divinity on St John's Street, hoping to catch a glimpse of 'my beloved' walking into or out of the building. It was a grim autumnal day — overcast and awash in a grey drizzle. Cars and buses continually drove past, enveloping me in exhaust fumes and speckles of dirty moisture. My face and hands stung with the cold. For about two and a half hours I remained there, enduring the rain and the suspicious glances of the St John's porters just across the road. Finally, around one in the afternoon, I shook my head and walked away, feeling as miserable and pissed off as I no doubt looked.

8.

A couple of weeks passed. Once again I began to go for long walks, returning to Fitzroy later and later at night. One Saturday I managed to reach as far as Huntingdon, a small market town some fifteen miles from Cambridge, where Oliver Cromwell was born in 1599. It took me five hours to get there, and six and a half to get back. On another occasion, I walked to Wimpole Hall, a country estate about seven miles south of the city. I had wanted to go there since the day I read in the 'Things to do' section of my Cambridge University Undergraduate Handbook that Wimpole Hall was one of the finest country houses in the East of England. But when I reached the place on a rain-sodden November afternoon, I was met by a plethora of 'Private property' signs and tall fencing, which meant that I could only see the house from the tarmacked hard shoulder of the A603, a single-lane trunk road connecting Cambridge to faraway Bedford. Not that I minded much. By this stage I did not really care where I was heading or what I'd be doing there; I was simply walking to tire myself out. In actual fact, I had noticed a subtle shift in what could be termed my walking frame of mind. When I first started going on my walks, I had only needed to be out for an hour or so for my mood to dramatically improve. After just three or four miles on the road, I could feel myself relaxing, switching off, leaving my problems behind — or at least pushing them away into the distant background. But now, in the last couple of weeks, all that had changed. Maybe it was because I was getting fitter and the walks no longer tired my body (and consequently calmed my brain) as much. Maybe it was because I now had a dollop of lovesickness thrown into the whole messy psychological mix. I am not sure. All I know is that, even on my long treks to far-off places like Huntingdon and Saint Neots, I couldn't stop obsessing about Melanie, Gibraltar, my corridor neighbours and my increasingly difficult French and Italian classes. Reflecting on it now, I suppose I was caught between two contradictory pulls. On the one hand, I missed Gibraltar and desperately wanted to return home. But on the other Melanie was in Cambridge and I couldn't abandon my course after having worked so hard to get here, could I?

Then one afternoon, as we reached the middle of term, someone knocked on my room door. As chance would have it, I was taking a piss in my washbasin at the time, which meant that the knock almost made me jump out of my skin. Drawing up quickly, wiping my hands on a small towel which I kept hanging from a cupboard handle, I zipped up and shuffled across the room to open the door. To my surprise, I found Angelle Price standing there before me in the corridor.

'There's someone wanting to speak to you on the phone upstairs,' she said without looking me in the eye.

'Oh, right,' I mumbled, feeling my cheeks go red.

I shut the door behind me and set off towards the second floor where the payphone was located. The only person who ever called me on the phone was my mother, and she always called me at the same hour on the same day of the week: seven o'clock on a Saturday morning, the only time when that cramped booth was free of girls chatting with their relatives and boyfriends. As I climbed the steps, I told myself that Melanie must have tracked down my number and was calling to arrange a meeting between us. But when I picked up the receiver a few moments later it was not a woman's voice on the line; it was that of Henry Portas:

'*Qué pasa, hermano?* How's my fellow Gibraltarian in Cambridge these days?'

I have to admit it: it was a shock. Although I had had a great time at Henry's party and been quite overwhelmed by his personal generosity to me, I had convinced myself that our paths would never cross again. There was nothing that he said or did which had created this impression. Actually, if there was a reason for it all, it was probably the sense of inferiority I felt when being introduced to his mates. They had all been so confident, after all, so self-assured, so full of interesting anecdotes and stories. And most of them looked so well off, too. Why would someone with friends like that choose to hang around with someone like me? In fact, I soon persuaded myself that he had only invited me to his place to prove to his mates that there was more to Gibraltar than just two or three old monkeys. That's what he had said that day at the party. 'My friends have somehow got it into their heads that there's only myself and a couple of monkeys resident in Gibraltar. They'll totally flip out when I tell them there's another Gibraltarian in the house!' Which in my eyes meant only one thing: I had been invited to his party solely for my 'novelty value'.

'I'm fine, Henry,' I replied, adjusting the receiver. 'How come you know this number?'

'You wrote it out for me on the night of my party, don't you remember?' he said with a low chuckle. 'Jesus, Brian, you just climbed out of bed or something?'

'I'm sorry. I'm not really used to anybody calling me, that's all.'

'Anyway, the reason I'm calling you is because I am being *forced* (I use the word in its most brutal and most coercive sense) to attend this ludicrous out-of-hours plenary lecture this evening at Magdalene College, which as you know is very close to Fitzroy, and I was wondering if you wanted to meet me at one of the bars on Bridge Street afterwards for some drinks. It's just that I really, really, really don't want to go to this stupid lecture on a Sunday evening and on regulatory compliance of all things — and I figured that the only way I could force myself to attend was if I knew beforehand that I was going to go out and get sloshed afterwards. You know what I'm saying, don't you, *compadre?*'

'I don't know, Henry,' I answered hesitantly. 'I have Italian Listening and Reading Comprehension tomorrow morning at nine o'clock. I've already missed two sessions this term. I'm going to get into real trouble if I miss tomorrow's session too.'

'Come on, Brian, don't be such a scaredy-cat! Come and get plastered with me and screw the consequences. *Qué será, será!*'

'I don't know, man.'

'Okay, okay. How about if we go out and just have a couple of pints? That way you'll never miss your reading and comprehension thingy tomorrow.'

'You sure you can stick to just a couple?'

'Hey, man, what do you take me for — an alcoholic or something? I'm a Portas — we are renowned for our self-control.'

In the end we met at the Mitre Tavern, an old-fashioned Victorian pub about two minutes away from Magdalene and a brisk twelve-minute walk from Fitzroy. I arrived there at ten to eight, fifteen minutes earlier than arranged. The interior of the pub wasn't so much odd as lop-sided, with a small lounge at the front and a much larger seating area located at the rear. Flat-capped locals sat on high stools by the bar, their faces bloated and reddened by liquor. A fat woman in a nurse's uniform was badgering them with a cone-shaped plastic collection box. In the hallway linking the two halves of the pub stood an unused snooker table, a thick fug of cigarette smoke floating stagnantly under its bright canopy-style lights. After buying a pint of Whitbread from a short-haired barmaid, I moved to the back room to look for a table. Surprisingly, Portas was already there. He was sitting on his own, with a half-empty pint glass in one hand and a copy of the *Guardian* spread out before him. A packet of peanuts lay on the table, half of its contents scattered messily across the wet mahogany surface. As I made my way towards him, I noticed a striking detail: his shirt cuffs were fastened with a pair of purposely bent paper clips.

'I thought your lecture didn't finish until eight,' I said, stopping beside his table.

'Man, you have no idea what it's like to have some boring old fart banging on about regulators and licensing regimes and superannuation funds and the rest of it. I just had to get away to preserve my sanity.... Anyway, take a seat. You're not going to drink your pint standing up, are you?'

I took off my jacket, sat down, then placed my glass carefully on a beer mat.

'So,' Portas began, putting his beer down, 'how's things, old boy? Everything okay on the northern side of the Cambridge Ring Road?'

I nodded and said that everything was fine.

'Glad to hear it. Your place is not far from Kettle's Yard, isn't it?'

I looked at him questioningly. 'Kettle's what?'

'Kettle's Yard. The art gallery that opened last year. There's a couple of stunning Christopher Woods in their collection.'

'Sorry, never heard of the place,' I said, reaching for my pint. 'You forget that I'm just an ordinary grammar school kid.'

'Yeah, right. That's why you're studying Modern Languages at Cambridge, you little ponce. Anyway, enough flimflam. Did you enjoy my party? That's what I *really* want to know.'

I replied that *yes, I had enjoyed his party very much.*

'I'm going to have another one after Christmas,' he said, looking pleased. 'You can come if you want.'

Brushing a blond curl from his forehead, he began telling me about the preparations for his next party: what music he was thinking of playing, what types of beer he was ordering, what people he had already invited. As he continued with his rambling monologue, I thought about Melanie and wondered whether she would be invited to the party too. Several times I was on the brink of asking about her, but each time I pulled back, too embarrassed to bring up the subject. Finally, I could not stand it any longer: I had to broach the matter somehow.

'You know, Henry, I still haven't thanked you for what you did for me that day at your party.'

'What do you mean, *compadre?*'

'Well, you introduced me to Melanie, didn't you? If it wasn't for you, then nothing would have happened between us.'

'Oh, man, forget it. That was nothing. We're both Gibraltarians, aren't we? You'd do the same for me if you could, I'm sure.... Besides, why are you even thanking me? It was you who pulled that bird, not me.... By the way,' he said, staring at me with an inquiring frown, 'you're not still thinking about that girl, are you?'

I blushed and looked down.

'Man, just forget about her, Brian,' Portas said, shaking his head. 'That girl's no good for you. Do you know that she has a boyfriend in Devon? Some heavily tattooed, semi-professional footballer whose father owns a hardware shop in Axminster or some other miserable backwater. Man, just be glad you got a snog out of her and forget her. If you want women, then come with me on a few nights out. I'll get you all the women you want.'

I said I'd consider his offer and then tried to change the subject by asking him for a cigarette. He brought one out of his packet, handed it over and lit it for me, keeping his eyes fixed on mine as he did so. The conversation then turned to his lecture and how much he hated studying Law. I told him that I didn't particularly like studying languages either, but it was the only thing I was relatively good at. On hearing this,

Portas shook his head and said that at least I was good at something. 'That's half the battle won, isn't it, my dear Manny?' Intrigued by these words, I asked him why he was studying Law if he was no good at the subject and hated it so much. Portas responded by shrugging his shoulders and saying that some people had little choice open to them. Blowing out a cloud of cigarette smoke, I asked him what he meant by this.

'It's my father,' he said, sucking his upper lip behind his lower one.

'What do you mean?'

'Mr Henry William Mathew Portas. MA (Cantab), CBE, MBE. Educated at Trinity College, just like his father and his grandfather before him. Three times president of the Gibraltar Chamber of Commerce. Special adviser to the Chief Minister of Gibraltar on the economy and other matters. He's the only reason why I'm studying Law here at Trinity.'

'I don't think I follow you.'

'Come on, Brian,' Portas said, suddenly very animated. 'Please don't be so *fucking dim*. You're supposed to be a student at Cambridge University, for Christ's sake! Do I really have to spell it out for you? Parental pressure, family tradition, the wonderful Portas sense of filial duty — that's what I'm talking about, man. I'm here studying Law because my fucking father wouldn't have it any other way!'

I rested my cigarette on the ashtray before me and looked steadily at Portas. For a second I thought about my own father, who had died of a heart attack when I was only twelve years old. A softly spoken dockyard machinist, he had always had a smile for his children and had never let his involvement with the

Trade Union Movement interfere with his family duties. Alfredo Manrique had always been there for us, *al pie del cañón* as we say in Gibraltar: taking a second job as a delivery man when we needed a new washing machine, scraping a few pennies from his measly wage so that he could buy my sister and me the odd toy, walking us to school in the mornings, driving us down to Eastern Beach and Catalan Bay in the summer months. I thought about all these things and then I thought about the scant respect with which Portas had spoken about his still living father. Grimacing to conceal my inner turmoil, I picked up my cigarette and took a slow puff.

'But surely you can't be forced into studying a subject you don't like, Henry? Didn't you tell your dad that Law wasn't for you?'

'I tried,' Portas replied in a quieter voice. 'I told him I wanted to do History of Art.'

'And what happened?'

'He just looked at me for a long time without saying anything.'

'And is that such a bad thing?'

'In my family, Brian, that is *the worst possible thing*.... Anyway,' he said, smiling despite the look of discomfort in his eyes, 'let's not talk about my family, shall we? The main thing is that we're both here in this grand old tavern having a drink. Two Gibraltarian Cantabrigians in the middle of this fair East Anglian city. Now ain't that something, eh?'

He hoisted his pint into the air and we clinked glasses. For the next hour we avoided talking about his father or his hatred of Law and focused instead on what both of us had done in the months before coming to Cambridge. I told him I had been either going to the beach or just staying at home chilling out and doing nothing at all. This was largely true, but it was not 100 per cent accurate either, since I had only been to the beach some three or four times during the entire summer and, rather embarrassingly, I had always gone there with my mother and my little sister Mariela. Portas, for his part, told me that he had spent most of the holidays smoking his way through an enormous fifteen-ounce bag of dope that Sandro, one of his public-school mates up at Stonyhurst, had generously left with him before leaving the college and returning to his native Chile. At the beginning of August, he had visited Gibraltar for three days to attend his second cousin's wedding. He said he could have stayed on a bit longer in Gib, but 'it just wasn't worth the hassle.' Hearing this, I asked him if he usually spent his summers away from Gibraltar. He responded by saying that he had spent three out of the last five summers almost wholly on the Rock, with only the odd four- or five-day outing to the Portas finca near Ronda in Spain breaking up these long stays. Seeing the blank expression on my face, he explained that the Portas family owned a large house set in thirty-five acres of land between El Colmenar and Opayar, two small villages about forty kilometres south of Ronda. His great-grandfather, he said with a disgusted smirk, had named the house *White Haven* and had even imported twenty tonnes of finest Cumbrian turf to reinforce the illusion of Englishness. The Portas clan, he went on, were always going there whenever they got a chance — even though it took them a whole day to reach the property. ('You have no idea how much hassle it all entails, Brian — starting up the launch at the Gibraltar Yacht Club, travelling ten nautical miles from Gibraltar to Tangier, switching over into *La Princesse du Nord*, our Tangier-registered boat, sailing *La Princesse* to Algeciras, berthing at Algeciras, passing through Spanish customs, walking to the private warehouse near the docks where we keep our Spanish Mercedes, and, last but not least, negotiating the seventy or so miles of perilous hairpin roads from Algeciras to Opayar!') He himself, though, preferred to stay in their house in Gibraltar, as he hated the 'totally predictable shit' that normally went on in their Spanish mansion. All that his father and his friends did, he said, was shoot birds or go horse-riding or talk about business in that curiously affected Oxbridge way of theirs. 'They think they're English country gentlemen,' Portas laughed, a spurt of cigarette smoke escaping through the side of his mouth. 'But they're not, of course. They're full-blooded Latins, just like everybody else in Gib. You should see the arguments they have in that house! Man, it's like something out of one of those comedies they show on *Televisión Española*, with everyone, from the old toothless grandmother to the last little brat, all swearing and shouting at each other! Absolutely fucking pathetic!'

For the last hour of the evening Portas turned his attention to a pair of girls sitting at a nearby table. Their names were Helena and Crystal and we learned they both worked as waitresses at The Red Snapper, a seafood restaurant on King's Parade. Within minutes my fellow Gibraltarian was in full flow — poking fun at their gelled-up hairstyles, rhapsodising about knee-high leather boots, asking if a mole on Helena's forehead was real or not, wondering if we would get a discount if we visited them one day at their restaurant, telling Crystal that she had 'eyes like Jane Fonda', asking them if they had ever met such 'a disreputable pair of foreigners.' In this masterly to-ing and fro-ing, it seemed to me, Portas was like a championship boxer — backing off on to the ropes one moment, then advancing forwards the next with a flurry of unstoppable counter-punches. Watching all this from the sidelines made me feel even more conscious of my own awkwardness with the opposite sex, but I can't deny that I was also strangely fascinated by the whole performance. Could this be the same guy who only a few minutes ago had sounded so bitter and cut-up about his relationship with his family, I wondered? Was it really possible for someone to switch roles as abruptly as this? The answer came just after last orders, when Portas disappeared together with Helena, and I was left alone at the table with a smiling but visibly ill-at-ease Crystal. I had, of course, been half-expecting this eventuality all along, but it still bugged me to think he could leave me *just like that*, with no more than a wink and a hastily mumbled promise that he'd be in touch soon. 'The bloody shit,' I thought, gazing uncomfortably at Crystal. 'He invites me for a drink, then buggers off with the first girl he sees!' A surge of indignation coursed through my veins, making me clench my fists in my pockets and inwardly vow never to see the stuck-up, self-obsessed toff again. But moments later, as I walked out of the bar with Crystal, something happened which not only made me forgive Portas for his disappearing act, but also left me trembling with excitement. For as we exited through the swinging wooden doors, Helena's mate suddenly threw herself into my arms and kissed me for a few seconds on the lips … before pushing me away and walking off in her tall stilettoes. For a moment or two I remained rooted to the spot, watching her clip-clop her way down Bridge Street in the direction of the Round Church. Then, wiping the taste of lipstick from my mouth, telling myself that perhaps it hadn't been such a bad night after all, I turned around and began to walk in the opposite direction, towards Castle Street and Fitzroy College.

9.

Two days later, I fished out the business card that Portas had given to me some weeks earlier and phoned him to arrange another drinking session. We met this time at the Baron of Beef, another Bridge Street pub. In contrast to our previous meeting, there were no distractions around us and we spent practically the entire evening chatting about Gibraltar and its many idiosyncrasies. For me that night was a real surprise. Up till then I had thought that Portas was one of those snobby, public school-educated Gibraltarians who pretend to be proud of their origins while secretly despising us ordinary folk under them, but as we sat drinking together in the back room of the Baron of Beef I realised that I had judged the guy unfairly. Portas may have been the scion of one of Gibraltar's richest families, but he was still 100 per cent *llanito.* He knew all about the Rock's history and its legends, its buildings and its places, its people and its politics. And it was not only official mainstream stuff that he was familiar with, either. He even knew about the half-hidden shingly paths that led from the back of Laguna Estate, where my mother rented our government-owned flat, to the large area of Upper Rock scrubland known colloquially as '*el jungle*'! Obviously, he wasn't acquainted with the names that we Laguna Estate kids made up for them — *el camino de Carlito, el sendero del soldao*, Tommy's Trail — but he could still describe all the paths in great detail! 'It's called exploration, my dear Mr Manrique,' he said, brushing off my attempt to find out how he knew so much about my neighbourhood in Gibraltar. 'Everybody should try it at some point, including you!'

In next to no time I was meeting Portas three, four, sometimes even five times a week. We mainly met in pubs, but also rendezvoused in cafés and tea rooms. Clad in his trademark cricket jumper and long black overcoat, he'd stride hurriedly into a venue before patting me vigorously on the back and greeting me with the same words: '*Qué pasa, hermano? Cómo estamos?*' He'd then saunter off towards the serving counter and come back with either two pints of beer or a couple of coffees, without once asking me for any money for his purchases. The first few times we met, I was always a little nervous and hesitant in his company, having to think hard before saying anything in front of him. This nervousness started to wear off after our fourth or fifth meeting, only for it to return in the guise of a more or less respectful awe once I began to know him better. The truth was that Portas was such a remarkable being that I could never be fully comfortable in his presence. On the outside, yes, he may have conformed to an old stereotype — the rich, neglected kid who hated both his father and the bourgeois expectations thrust on him — but once you saw past that side there was nothing stereotypical about the guy. First, there was his unpredictability, his capacity to confound. Although he was always telling people, for instance, that he was too thick to be studying Law, his mind was a repository of the strangest and most curious facts, which he loved to bombard you with at unexpected moments. Who else but Portas could have told you which out of the Fitzwilliam Museum's two thousand-odd paintings was Charles Darwin's favourite? (A rather insipid *Venus and Cupid* by Palma il Vecchio, apparently). Or from which Trinity College window a drunken Vladimir Nabokov puked his guts out after hearing that his mother's estate in Siverskaya, just south of Saint Petersburg, had been confiscated by the Bolsheviks? (The third window on your right as you enter Trinity Lane from St John's Street). Or given you a step-by-step account of what happened to the Swiss reformer Martin Bucer's cadaver after his death at Cambridge in 1551? (Buried honorifically in the Church of Saint Mary the Great under the ultra-Protestant Edward VI, exhumed and hung up from the church's entrance gates under the ultra-Catholic Mary I, then finally taken down and reburied with slightly less fanfare under the moderately Protestant Elizabeth I). But it was not only his ability to spout anecdotal remarks that made Portas such an interesting character. There was also the fact that the man himself was a veritable box of surprises. Take the time some guy came up to our table at the Mitre and said, 'Hey, Henry man, when are you going to come down to see us at the Grange? Flintie recently fractured his cheekbone while doing the King Street

Run and old Crokey's going out of his head looking for a decent left-winger. I reckon the old pot and pan would have you back in a flash if you showed your face around the clubhouse one day.' When I asked Portas a short while later what all this was about, he told me that he had attended the Cambridge University rugby trials a few weeks earlier and been selected for the Varsity team, but had yet to show up for a training session. When I asked why, he put his pint down, tucked his hands into his coat pockets, looked me in the eye and, ignoring a fly that had just landed on his left cheek, said, 'Come on, Brian, do I look like the kind of bloke who'd be arsed with regular Monday- and Thursday-evening rugby training with a load of big, sweaty fellas?'

There were other incidents like that. One day I'd learn that he had won a bronze medal at the 1969 All-England Schools Judo Championships. Another evening that he had been mentioned in the *Cambridge Evening News* for rescuing an eighty-eight-year-old pensioner from the River Cam. A few days later, something that both surprised me and didn't surprise me: that during his time at Stonyhurst he had almost been expelled from the college for running around the central courtyard in a stolen cassock and shouting '*Futue te ipsum!*' and '*Filius tu canis et cameli!*' ('Go fuck yourself!' and 'Son of a dog and a camel!') Possibly the most shocking revelation (and the last thing that I am going to mention, seeing that this is now sounding positively hagiographical) came when I entered the back room of the Baron of Beef one evening and found him reading an old cloth-bound book that looked like it was about to crumble in his hands. Not wishing to disturb him, I sat down and watched him for a second. His head was tilted forward and his eyes were avidly scanning the open tome. The ceiling fan was noiselessly stirring a lock of his hair. By inclining my head and focusing hard, I could just make out the book's title — *The Night Climbers of Cambridge by Whipplesnaith.*

'That's an unusual name for an author, Whipplesnaith,' I finally said, starting to get bored.

'Mmm-mmm,' he replied, too engrossed in the book to look up.

'Is it a real name, or a pseudonym?'

'Mmm-mmm.'

'Must be a real riveting read for you to ignore your mate who's just come in to see you.'

'Mmm-mmm.'

'*Henry!*' I bellowed angrily.

'Yes?' he asked, lifting his head.

'I've been asking you about your book.'

'My book? What about it?'

'Well, you tell me,' I said, 'seeing that you seem to find it more interesting than my company.'

He smiled and nodded. 'This, my friend,' he said, holding up the book with a look of pride, 'is the Cantabrigian stegophilist's Holy Grail.'

'A stego-what?'

'A stegophilist, my dear boy, is a person who, purely for the love of what he is doing, often in the face of great hostility from the authorities, and relying solely on the dexterity of his own feet and hands, climbs the outside of famous old buildings.'

He explained that he had been interested in stegophily since his days at Stonyhurst. He had not known it at the time, of course (until recently he had never even heard of the term), but looking back it was clear that he had been *a stegophilist all along*. At first, he said, it was simply a matter of climbing out through his window in the evenings so that he could enjoy a cig without stinking out his room. Then it progressed to crawling up the sides of the block's sloping lead roof. Not long after that, he was climbing the college's famous Eagle Towers, struggling up their narrow fluted columns before clambering onto their ancient leaden cupolas. He said he undertook the climbs because they helped him unwind, because they cleared his head of unwanted thoughts. You could be worrying about exams, he said, or pondering how to ditch your girlfriend. Fretting over world peace or stressing about your latest row with your parents. The moment you were up there, standing on a corbel or holding on to a flying buttress, *whoosh!* — all of it disappeared as if by magic from your brain. So far at Cambridge, he had only climbed the Trinity College gatehouse (and almost got caught by one of the porters in the attempt), but he was planning on doing the 'Wedding Cake' (as the octagonal clock tower at St John's New Court was widely known) one of these days. He had even devised a strategy to reach the top of the 'Cake'; it involved (from what I can remember) scaling a drainpipe near the main entrance into St John's, climbing an emergency staircase located just outside the Senior Bursar's room, scrambling up the lead roof to the base of the tower, then using a chimney climbing technique to push his way up between the side of the clock tower and the neo-Gothic buttresses and pinnacles clustered around it. 'Not the easiest of climbs,' Portas admitted after describing his plan, 'but by no means totally impossible either.' Listening to him speak like this, I had the awful feeling that Portas would make his attempt later that same night. However, when we left the pub after last orders, he clambered into the first taxi we came across on nearby Jesus Lane and repeatedly 'V-signed' me as the vehicle pulled away — a jesting mannerism of his that always irritated me, but which, that evening at least, filled me with a sense of relief. In fact, for the next few days nothing more was mentioned about stegophily, the New Court clock tower or any of the other stuff we had talked about that night, leading me to think that, for once, I must have overestimated Portas's capacity for mischief and tomfoolery. Then one day, about five and a half weeks later, just after coming back from the Christmas holidays and having all but forgotten our conversation that evening at the Baron of Beef, I read in the Cambridge student newspaper *Varsity* that an unknown person had climbed the New Court clock tower in broad daylight a week earlier. 'Such a remarkable feat,' wrote the paper's correspondent, 'may well remind some of our more historically minded readers of the scandent escapades of Lord Noël Howard Symington and his coterie of infamous Night Climbers. But it is this reporter's belief that the achievements of this unknown climber — henceforth to be known as the Mountain Goat of St John's — actually supersede those of his Roaring Twenties predecessors, since, as far as we are aware, none of the Bright Young Things (God bless their cloche hats and their *très chic témérité*) ever attempted a feat like this at five o'clock in the afternoon, with a full complement of freshers, bedders, porters and other individuals assembled in the courtyard below.' The article went on to describe how the anonymous student — who had worn a cowboy hat and a black Zorro mask to protect his identity — had eventually been chased away from St John's by a mixture of fire, police, ambulance and city council personnel, but had managed to evade capture by jumping into the River Cam and emerging from the water, it was believed, somewhere near Magdalene Bridge. 'A good job too,' the student reporter added archly, 'since the Mountain Goat's apprehension would have surely led to a dressing down of the worst sort!' When I asked Portas later that evening at the pub whether he in fact was the Mountain Goat of St John's, he shook his head and looked down, earnestly protesting that no power on earth would have made him jump into the River Cam in the middle of January. Something in his eye, however, told me that he wasn't being straight with me — so for the next few hours I badgered him for a confession. Finally, just before last orders, my persistence paid off. 'God, that water was cold,' he said, putting down his pint glass and winking roguishly. 'And you should have seen the look on the little old lady who saw me come out of the water where the punts are kept near the bridge. I'm not kidding: it was like she had seen the Loch Ness monster!... Actually, Brian, I don't even know why I bothered escaping from those coppers. Would have been mega-fucking funny if my father had found out that his son was none other than the infamous Mountain Goat of St John's, don't you think?'

10.

But I am getting ahead of myself. Portas's act of free-climbing daredevilry occurred on the fifteenth of January, five days before the start of the Lent term. In between this event and the day that he had given me the 'V' from the departing taxi, there was the small business of my Christmas vacation in Gibraltar to get through. This started on the twentieth of December, the day after my final lecture for the year, and lasted until the nineteenth of January. Disappointingly, the trip did not go well. Although I had been counting the days to Christmas practically since my first week in Cambridge, once I got to Gibraltar and found myself stranded in our Laguna Estate flat, with nothing to do except work on my various university assignments and listen to *Simplemente María* and other of my mother's Spanish *radionovelas*, I began to feel bored and restless. To relieve the monotony I'd leave the flat every now and then and go for long walks along Sir Herbert Miles Road, heading past Catalan Bay and the water catchments, until I reached the road running above the inaptly named Sandy Bay. While negotiating the constant bends in the road, I'd sometimes catch glimpses of the sea pounding against the coastal rocks and spraying its frothy discharge high into the air. Its terrible power would always bring to mind the opening of Charles Baudelaire's *'L'Homme et la mer'*, one of the poems I had recently read for my French Romantic Literature module:

Homme libre, toujours tu chériras la mer!
La mer est ton miroir; tu contemples ton âme

Dans le déroulement infini de sa lame,
Et ton esprit n'est pas un gouffre moins amer.

On reaching the MOD police post at the end of Sir Herbert Miles Road, I'd turn around and begin the slow hike back home, wondering why they allowed cars to continue past this point and travel around the Rock, but not us poor pedestrians. If I was feeling adventurous, I'd walk down the access ramp into Sandy Bay itself and zigzag my way through the tangled mass of driftwood, oil drums and pebbles scattered on the mostly sandless beach, keeping an eye out all along for the waves crashing on the shore and racing to the top of the cove. Inevitably, at some point my thoughts would turn to Cambridge and all the things I had left behind there — Portas, my long walks at night, my flatmates at Fitzroy, my French and Italian classes. How distant it all seemed, how much like a half-recollected dream. It was hard to believe that I, Brian Manrique, the same person who was walking on this desolate beach with his collars turned up against the piercing easterly wind, had really experienced all that, that it had all been lived by me and not by some character in a dismal B-movie. I tried telling myself that I felt like this because I had no love for Cambridge and didn't want to be there, but deep down I knew this was only a half-truth. Cambridge may not have been my cup of tea, but being stuck at Laguna with my mum was no joyful experience either. Look at all these walks. Look at how bored and fed up I was back at our flat. Look at the way I couldn't stop thinking about the people and places I had left behind in East Anglia. If my original problem had been simple homesickness, then why did I feel just as shit here as back in the UK?

11.

I returned to Cambridge on the eighteenth of January, two days before the beginning of the new term. Portas, who had spent the entire Christmas on his own in his house in Trumpington, came to see me some days later and we went for a few beers at the Mitre Tavern. As we clinked glasses, he asked me how I had enjoyed my trip and I said it hadn't been the best of Christmas holidays. He laughed and said I was starting to sound like him. Ignoring this last remark, I asked him how his own Christmas had gone. 'Not bad,' he replied with a smile. 'There were hardly any birds around, which, as you know, is never a good thing. But there is something to be said as well for quiet pubs and not having to queue forever at crowded bus stops.' Later that evening, I heard about his New Court clock tower exploits and his freezing swim in the Cam. He also told me about two other stegophilistical 'jobs' that he had pulled off — the tower of Great Saint Mary's on the twenty-sixth of December, and the spire of the Bodley church on Jesus Lane on New Year's Eve. Neither of them were particularly difficult climbs, he explained, but their location on main roads made up for their relative lack of complexity. 'The Church of Great Saint Mary's, for example,' he said, picking up his pint glass and holding it an inch or two from his mouth, 'well, it's a real bugger, isn't it? There are always people streaming past the bloody place. Townies during the day and drunken students from Gonville and Caius at night. The only time when you can realistically have a shot at the damn thing is at night during the middle of the holidays, when there are hardly any student revellers out in the streets. Even then you have to be very quick about it, since, being so close to the shops and the offices of the City Council, the place is always swarming with cops and security guards. Ten to twelve minutes max to get to the top and back. I don't think I've ever scrambled up and down a building *as quickly as that!*'

Over the following weeks I saw Portas regularly at the Baron of Beef and the Mitre Tavern. These meetings were similar to the ones we had before Christmas, inasmuch as I kept discovering strange and fascinating facts about him. Among other things, I found out that he had once run the 100 metres in 10.9 seconds. That he used to keep pet tarantulas in his room at Stonyhurst. That he had once walked from Clitheroe to Burnley and back just to win a two-shilling bet. All these revelations were interesting enough, but what really fascinated me was why Henry ended up doing these things. Was it pure rebelliousness? Was it his way of spiting his straitlaced bourgeois father? Or was there an element of madness lurking behind it all? Looked at dispassionately, it was clear there had to be a pronounced rebellious streak within his character. But could rebelliousness alone, I wonder, help you run the 100 metres in 10.9 or perform astonishing feats of free-climbing? Can hatred of someone or something make you develop extremely difficult skills and talents? For a long time I thought about all this without being able to reach a definite answer. Then, slowly, painstakingly, by constantly taking note of what Portas said about his family and then analysing it in the light of his 'foibles', I developed my own personal theory: not only was Portas rebelling against his dad, but every single act of rebellion, from keeping pet tarantulas at Stonyhurst to walking fifty miles for the sake of a two-shilling bet, was itself a direct reaction to some behavioural trait of his father's:

Portas Snr: *Miserly, pragmatic, doesn't do anything for anyone unless there's a chance of substantial financial gain.*
Portas Jnr: *Walks fifty miles for a two-shilling bet. Always giving money away.*

Portas Snr: *Says that all animals except horses and dogs should be shot.*
Portas Jnr: *Keeps pet tarantulas. Calls them Antonio, Freddie and Passepartout.*

Portas Snr: *Considers televised sport 'the opium of the masses.' Boasts that he has never watched a full football or rugby match.*
Portas Jnr: *Runs the 100 metres in 10.9 seconds. Gets selected for the Cambridge University rugby team.*

Portas Snr: *Doesn't read. Hates art.*
Portas Jnr: *Loves painting and sculpture. Keeps a bust of Michelangelo on his bedside table.*

Portas Snr: *Never takes risks of any kind, either financial or emotional.*
Portas Jnr: *Constantly risking life and limb as a stegophilist.*

Portas Snr: *Impeccably dressed at all times. Believes that clothes 'maketh the man.'*
Portas Jnr: *Scruffy, unshaven, always wears the same white cricket jumper and black navy-style overcoat.*

12.
But it would be a mistake to think that Henry Portas Jnr. was just some kind of amateur psychoanalytic project for me. I really *did* enjoy the guy's company. Always looked forward to spending time with him. If he called me while I was writing up a home assignment, I'd drop everything to go and meet him at the Baron of Beef or the Mitre Tavern. If he asked me to attend some late-night party with him, I would say yes even if I had a supervision at eight-thirty the next morning. Was there an element of hero worship in all this? Probably. But there was another factor, too, that made me carry on wanting to see him: the many and assorted benefits that his friendship offered. Take the way my flatmates at Fitzroy had stopped shunning me and badmouthing me. This was *entirely down* to Henry's occasional visits to the flat. Appearing at Fitzroy once or twice a week, he charmed and flattered my flatmates to such an extent that before long the buggers began to smile and say hello and sometimes even share a few words with me in the corridor. Incredible, really. You are friends with someone who is popular and, purely by moving in their sphere of influence, you yourself become popular too! How crazy is that?! And what does it say about the superficiality of human beings? A similar alchemical process, in fact, also transformed my dealings with the opposite sex. Although I was never the most confident guy when engaging with women,

being Henry's friend really helped me in that department. Obviously, I was nowhere near as successful as he was (What can I tell you? Portas was in a completely different league!), but there were still plenty of opportunities nonetheless when I was able, as it were, to 'bask in his reflected glory.' And what a remarkable and magnificent 'glory' it was, too! In common with most Lotharios, Portas could stroll into any discotheque or house party and within moments there'd be a bevy of girls at his side. I saw this happen time and again and it never ceased to amaze me. How can a man walk into a room where the music is playing at eardrum-splitting levels, and where you can hardly see because it is so dark, and still attract so much feminine attention? No doubt, in Portas's case, part of the answer could be found in the rugged masculinity he exuded, in his physical presence. But I don't think physicality alone can fully account for the situation either. There was also something about Henry himself, some mysterious, inexpressible aura, which attracted people, and especially women, to his side. What this quality was I'll never be sure, but I do know what it was that kept them tethered to him once they came to him: it was his frankness, his almost childlike spontaneity. Yes, he never slept with the same woman twice and, yes, he never stayed in touch with any of his conquests, but when he was engaged in the process of wooing a girl, he'd lavish on her all the charm and attention that only someone as emotionally deprived and neglected as this magnate's son could muster. You could feel it radiating from him — this intensity, this heartfelt sense of passion. I think it was this more than anything else that women found so fascinating about him.

Till now I have speculated on the reasons for Portas's behaviour and why people always responded to his charm. But there is one final area of speculation which I must consider before proceeding with my narrative — and that is why someone like Henry Portas chose to be friends with somebody like me. For the first few weeks I thought that the only possible reason had to be our shared *Gibraltarianness*, there being no other qualities or attributes linking us together. Then, as I got to know Portas better, I told myself that perhaps he liked my company because we were both outcasts of a sort (he from his family; me from society in general). Some weeks after this, I changed my mind yet again and convinced myself that he had only befriended me because of my working-class background, and that our friendship was an act of rebellion against his father. This line of thinking, it is true, probably said more about my own hang-ups and insecurities than anything else, but the fact still remained that there was no way that someone like him — rich, urbane, public school-educated — would have consorted with a Laguna Estate kid like me had we both lived in Gibraltar. It just wouldn't have happened. Then, after considering the matter further, I reverted to my original position and surmised that we had to be friends simply because we were both Gibraltarian. National bonding of this kind often happens at university. Visit any college or polytechnic dining room and you'll see it for yourself: the Greeks at the 'Greek table', the French at the 'French table', the Germans at the 'German table', the Israelis at the

'Israeli table.' The members of each national cluster will have different characters and interests, but the fact that they speak the same language and share the same cultural background makes them cling to one another. It is just a form of self-defence, I reckon, a way of insulating themselves from the strange new laws and customs around them. Once back on their native soil, they'll go their separate ways and have nothing to do with each other.

13.

Some weeks passed. Life continued more or less as it had done before Christmas, with boozy sessions at the Bridge Street pubs and impromptu parties in the evenings (and throbbing hangovers and unbearably boring lessons in the mornings). In the final week of February, Portas bought a second-hand car — a battered but nonetheless very impressive Citroën DS Super Cabrio. Driving through the narrow streets of town in that oversized convertible was one of the highlights of that first year at Cambridge. Laughing like *gilipollas*, crouching half-frozen behind the Citroën's low windscreen, taking occasional puffs of the joint which Portas kept hidden under the dashboard, we'd trundle down King's Parade like we were the absolute rulers of the place, waving with mock solemnity at all the shoppers and students streaming past. *Girlwise*, too, the car turned out to be a splendid investment. A 'babe magnet' capable of attracting all sorts. Tall girls. Thin girls. Fat girls. Slim-hipped girls. Girls with bad breath. Girls with braids in their hair. Girls with boots up to their knees. Girls who said they had psychic powers. Girls with pretty eyes but *off-puttingly* square jawlines.

Girls with more *cojones* than Joe Frazier or George Foreman. Girls who could recite every single sonnet written by Shakespeare. Girls who wouldn't look you in the eye, but then turned out to be real sex-maniacs. Girls who wanted to save the whale and the Third World. Girls who went around quoting Wittgenstein and Heidegger. We'd pick them up outside the entrance to Sidney Sussex College, or by the back of St John's, and then take them for a picnic or an in-car lunch somewhere beyond the city. To Madingley, maybe, or to Yaxley further up Saint Neots Road. The itinerary of these rural outings was always the same: champagne, strawberries, a couple of spliffs, a few bawdy jokes, a bit of the old *slap and tickle*. If Portas really liked our female companions, we'd leave Cambridgeshire altogether and venture further afield — to Cromer on the Norfolk coast, perhaps, or to the ancient market town of Saffron Walden in Essex. Getting to these places was always an adventure in its own right. Hunched over the wheel, continually pushing his long blond hair out of his eyes, Portas would either puff away at his joint, or else ramble on about the passing scenery. 'You see those cliffs to your left, people? Those are the famous Hunstanton cliffs. Patrick Hamilton's novel *Hangover Square* starts off with its protagonist, George Harvey Bone, trudging along the top of these cliffs in a murderous daze. There's also a fantastic chippy at the end of this grassy stretch here, just in front of the abandoned old lighthouse. Can you see it, people?' Once, as we were coming back from Bury Saint Edmunds, we got stopped by a copper in an unmarked police car. Youngish guy. Thin moustache. A constellation of sandy freckles scattered across his neck and face. The Cabrio's roof was down at the time and the car stank to high heaven of cannabis. Ominously, the policeman asked Portas to step out of the vehicle and, after making him put his hands on the back of his head, began to frisk him. As I watched the scene unfold from the front passenger seat, I thought that we were done for, that the four of us would end up in jail. In my mind I was already playing out the worst possible sequence of events: arrest, imprisonment, expulsion from the college, deportation to Gibraltar. But then, just as I thought that the handcuffs were about to come out, something extraordinary happened: the copper grinned, Portas put his hands down and they both walked a couple of paces away from the Cabrio. Smiles and nods, relaxed gestures, an increasingly affable exchange of remarks. Finally, the policeman returned to his grey Ford Escort and Portas strode back to the Citroën. Filled with relief, I asked my friend what had just gone down. 'It's no big deal,' Portas said, casually waving goodbye to his new mate. 'This guy Jim — that's the copper's name — asked me if I had smoked any drugs and I said I had only smoked a small joint. He then began to tell me, all formal and copper-like, that driving under the influence of drugs was a serious offence and that he was going to have to search me and quite possibly arrest me. As he rifled through my pockets, I noticed that the bunch of keys clipped to his belt had a small Norwich City key-ring attached to them. I thought, *aha, that's your Achilles' heel, old chap, is it?* So, *sin pensármelo*, as we say in Gib, I asked him if he thought Graham Paddon was staying at the club or going to

Watford like the fans are saying. Next thing I know we're there chatting about last year's league campaign and whether Ron Saunders was any good as a manager. We're having a proper debate, too — talking about Doug Livermore's sense of tactical awareness and Ken Foggo's lack of dribbling skills and all kinds of related things. Anyway, in the end Jim told me that, seeing that I had only smoked a small joint and that he hadn't found anything on me, he was going to be nice to me and let me off with a warning. "Just stop off somewhere and give the skunk a few hours to flush out of your system," he said. "Go for a walk or something," he said. "Do you good to park up and get some fresh air." Thank Christ he didn't look in the glove compartment and see the colossal fuck-off stash we've got in there, ha ha ha!'

The weeks passed and soon the second term was coming to an end. It seemed incredible to me that it had gone by so quickly, but I was only nineteen years old and I had no notion as yet of the fickleness of time — slowing down, as it does, when you are depressed, and speeding up, conversely, when, for once, things are going well. All I can say is that I didn't really want the term to end. Nor was I keen on returning to Gibraltar. What was there to go back to, after all — long solitary walks to Sandy Bay and endless Spanish *radionovelas?* So I decided to look for a part-time job that would give me the funds to stay in Cambridge for the Easter vacation. The post I eventually found was that of shelving assistant at Cambridge University Library. As the job title indicated, I had to go around the building with a trolley looking for books that hadn't been returned to their proper place and then restore them to their original shelves. It was neither the best paid work nor the most intellectually demanding, but it still covered my living expenses. Plus — rather handily — I could choose the number of hours I wanted to do each day. Moreover, there was something pleasing about pushing my trolley through the labyrinthine passages of the library in the quiet of the evening. Something strangely satisfying. I'm not sure how to explain it, but it was almost as if, surrounded by so many books, girded by all that knowledge and information, you felt cocooned from both your own personal problems and the harsh realities of everyday life, magically insulated from all mundane concerns. On the days when I didn't finish too late, Portas would sometimes be waiting for me outside the library in the Cabrio. Portas being Portas, he often had people in the car with him: a course mate one day, a Law professor of his the next, his next-door neighbour at Trumpington a week later, a couple of girls the day after that. As a lifelong loner, I couldn't help feeling both impressed and perplexed by all this. I even began to wonder if human beings could be divided into two fundamental types: those like me, who have to fight tooth and nail to form and sustain any sort of relationship; and those like Portas, who end up attracting people *even when they don't want to.*

After the Easter vacation, I quit my job at the library and returned to being a full-time student. Just before I left, the holdings supervisor told me I had done a good job and that she'd be happy to take me on again if I needed some work in the summer. In the meantime, the weeks passed and suddenly we were near the end of our first year and approaching the first part of our Tripos examinations. Portas, the eternal pessimist when it came to his studies, was convinced that he'd fail every single one of his exams, but didn't seem bothered by the prospect. ('See here, my dear Manrique, there are many benefits associated with failure — the finest among them being that it will really piss off grouchy old Moneybags back in Gib!') I wasn't feeling too confident either. My average essay grade throughout the last two terms had been III, well below the year average and the marks obtained by the other students in my weekly supervisions. I had also skipped so many lessons and lectures that I had already received two formal letters of warning from the college authorities. Fearing that I was about to fall flat on my face, I temporarily stopped seeing Portas and went on a last-minute cramming offensive. I started going to the library every morning and remaining there till late in the evening, head buried in books and constantly yawning, trying not to think too much about Portas and his Cabrio and his posse of girls as I struggled to master the indefinite and partitive articles in French and improve what one of my tutors had — half-jokingly, half-seriously — described as my 'excessively Hispaniolated' pronunciation in Italian. It was all very tough on the nerves and fatiguing. But in the end the cramming was worth it. Against all odds, I scraped through my orals and language papers (obtaining low 2:2s all round), and even managed to do well in my two semi-optional scheduled papers (which I chose to write, don't ask me why, on 'Paris and the Commune of 1871' and 'The History and Literary Representation of World War Two in Italy'). Meanwhile, I found out that Portas had also passed his exams — squeaking through with low IIIs in Civil Law, Criminal Law and the Law of Tort, but, quite unbelievably, obtaining the third-highest grade of his year in Constitutional Law. Perhaps, I told myself with pride, we Gibraltarians are not such slackers after all.

14.

The summer following our first-year exams was long and balmy and, in retrospect, probably the happiest period of my life. At the end of June, most students left Cambridge and were replaced by hordes of foreign tourists. I'd often see them on my way down to Bridge Street, masses and masses of Swedes, Americans and Japanese, all of them loitering outside Trinity and St John's with their bright baseball caps and their expensive Nikon and Canon cameras. Once more I was back at the library, this time doing between twenty and twenty-five hours a week. In theory, this increase in hours should have translated into a lot of work, but the library was so empty and quiet that there were hardly any books needing shelving. In point of fact, things were so dead that I'd often lock myself in the toilets and spend twenty minutes or even half an hour sitting back and relaxing. *Properly unwinding,* I liked to call it. In the afternoons, once I'd finish for the day, I'd meet Portas at the Baron of Beef, or else he would pick me up and drive us out to the Green Man, his local at Trumpington. I suppose we didn't really do much those evenings except drink and smoke and moan about the lack of female students in town, but it was nice enough all the same — sitting there with our pint glasses and our cigarettes, with none of the usual worries or distractions.

There is not much else to say about those summer months. Each week mirrored the week we had just left behind, each day felt like a replica of the preceding twenty-four hours. Under the agreeable glow of a North European sun, my life became anchored to a series of places and routines, constantly shifting as I did between the university library, the beer garden of the Green Man and the periods I'd spend faintly hungover in my bed every morning. Only one incident from this time is worth mentioning in any detail. One day, while we were boozing it up at the Green Man, Portas told me that his kid sister might be coming to visit him soon. He said this through pursed lips and with a disgusted expression, as if he had just detected an unpleasant odour in the air. Since he never mentioned the subject again over the next few days, I assumed that the visit must have been cancelled and that Portas would avoid seeing his obviously detested sibling. Imagine my surprise when, on leaving the library one evening a week or two later, I climbed into Portas's car and there she was sitting defiantly in the back of the Citroën. A short, scruffily dressed thirteen-year-old schoolgirl. Same nose and facial shape as Portas. Large phlegm-green eyes brimming with hostility. She was chewing gum and picking at a scab on the side of her neck. The only significant difference between the siblings was that the girl's hair was long and intensely black in colour, quite unlike my friend's tangled blond mop. 'This, my dear Manrique,' Portas said, amused by the look on my face, 'is Sophia, *mi queridísima amada hermana*.' A little discomfited by his sarcastic tone, I turned around and smiled warmly at his sister, but the miniature Portas replica glowered back at me, unimpressed by my diplomatic offering. Later, once we had dropped off the girl at his house and walked over to the Green Man, Portas explained that his sister had come down from her school in Leicester, where she had spent the last few weeks as a summer boarder. He said she had boarded there every summer for the last five years.

'I'm sorry she was so damned rude to you earlier,' he continued, taking a sip of his beer. 'She just can't help herself, I'm afraid. Most of the Portas family are like that. Have no idea whatsoever about social graces.'

'It's no problem,' I said.

'She's only here for one night, thank Christ,' he went on. 'My uncle James is picking her up tomorrow and driving her down to Heathrow. She's flying out to Boston to attend some sort of summer camp for girls. My mother's idea, by all accounts. Thinks that if Sophia socialises with other girls at one of these camps her temperament will somehow mellow out. Fat chance of that happening, but anyway, we've got to spend our mountains of Portas cash on something, haven't we?… You've got a kid sister, too, by the way, haven't you, Manny?'

'Yes, I have.'

He looked at me with his pint glass suspended under his mouth. 'And is she as problematic as our little lady Sophia?'

I shook my head with a smile. 'Nah, Mariela's a nice kid. Really straightforward. Never gives us any trouble.'

'Don't get me wrong,' Portas said, sounding surprisingly defensive. 'I do love my sister in my own way. She may have her faults, but at least she's not a schemer and a manipulator like the other members of my family. If anything, she's gone the other way: she wears her heart on her sleeve all the time and just can't conceal her feelings.'

'That's not a bad thing, surely?' I asked.

'Well, no — but she's got to be careful. You cannot afford to be so unguarded and emotional when you're going to come into a lot of money one day. I think she's the type who could be easily manipulated, who could be taken advantage of. Which reminds me: don't think I didn't notice the way you were giving her the eye before.'

'You what?'

'Sizing her up for when she grows a little bit older, were you, you disgusting filthy rat? Or do you perhaps have a thing for little girls?'

'Pero qué dices?'

'Either way, I would stay well clear, mate. Cos if you don't, *I'll break every single fucking bone in your fucking puny little body!'*

I assumed that Portas had to be joking, that he couldn't possibly believe that I was interested in his thirteen-year-old sister, but the look on his face was so sinister and threatening that … well, I just wasn't sure any more.

'You're kidding, Henry, aren't you? You are, *aren't you?* Please tell me you aren't being serious!'

Portas looked at me with the same malevolent expression for a few more seconds, then burst out laughing. 'Course I'm kidding, you silly oaf! What do you take me for? Some kind of overprotective psycho older brother? Come on, finish your pint. I'll get the next round in for having wound you up!'

Slowly the rest of the summer ebbed away and before we knew it we were reaching the end of August. Unlike the majority of returning students, I was not looking forward to the start of the new Michaelmas term. Not only would it spell the end of those carefree summer days, but, what was even more of a drag, I was also supposed to be going on my obligatory year abroad. This was not an enticing prospect. Moving away from Cambridge would mean dislocation, it would mean unnecessary disruption, it would mean having to begin all over again in a fundamentally alien place. Financially, too, it would stretch my meagre resources to the limit. I therefore approached the college authorities and naively asked if I could be exempted from doing my ten-month stint abroad on the grounds that I found it difficult to adapt to new places. I tried every tactic I could think of: that it had been difficult enough settling down in Cambridge; that I suffered from violent homesickness; that I came from Gibraltar, where people were not used to overseas travel. Unsurprisingly, the college deans were having none of it. The best they could offer me (and they made it clear that this was a big concession) was the possibility of doing ten whole months in Italy instead of spending five months in Italy and then five months in France like I was supposed to. Obviously, I'd have to attend extra classes in French while in Italy, I was told, but the university would help me arrange this. Furthermore, there were only three places where they'd allow me to do a ten-month stint of this nature: Venice, Trieste or Rome. At first I couldn't see the point of doing a ten-month placement instead of two five-month ones; both options seemed just as unpalatable to me. But after thinking of the turmoil that I had gone through when first coming to Cambridge, I changed my mind. Better to move once and get it all over and done with, I thought. Less hassle. I also decided that I'd find things less stressful in Trieste — not because I had any particular interest in the place, but because, being smaller and less well known than the other two, it was bound to be quieter and easier to settle in. However, I had not been counting on Portas's opposition to my plans. When he heard that I was intending to go to Trieste instead of Venice, he kicked up such a stink that I seriously thought he was going to sock me one on the jaw.

'Let me get this straight, Manny,' he said, almost knocking over his pint glass. 'You're telling me you've been given the opportunity to spend nearly a year in Venice and you want to go to Trieste instead? Man, wise up, will you? This is Venice we're talking about, the Queen of the Adriatic, the City of Bridges, *la gloriosa serenissima.* Anyway, what are you going to do in shitty old Trieste for ten whole months — wander through the corridors of Miramare Castle like poor old Maximilian's ghost? Yes, Joyce spent some time there in self-imposed exile and Italo Svevo tried to escape the drudgery of working for Generali by getting drunk and chasing after the local seamstresses and milliners — but that's about it! There's not even a decent beach there, for fuck's sake. It's just an old, decaying, bourgeois city that was once very important commercially, but now lies forgotten by the rest of the world. No, man, this is an opportunity you cannot afford to miss. You *have* to go to Venice. The place oozes atmosphere, it is the embodiment of everything great and noble in Western civilisation. Not to mention the fact that you'll be near two of the greatest paintings in the history of Western art!'

I looked at him as if he had sprouted a second head.

'Well, aren't you even going to ask me what these paintings are?'

'But I'm not an art lover, Henry,' I protested, taking a puff of my cigarette. 'You know that art and painting leave me cold.'

'But you *will* become an art lover once you get there,' Portas shouted. 'I give you my personal guarantee. How could you not, when you will be caught between Bellini's *Madonna Enthroned with Child and Saints* at San Zaccaria on the one side and Titian's *Assumption* at the Frari on the other? Even one of our bloody Rock apes would become an art lover if it spent some time in Venice!'

I picked up my pint glass and took a short sip. 'You're not convincing me, Henry,' I said.

'In any case, there are other reasons why you should go to Venice.'

'Such as?'

'Well, there's all those wonderful beaches on the Lido, for instance.'

'You already know I'm not keen on beaches, Henry.'

'And there's all that lovely Venetian food. *Bigoli, casunziei, sepe al nero* and the *cicchetti* from the little *bacaros*.'

I shook my head with a grimace. 'Mate, you know I'm the sort of bloke who lives off tinned ravioli and cold baked beans.'

'Anyway, there's one last reason why you should do your ten-month stint abroad in Venice.'

'Yeah, what's that?'

'Well, what do you think?'

'Go on, surprise me.'

'If you go to Venice, I will come and visit you once a month.'

'You what?'

'You heard. If you go to Venice, I'll come and visit you once a month.'

15.

I arrived in Venice on the twenty-eighth of September 1972. It was very hot and muggy, one of those stifling, windless afternoons when most of the Venetian Lagoon lies wreathed in a bluish-grey fog. It had not been the easiest of journeys getting there. First of all, I had to board a National Express coach which stopped at every Godforsaken little dump across Hertfordshire and Greater London and took five hours to reach Heathrow. Then I had to catch two back-to-back flights: first to Brussels with British Caledonian and then on to Roma Fiumicino with Alitalia. Emerging from the customs area at Fiumicino with my rucksack and two small PVC suitcases, I paused to ask for directions and then crossed the road to the adjacent railway station. There I caught a train to Roma Termini, where I spent five and a half sleepless hours propped up against a hoarding for Nazionali cigarettes. Pigeons continually approached me looking for food.

Vagrants and pickpockets eyed up my battered plastic suitcases. When the train for Venice Santa Lucia finally opened its doors just before seven in the morning, I loaded my stuff into one of the second-class carriages and then, once safely tucked away from the assorted cutpurses and *delinquenti* who prowl Termini at night, promptly fell asleep. When I eventually woke up, it was half past twelve and we were leaving the town of Ferrara, approximately eighty miles south of Venice. Bleary-eyed and disorientated, struggling to dislodge some phlegm from the back of my throat, I looked through the carriage window and saw the red-bricked turrets and rooftops of Ferrara looming over the walls of its train station. Yawning, still more asleep than awake, I sat up and groped for the cheap Halina in my rucksack — but by the time I had retrieved the camera, the old buildings had been replaced by a bunch of tower blocks 'decorated' with washing lines and TV antennae. *Mierda puta!* A good photo opportunity missed! For the next hour and a half I sat upright on my seat with a book about Venice that Portas had given to me as a present in Cambridge a few days earlier. I could not make much sense of what I was reading — it was far too philosophical and poetic for a mere languages student like me — but it had a pleasing cadence all the same:

> *So the Venetians settled into island life, and there they've remained – still distinct, still carrying the quiet melancholy of those who once fled their homeland.*

A short while later, we reached Mestre, Venice's ugly sister on the western side of the Venetian Lagoon. As we crossed the thin brick causeway linking one city to the other, I could make out the smudgy, half-formed silhouettes of domes and bell towers in the distance. So this is Venice, I thought to myself, bringing out my camera once again and this time managing a few shots.

Despite this atmospheric beginning, I can't say that I really enjoyed my stay in *la serenissima*. For a start, I found the Venetians too cautious and reactionary, too obsessed with things like good manners and family trees and antique furniture and other vaguely right-wing stuff. My *ostello dell'allievo* was located in the *sestiere* of Santa Croce, not far from Santa Lucia Railway Station itself. Housed in a former Benedictine monastery, it had large, high-ceilinged rooms with double-shuttered windows through which one could see the scummy green waters of the Canal of Santa Chiara and hear the unceasing din of buses and scooters coming from Piazzale Roma, the vast, characterless square attached to the Ponte della Libertà causeway. About 75 per cent of the hostel's 220 residents were Italians who weren't native to Venice, with the remaining 25 per cent divided between Germans, French, Brits and Scandinavians. With such huge numbers of *Italiani* around, you would have thought that the place would be dominated by our good hosts, wouldn't you? But in fact the Italian students, some of them coming from no further than Mestre and Treviso on the other side of the Venetian Lagoon, were always scooting off home whenever they had a chance, leaving the hostel more or less in the hands of the international visitors. Not that you could blame our Italian neighbours for such behaviour. Since the *ostello* was not affiliated with any one local educational institution but had instead developed tentacle-like connections to every language school and college of higher education in the city, it attracted the most varied collection of foreign residents, from PhD candidates studying Tintoretto's Madonna dell'Orto paintings to fifteen-year-old 'summer schoolers' whose Italian vocabulary was limited to words like '*gelato*' and '*cornuto*', all of them living cheek by jowl in a building that, to make matters even more surreal, had a working chapel dedicated to the Virgin Mary in its basement. Yes, they were a curious bunch all right, those foreign students. You had bespectacled social scientists from Hannover and long-haired linguists from Uppsala. Short-haired lesbian architects from Essex and beret-wearing but chronically shy art historians from Paris. Noisy foul-mouthed teenagers from Brighton and studious pipe-smoking types from Bremen. Every morning they'd all walk through the *ostello's* arched medieval doorway and disperse to different points across the city — some to the San Sebastiano Campus on the Dorsaduro, others to the Faculty of Economics and Business Management at Cannaregio, others to the *Istituto Venezia* Language School near the Ponte di Rialto. In the evenings they'd all return to the hostel and hang around in the massive lounge on the ground floor, smoking imported cigarettes or playing Paul Simon and Bobby Vinton LPs on the communal record player. Once or twice — for by this stage I was not as anti-social as I had been when I first arrived at Cambridge — I did go out with some of the Germans to *Filovia*, a shabby little bar just around the corner from the *ostello* in Piazzale Roma. But I never really enjoyed these outings. All that the Germans seemed to do was sit there with a single bottle of Valpolicella between them, bitterly complaining about the dirty streets or the smell of the canals or the mounds of uncollected refuse or whatever else was not as good or as clean as in Germany. Not this Gibraltarian student's cup of tea, I'm afraid!

Several weeks passed without much happening. The Germans kept moaning about the foul smells, the *Istituto* teenagers continued getting drunk at night and running down corridors, and the Italians, the cleverest of us all by far, carried on performing their regular weekend disappearing acts. Depressed by the monotony of it all, I sought solace in solitude and went for long walks around the city. Usually, I'd start by heading up towards Cannaregio, where I'd spend some time exploring the crumbling alleyways of the Jewish ghetto, before zigzagging through the shadowy streets of Castello to the old Arsenale, at which point I'd turn around and head in a south-westerly direction, past the tourist-stuffed environs of Saint Mark's and the Doge's palace, until I crossed the wooden Accademia Bridge into the *sestiere* of Dorsoduro, from where I'd reluctantly trudge back into Santa Croce — a journey of about ten kilometres, or just under two hours. Sometimes, when I felt in need of a little pampering, I'd catch the vaporetto at Piazzale Roma and travel down the Grand Canal to the islet of Giudecca, where I'd treat myself to a dish of *sepe al nero* (cuttlefish cooked in its own ink) at a small tavern called *Ai Cacciatori.* I admit it: I didn't mind Giudecca. If you got off the vaporetto at Zitelle instead of at Redentore (which was always busy with tourists), you could make your way down the Via Michelangelo until you reached a rickety wooden pier on the southern side of the islet. Here you could sit for hours and hours in total isolation — watching the murky but always restless waters of the lagoon, listening to the gentle sounds of the sea lapping against the oaken mooring poles, swiftly forgetting you were only a mile and a half from one of the noisiest, most densely crowded squares on earth.

November brought a rapid decline in temperature, but I still carried on strolling through the Venetian backstreets. I was aware that I was striding past famous and historical buildings, but I confess that I never showed much interest in them. Occasionally, whenever my feet hurt from going up and down bridges, I'd enter a church and sit there for a few minutes, my senses temporarily numbed by the smell of incense and freshly cut flowers, wondering how Venice could maintain so many churches when almost no one prayed in them — but that was as much as I ever thought about the buildings around me. Once, on learning that my lessons had been cancelled because of a last-minute university lecturers' strike, I caught the train and went to Trieste for the day. To my surprise, it was really nice there. Like Venice, Trieste had a melancholic air, but the melancholy there was quiet and understated, very different to the loudly trumpeted, almost theatrical love of decay that stirs in the breasts of the good *Venezianos*. I especially liked the city's tranquil back alleys, its impressive but hardly visited castle, the fact that you could walk around for hours and hours and — miracle of miracles! — never bump into any backpackers. Inevitably, those half-deserted streets made me think about Portas, who had persuaded me to forget about Trieste and travel instead to Venice, and the life I had left behind at Cambridge. Despite his promises to come and visit me every month, the bastard had never kept in touch. In fact, I had written several times to his address at Trumpington and never received any answer to my letters. What a strange guy, I thought to myself as I walked past Trieste's old town hall. What an enigma. He persuades me to come to Venice on the pretext that he'd like to visit me and then he cuts me out of his life as if I never existed. And yet, if I am to be completely honest, it's not as if I expected anything less. Unreliability and the capacity to confound were not just minor, occasionally surfacing strands of Portas's persona; they were a dominant part of his being.

Then one day in February 1973 I received a real surprise. Returning to the *ostello* from my afternoon lessons at San Sebastiano, I found Portas sitting on one of the tattered leather sofas in the hostel lobby. He was smoking a cigarette and scratching his nose, one leg crossed over the other. A pallid girl in a black leather jacket and lacy dress was seated beside him. At first I wasn't sure if there was any relation between them, but when Portas got up and the girl followed suit I realised they must have travelled together.

'Hello, Manny,' Portas cried, moving towards me and crushing me in a bear hug. 'Bet you never expected to see me here like this, did you, *compadre?*... Come and meet my friend Victoria, *anda*. She's been dying to meet you, our Vicky lass has.'

'Our Vicky lass', however, couldn't have been less interested in talking to me. Mumbling some words which I couldn't make out, she stood there gazing at me with a half-smoked fag in her mouth and a look of disgust on her face — and only took my extended hand when Portas, finally losing patience with her, nudged her in the ribs and told her to 'get on with it.' After this bizarre turn of events, I ushered them out of the lobby and led them upstairs to my room on the third floor. As we laboured with their cases up the *ostello's* steeply inclined stone steps, I asked Portas how long they were planning on staying in Venice and he said no more than two or three days — 'that is,' he added with a laugh, 'if you don't kick us out of your place earlier.' Patting him warmly on the back, I said they were both welcome to stay with me as long as they liked.

Once at the room, I moved my sofa into the en-suite bathroom and told Portas I'd sleep there while he and Victoria borrowed my queen-sized bed. This operation accomplished, I put the kettle on and Portas began explaining what had made them come to see me. It had been 'a totally spontaneous decision,' he said. One Saturday afternoon the pair had been boozing back at the Green Man in Trumpington when Bert Foord appeared on the pub's telly, all deadpan and respectable as always, saying that it was going to be grey and miserable over the next few days. 'Hey, baby,' Portas supposedly piped out to Victoria, who according to him was half-Italian, 'I know this guy down in Venice. Why don't we go there for a couple of days and you can blow my socks off with the sheer sexiness of your spoken Italian!' Next thing they knew, he said, they were both sitting on an Alitalia plane sipping grappa and heading for 'sunny southern climes!' As he spoke, Victoria stood against the wall radiator, with her hands clasped behind her back and her knees turned towards each other. She was staring at the travertine marble floor tiles. She had the vacant look of a drug addict, I thought, or at least someone who was heavily stoned, her pink, fleshy, slightly swollen upper eyelids veiling most of her eyes. She was not completely unattractive — indeed, when at one point she raised her eyes from the floor and turned towards the window, she reminded me of a sickly Audrey Hepburn — but make no mistake: she was by no means the type of knockout blonde that Portas normally plumped for. I couldn't help wondering where the pair had first met.

At half past six, we went out. I wanted to catch a vaporetto at Piazzale Roma and take them to my hidey-hole in Giudecca, but Victoria, who seemed to have come to life under the cold February sun, insisted on going to a bar and having a drink first. As a result, we ended up in *Filovia*, the shabby little bar frequented by taxi drivers and tour bus conductors which stood just around the corner from the *ostello*. Here we ordered seven (yes, seven!) bottles of Chianti, which Portas and Victoria wasted no time in knocking back while indulging in the most hysterical laughter. To make matters worse, the pair constantly kissed and pawed at each other, causing even the easy-going Italian punters to grimace and pull disapproving faces. My discomfort was great — so great that, even though I must have polished off two of the bottles myself, I was stone cold sober and could not think about anything except how long it would take one of the Italians to say something to us and Portas to tell him *to go fuck himself.* Thankfully, at around half past eight, Victoria hiccupped and pushed aside her tenth or eleventh glass of wine. 'God, I'm Hank Marvin, Portie,' she slurred. 'That dago red don't half make you peckish!' Right on cue I told Portas there was a smashing *trattoria* down the road which served top-notch Venetian food. This was not strictly true — the 'smashing *trattoria*' was just a small kiosk run by a permanently surly Libyan on the other side of the square — but it was all I could think of to make them get up and leave the bar.

Outside the usually gridlocked *piazzale* was quiet and a light drizzle was falling. A few lamp posts had already been switched on and squiggles of reflected light were dancing tremulously on the damp tarmac. Crossing thc square at a brisk pace, we reached the kiosk and ordered three portions of *fritto misto di mare.* While we waited for the food, Victoria flirted with the white-hatted Libyan, asking him what his name was and where he originally came from. I looked at Portas to gauge his reaction, but he was just staring at Victoria's scrawny denim-clad buttocks with an imbecilic smile on his face, as if in some kind of trance. Once the man handed over the food parcels, we zigzagged our way back to the *ostello,* trying to seek refuge in different doorways from the rain, which by now was pelting down. We also munched through our newspaper-wrapped *fritti* — a distinctly unmemorable experience. I had been planning on offering them a cuppa once back at the residence, but as we ascended the *ostello's* staircase Portas and Victoria became so disgustingly amorous that, when we reached the room, I merely wished them good night and retired to the bathroom, hoping to erase the pair from my thoughts. What a vain hope, alas, that turned out to be! Although I managed (possibly due to the influence of all that Chianti!) to doze off within minutes, I was soon woken up by an infernal racket which sounded like the musical accompaniment to an Amazonian rain dance, but which was the noise produced by the combination of Victoria's grunting and the bed's headboard banging against the wall. The shameless pigs, I thought. Screwing on my bloody bed! Astonished by their audacity, I put one of the sofa cushions over my head to block out the sounds of their drunken fornication, but it was no use: I could still hear the bastards. Finally, after about an hour, the racket subsided and everything went quiet again. For a while I turned and twisted on the sofa, trying hard to make myself comfortable. Then I closed my eyes and somehow managed to fall asleep. However, even then there was no reprieve. For around a quarter past two the bathroom door creaked open and in strode a barefoot and tousle-haired Victoria, saying that she had to use the loo. She looked even more emaciated than usual and her face had acquired a cadaverously green pallor under the bright bathroom lights. When I stood up to leave the room, she gazed at me drowsily for a few seconds, then shook her head and staggered zombie-like to the toilet. 'Relax, matey,' she said, hitching up her nightie and sitting down. 'I'm only going for a wazz, not a shit.'

16.

I wish I could tell you that things calmed down after that first night, but sadly they didn't. As soon as we got up the next morning, it was back to the same shenanigans — with more drinking, more pawing at each other, more staggering around, and, worst of all, more loud fornication in the evenings. Coping with all this was not easy. With every hour that went by, I felt more and more fed up and irritated with their company; more and more tempted to tell them *to fuck off and leave me alone.* In the meantime, Portas and Victoria continued their drunken rampage through the streets of Santa Croce — arguing with a security guard outside the Church of San Giacomo dell'Orio, picking a fight with a waiter who overcharged them for a plate of artichokes and Parma ham, mooning some kids who heckled them for leaving an empty wine bottle on top of a postbox and (what was almost funny, I have to admit) nearly falling together into a canal when they asked me to take a photograph of them balanced on a stone bollard. One particularly irritating episode occurred as we were leaving *Il Cantinone Gia' Schiavi*, a *bacaro* near the Accademia Bridge on the Dorsoduro. As we trooped out of the bar's cramped entrance, Portas turned around and, rubbing his head like he had forgotten something, said he needed to go back inside to use the bathroom. Victoria pulled a face, saying there had to be something wrong with his bladder. 'You keep on doing this,' she sniggered. 'You really are the King of the last-minute wazz, aren't you?' 'That's me!' Portas replied with a smile, walking into the bar. 'The Emperor of the impulsive wee-wee!' While we waited for him on the narrow *fondamenta*, Victoria first of all made a clucking sound with her tongue and then sat down on the low stone wall opposite the *bacaro's* entrance. She began to scratch her wrist, her skin reddening and erupting into little lumps. She looked thoughtful and abstracted, detached from her surroundings. Suddenly she stopped what she was doing and turned towards me:

'Is it true you come from some shitty council estate?'

'Excuse me?'

'I've heard you come from this horrible skanky council estate full of peasants who can hardly speak English.'

'Is that what Portas has been telling you?' I asked.

'No, matey, I read it in *Il Gazzettino*, didn't I?'

I looked at her for a moment in silence, scarcely believing what I was hearing. 'There are no council estates in Gibraltar,' I finally mumbled in the calmest voice I could muster. 'And everybody speaks perfectly good English.'

'Yeah, I'm sure. Anyway, how you doing in *dees* place? You bagged yourself any bitches yet?'

'You what?'

'You banged any gongs, matey? Portie says he don't think you have, but *mi mama è de Orvieto* and I know what these Italian floozies are like.'

'I don't think that's any of your business,' I said, the colour rising in my cheeks.

'He's right, isn't he?!' Victoria screeched. 'He's fucking right! Don't worry, matey. I know things can't be easy for a weird little bloke like you.'

I crossed my arms and looked down at the ground. 'I don't know what you're on about, Victoria.'

'*You*, matey,' she bawled, 'that's what I'm on about! *You!* Portie says you were like a babe in swaddling clothes when he first met you. One of life's innocents — that's how he described you.'

I looked at her eyes and saw that they were glistening with malice.

'He says you were as shy as a baby squirrel and that you'd have never lost your cherry without his help. Is it true, matey? Were you as fucking useless and pathetic as all that?'

'Well … it's a complicated matter, isn't it?' I said rather idiotically.

'Oh, is it now? Ha ha ha. I see it another way, matey. A matter of simple hydraulics. That's what it's all about. Attraction and repulsion. Insertion and ejection. Inclusion and expulsion. A model of simple uncomplicated gravitational motion…. What do you think, darling Portie-Bortie?' she laughed, turning around to face the re-emerging Portas. 'Are we talking *grande passione,* or simple hydraulics here?'

'Oh, hydraulics,' he said, bringing her close to him and kissing her on the mouth. 'Definitely hydraulics.'

She did not talk to me any more after that, but her indifference towards me now carried an element of unspoken hostility, an undertow of resentment. I wondered whether she was jealous that Portas and I had been good friends in the past, or whether there was some other reason for her enmity. I was also deeply puzzled by what she had said about Laguna Estate. Had Portas really told her such spiteful things about my hometown neighbourhood? Or had she pounced on an unthinking remark of his and viciously twisted it out of all recognition? At last, after seventy-two hours of dealing with their eccentricities, the blessed hour arrived: it was time for them to go. Racked with anxiety, I accompanied the pair to Piazzale Roma to help them flag down a taxi. It was an unseasonably warm evening and the square was filled with buses and lines of queuing Mestre-based commuters. Street vendors wove their way through the chaos, hawking cigarettes and sweets. Diesel fumes thickened even further the already acrid Venetian air. After a few unsuccessful attempts, I managed to locate a vacant taxi and Portas and Victoria climbed into it, laughing and pulling faces at each other like a pair of unruly children. I watched them from a traffic island, my heart beating frantically in my chest. 'Goodbye, Manny, you boring old sod!' Portas shouted through the car window seconds later. 'Hope you finally get some Venetian pussy!' 'Too right!' Victoria hollered beside him. 'Get busy and get humping, mate!' As the vehicle sped out of the square, I felt such a huge surge of relief that I had to lean against a lamp post to steady myself.

However, as soon as they had gone, my relief gave way to a torrent of anger. Yes, I was livid. I was bloody furious. Peculiarly, what made me so angry was not so much what had happened over the last couple of days, but the fact that for months I had been *so eager* for Portas to come and visit me. *God almighty, Brian, you are such a patsy sometimes!* Seething with self-hatred, I left Piazzale Roma and headed down to the Canal of Santa Chiara. As I expected, it was very quiet there — with no one to be seen except for a lone postman far away in the distance. A thin mist had settled over the dirty lime-green waters of the canal and a couple of seagulls rested on a metal lifebuoy housing. A solitary rat was swimming close to the opposite bank, its soggy arrow-shaped head just poking out of the water. Eventually, after walking for about two hundred yards, I came to a small bridge with a pair of gondolas tied beside it. Someone had left a few bags of rubbish at the foot of the bridge, together with some kind of rusting electrical generator. Monstrous old thing. Probably dating back to before the war. Without thinking, I picked up the generator and hurled it against one of the moored gondolas, damaging the top of its *fèrro*. For a second or two I remained standing there, breathing hard through my mouth, my vision dimmed by the tears gathering in my eyes. Then, glancing from side to side to check that no one had witnessed my actions, I turned around and scuttled away from the scene of the crime.

For the next couple of days I was in a devil of a mood. I ate little. I did not attend my lessons. I stopped going on my long walks. Hanging over everything like a black cloud was the memory of Portas's visit and the mindless act of vandalism I had committed after his departure. Why had he come to Venice with that moody sot? And what had possessed me when I threw the generator against the gondola? I know that this may sound a tad unreasonable, seeing that he had not even been there when I picked up and hurled the damn thing, but I blamed Portas for what had happened that day down by the canal. Blamed him and also hated him for having pushed me to what in effect was my first ever criminal act. At length, after a period of agonised deliberation, I came to a decision: I would have to cut Henry Portas out of my life. There was no other alternative. As much as I had once enjoyed his company, he had let me down badly and that was something that couldn't be tolerated. So, clenching my fists, telling myself that from that moment onwards I would have nothing more to do with him, I dismissed the guy from my thoughts and slowly went back to my old routine.

Meanwhile, time passed. Spring arrived and Venice was once again crawling with tourists. To escape the crowds, I often went to the pier on the other side of Giudecca, where I'd spend hours staring at the gently rising and falling sea. I also began to travel by vaporetto to the Lido, the famous barrier island in the Venetian Lagoon. Decent public beaches on the Lido were few and far between, but I found a relatively peaceful stretch of coast at the southern end of the islet, a twenty-minute walk from the Santa Maria Elisabetta vaporetto stop. The name of this beach was *La spiaggia degli Alberoni* and most afternoons I'd be there with my language books and my transistor radio, immensely glad that in Italy they have the good sense to finish lessons early during the warmer months. One afternoon there was an American girl sunbathing next to me. Her name was Lucy and she was studying Art and Architecture. Sun-bleached blonde hair. Healthy brown Texan tan. An interest in Sylvia Plath that seemed (in my mind at least) strangely at odds with her Houston drawl. She had been in Venice for the last two months, she said, and was flying back to the States at the end of that same week. I wouldn't go as far as describing our coming together over the next few days as a holiday romance, but it was pleasing nonetheless and I did feel a little sad when she eventually went home. Then, with only a couple of weeks left before I was due to leave Venice, something unexpected happened. Something unnerving and weirdly gratifying. On returning to the *ostello* after a drowsy afternoon at the Lido, I found Henry Portas standing by the door to my room.

'Hello, Manny,' he said, taking out a wrapped bundle from his rucksack. 'I thought you might like some Trinity Burnt Cream?'

I unlocked the door and invited him inside. I could feel my heart racing in my chest and my body stiffening with rage. 'The arrogant tosser,' I thought, unfastening the window shutters. 'How dare he present himself back here with a bag of cakes?' And yet — paradoxically, exasperatingly, for God knows what reason — I cannot deny that a part of me was pleased to see him there.

'So how did you get here this time?'

'I caught a flight down to Paris and then I bought a ticket for the Orient Express.'

'You caught the bloody Orient Express?' I asked, moving back to the centre of the room.

He smiled and shifted to where I had just been standing. Placing the wrapped bundle on the projecting brick sill, he looked out of the window and in a sad voice said:

'That girl was something else, you know. Really something else.'

'You mean Victoria?'

'She's the daughter of an Earl, you know.'

'You're kidding me?'

'Lady Victoria Allegra Malmstead Clements, youngest daughter of the Earl and Countess of Rochetown and Blandbury.'

'But she seemed like such a-'

'A fucking nutcase? That's probably why we got on so well, my dear Manny. Actually, Victoria and I had a lot in common with each other. Overbearing fathers, lonely childhoods, all sorts of mindless, fucked-up expectations thrust upon us…. Anyway, it's all over now. We decided to split up. Things would have never worked out between us. We were too similar. Too self-destructive for our own good. Better to recognise as much while you can and move on, don't you think, *amigo mío?'* he said, walking away from the window with a weak smile.

17.

The long weekend that followed was one of the strangest I ever spent in Portas's company. Acting like he wanted to atone for the excesses of his last visit, my friend was quiet and mild-mannered and insisted that we spend our time visiting churches and museums. Tramping around cities looking at old buildings has never been my idea of fun, but doing so with Henry Portas wasn't so bad. Firstly, it was refreshing to see the guy without a beer or a glass of wine in his hand. Secondly, I enjoyed discovering what lay behind some of the buildings I had walked past every morning without batting an eyelid. Take the Calle Tintoretto Cannaregio, for example, one of the roads I followed every day to get from Santa Croce to the university campus in Dorsoduro. A large (by Venetian standards, anyway) thoroughfare lined with seedy little cafés and crumbling scaffolded palazzos, it had seemed to me just like any other street in the city. True, there was always a line of people queuing outside one of the three, virtually identical *palazzos* in the widest part of the road. But so what? If there was one thing you saw *everywhere* in Venice, it was people queuing for something or the other. Thanks to Portas, though, I found out that behind that particular palace's walls lay no less than twenty-two paintings by the Venetian master Tintoretto, including his sprawling, six-yard-long *Crucifixion*, one of the most influential depictions of Christ's death ever painted, according to my learned guide. Even so, the greatest shock that weekend came when we entered the Basilica di Santa Maria Gloriosa dei Frari, just around the corner from the Scuola di San Rocco. I had often sauntered past this church during the last few months, but never paid any attention to it. To a cultural ignoramus like me it was just a big lump of a building — quite uninteresting, really, when set beside the flashy Baroque jewels in the immediate neighbourhood. And in fact, when we first walked through the basilica's ageing oaken doors, I was very surprised that Portas had been so keen on coming here — so empty and barren did this church seem compared to the marbled interior of Santa Maria dei Miraculi and some of the other places we had visited earlier that day. But when I strolled halfway down the nave and looked through the carved wooden doors leading into the choir, I almost couldn't believe my eyes. 'Wow,' I gasped, turning to face a grinning Portas. 'That's some painting, that is!'

'That, my friend,' said Portas, still grinning, 'is Titian's *Assumption of the Virgin*, the largest altarpiece in the city and, according to Oscar Wilde, the most beautiful picture of the sixteenth century.'

I looked at Portas for a moment and then focused again on the altarpiece.

'It was painted in 1516,' Portas continued in a reverential whisper, 'when Titian was just twenty-six years old. It was his first major commission in the city and the painting which established him as Venice's foremost artist.'

'Why am I not surprised by that?'

'There's only one other painting in the city, in my opinion, which can compete with it,' Portas said under his breath, 'and that's Giovanni Bellini's *Madonna Enthroned with Child and Saints* at San Zaccaria, close to the Arsenale. Another great, great painting, that Bellini. I like to think of the Bellini and the Titian as two gigantic dynamos, radiating waves of invisible but pulsating energy. I know that this is a bit bonkers, but there've been times when I've felt the Titian's presence all the way from the other side of the Grand Canal. Kind of like this fine static in the air. An ultra-faint humming. Calling me towards it, whispering my name, drawing me in. What do you think of it? Does it get the Manrique seal of approval or not?'

I stroked my chin for a few seconds and tried to put my thoughts into words. 'Well, it's the red, isn't it?'

'The red?'

'Yeah, that red.'

'What do you mean, old boy?'

'The red on the Virgin's tunic. It's so intense, so eye-catching, so overpowering. It sort of arrests your attention the moment you enter through the choir doors, doesn't it? Grabs you by the throat and doesn't let go. That's what makes it such a brilliant painting, I think.'

Portas turned towards me with a beaming smile. '*No ves*, Manny, old chap,' he said, patting me on the back. 'I told you you were an art lover deep down, didn't I?'

18.

Portas returned to the UK two days later. I stayed behind in Venice for the last two weeks of the academic year and then flew via London to Gibraltar, where I spent five boring and rather sweaty weeks in my mother's Laguna flat during the height of summer. At last, on the thirteenth of August, I arrived in Cambridge again. It was early in the afternoon when I reached the city and — predictably enough — it was raining. A heavy grey mist had drifted in from the Fens, reducing both modern and ancient buildings to an impressionistic blur. Pedestrians shuffled hurriedly down Northampton Street, their features hidden by large black umbrellas. After a few days, I found a vacancy at the library (this time inspecting new books and transcribing their details into the card catalogue) and gradually settled back into my old routine. As in the previous summer, I saw Portas regularly and we'd spend whole afternoons sitting in the Green Man, slowly getting drunk and bemoaning the lack of female 'talent' in the half-empty city. The weather was typically English in its variability: rain one moment, sun the next, then back to rain a couple of hours later. The only constant among all this changeability was Portas's old cricket jumper, which (it gratified me to see) he still wore every day — even if its cuffs were now disfigured by tangles of unravelling yarn. On two occasions we drove out of Cambridge in his Citroën

— the first time to a church in Cheadle, near Stoke-on-Trent, which Portas said was the finest religious building in England, and the second to some eerie memorial chapel in Berkshire covered in First World War paintings. At times I thought Portas seemed calmer and more subdued than he had been the previous summer, but then he'd suddenly do something crazy like climb onto the roof of his house, or drive his car down a one-way street, and I'd be left to wonder how such an idea had crept into my head in the first place. Meanwhile, the new Michaelmas term arrived and Portas and I found ourselves starting our final and penultimate years at Cambridge respectively. It was strange to think that in less than nine months Henry would be leaving university with his Law degree certificate, but as I had already discovered time moves exceedingly fast when you're a student. It's just one of those things. You think you have all the time in the world before you need to worry about jobs and other grown-up stuff and then, bang, you are striding into the exam hall for your finals with a mild feeling of sickness in your stomach. *An almighty sleight of hand*: that's the best way to describe it.

But enough of these pseudo-philosophical speculations. For the first two terms it was very much business as usual, my life as a student once again transformed into an endless round of pubs, girls, cigarettes and constant parties at Portas's house in Trumpington, with a few hours of part-time work and catch-up study squeezed in here and there. If I had to pick a highlight, it was probably watching Portas climb the colonnaded facade of the Fitzwilliam Museum on a whim late one Saturday evening. (Good job I was drunk out of my head at the time, as otherwise I wouldn't have dared to watch!) Or maybe seeing him turn up one afternoon at Fitzroy with some vaguely famous BBC children's TV presenter. (I cannot remember her name; all I recall is that she was buxom, witty and wore red leather stilettos, with a line of pink crystals glued onto her heels.) When I think about those first couple of terms during my third year at university, I am invariably faced with a set of hazy, unrelated, cannabis-infused, alcohol-drenched impressions that cannot be arranged into any sequential order. Everything feels blurred and distorted, weirdly out of shape. The only incident that I remember with absolute clarity, in fact, the only thing that I am able to mentally relive as if it happened yesterday, was the night in early April when, seated at our usual table at the Baron of Beef, Portas lowered his pint glass and, calmly, almost in an undertone, said that he was going to take things easy for a while so that he could prepare for his final exams.

'So you're really going to buckle down and study?' I asked, finding it hard to believe that Portas, the legendary Portas, the craziest, most carefree, happy-go-lucky devil in all of Cambridge, had come up with such a sensible statement.

'Yup,' Portas grinned. 'I know it's hard to believe, Manny, but I've decided that it's better to come out of this place with a degree that will help me get a job and make me financially self-sufficient than to flunk my exams and be forever beholden to the old ogre and the rest of the Portas clan.'

'Wow,' I said, absently reaching across the table for some dry roasted peanuts. 'I don't know what to say. I never thought I'd hear you say something like that.'

From then on, I saw Portas once or twice a week and never for more than twenty minutes to half an hour. Ashen-faced and frowning, carrying a large blue folder stuffed with handwritten notes and held together by an elastic band, he'd down two or three beers in quick succession, then get up and say that he had to be going, promising to 'make it up to me' once the exams were over. I don't know if this will make any sense, but the Portas I saw during those weeks was the least 'Portas-like' of all the different Portases I had encountered over the last two and a half years. It's hard for me to describe what I mean by this, but it almost felt as if the person who came into the Baron for those speedy pints of Watneys was no more than a hologram, a mere photostat of the character I had once known. Then, with only a couple of weeks left to his first exams, Portas stopped coming out altogether. He simply vanished from sight. For a while I assumed that he was cloistered at home with his books, cramming up on Jurisprudence and Tort and Family Law and all those other subjects he hated so much. Part of me wanted to ring him up, to check on him and ask him if he was okay — but at the same time I felt reluctant to drag him out of the isolation he obviously needed to prepare for his finals. So in the end I just let him be. Told myself that larger-than-life characters like him needed their space before their exams. All the same, once the examinations finished in late May and there was still no sign of him anywhere, I could no longer carry on being so blasé. Something's not right, I thought. This is not normal Portas behaviour. Hesitantly, weighed down by all sorts of apprehensions, I plonked a baseball cap on my head and walked from Fitzroy to his house in Trumpington, where I found an empty drive and a 'For Sale' sign planted in the front lawn. Peering through one of the bay windows, I saw that the living room had been emptied of its contents. Puzzled and worried, fearing that something terrible might have happened, I went round to the neighbour's and asked her if she knew anything about Portas's disappearance. 'Well, young man,' the neighbour, a slender, grey-haired lady, said, 'I'm afraid I know just as little as you. One day Henry was saying "Good morning to you, Jill" in his polite and cheerful manner; the next the removals men had moved in and there was not a sign of him anywhere. That must have been around two, three weeks ago, I'd say. Something must have been really bothering the poor lad, for him to have left without even saying goodbye.'

That same afternoon I went to the Faculty of Law on Mill Lane and asked them if they could tell me whether Henry Portas had completed his final exams. As I had half-anticipated, they told me that they could not divulge this information as they were bound by faculty regulations to respect the privacy of their students. I replied that Portas was a childhood friend and that I was worried about him because I hadn't seen him for a while. 'I'm sorry,' the old guy standing behind the counter responded, 'but the rules are there for a reason.' Irked, I was about to march out in a huff when who should come through the revolving glass doors but a weedy, long-haired guy called Jez whom I knew to be one of Portas's classmates and who had once or twice attended some of my friend's parties. Breathlessly, I pounced on him and asked him if he knew anything about Portas's whereabouts. 'What — you haven't heard?' he sneered. 'The crazy cat didn't turn up for his finals. Flew back home at the last minute. Family trouble, apparently. Something to do with his father. Not sure about the ins and outs, but they say it was serious stuff. You know what these temperamental Latin types are like — always quarrelling and fighting with each other. All I can tell you is that that cat will live to regret it some day. Bunking out of Cambridge at the last minute! Some people are born with a penchant for self-sabotage!'

I thanked Jez for the update and went back to my room at Fitzroy. I was feeling pretty demoralised and I couldn't stop thinking about Portas and his decision to bail out at the eleventh hour. What had made him do such a reckless thing? Had exam stress got to him? Was this his way of spiting his father? Or was there some other reason for it that I did not know about? Determined to find out, I rang my mother that night from the payphone on the second floor and asked her to fetch me the address for Portas and Sons from the Gibraltar Telephone Directory. Afterwards I sat down at my desk and wrote a long letter to Portas, asking him if he was okay and whether he was planning on returning to Cambridge to repeat his final year. I told him that my own exams hadn't gone well and that my French oral, in particular, had been an absolute nightmare. I also assured him that I'd always be ready to help him in any way that I could. Then I put the letter in an envelope, sealed it and took it to the post office on Huntingdon Road.

19.

But Henry Portas never received my letter — or, if he did, he never bothered replying to it. In the meantime, I heard that I had scraped through my own end-of-year exams and soon afterwards I started my full-time summer job at the library. On this occasion I was assigned to the Japanese Collections on the first floor. Fairly small set of rooms connected by swinging glass doors. Recessed panel lighting. One or two framed *kakemonos* brightening the aseptic surroundings. My job was to go around the section looking for books and bound periodicals that readers had taken to their desks and forgotten to return to the appropriate stack or bookcase. The number of items that needed shelving was not as large as in other parts of the library, but because many of the books and volumes had their titles printed in kanji I couldn't identify them at first sight and was often forced to rely on the faded, sometimes partially peeled-off information stickers on their spines. A bit of a pain in the sphincter, to use one of Portas's old phrases.

I am not sure what else to say here about the next few weeks. In Portas's absence, I began to work very long hours at the library and there were times when it seemed as if all I did was sleep, push my basket trolley and shuttle back and forth between the library and Fitzroy College. Trapped in this Möbius strip of a routine, I often thought about quitting my job and flying to Gibraltar to seek out my absconding friend. Perhaps I could talk to him and find out what had happened. Maybe even convince him to come back to Cambridge and repeat his final year. In the end, though, I'd always stop myself from making a flight booking. One, there was no guarantee that Portas wouldn't be cooped up in his family mansion in the Andalusian mountains. And two, I didn't fancy the prospect of spending July and August stuck in my mother's airless flat. Accordingly, I put all altruistic feelings out of my head and tried my best to focus solely on my misplaced Japanese books and periodicals.

Soon a terrible monotony set in. The pattern was much the same each day: eat, go to bed, sleep, wake up, have a shower, shave, head off resignedly in the direction of the library. During my lunch hour I'd sometimes plod over to either the Mitre or the Baron of Beef and sit there with a pint of Double Diamond, reminiscing about former days. Other times I would cross Queen's Road and wander down to the Backs, where I'd choose a tranquil spot, lie on the grass, tilt my baseball cap over my eyes and try to forget about the stream of kanji characters spinning in my head. Birdsong, rustling leaves, the unceasing *bons mots* of the Cambridge punters, the adenoidal laughter of easily amused American tourists, the soft and rhythmic plosh of punting poles sinking into, and then pulling out of, the murky river waters. In the evening, after I had shelved the last of my Japanese books, I'd saunter back to Fitzroy, stopping en route at the corner shop between Castle Street and Northampton Street to grab some beers for the night. Worthington E. Four cans for thirty-six pence. A belter of a bargain. Back at the flat it was always very quiet — and awfully boring. The only other student who had stayed on in my corridor for the summer was Martin Bernstein, a twenty-eight-year-old postgraduate geographer from Ontario,

Canada. Ponytailed guy. Sunken veiny eyes. A predilection for grey socks and leather sandals. I think I saw him about seven times in the space of two months — usually in the act of closing his room door. Once, just after I had come back from a ten-hour stint at the library, he knocked on my door and asked me if the electrics had also gone in my room. 'No,' I said, shifting slightly so that he could see that my study light was still on. 'My room's okay.' 'Okay, thanks,' Bernstein replied, already heading back to his room. 'Must be a fault in my room, then.' And that was that: he never spoke to me again.

The high point of my routine was probably my weekly telephone conversation with my mother. Normally, she'd call between seven and eight o'clock every Sunday evening. I'd always leave my room door ajar and prop open the door at the end of the corridor with one of my trainers so that I could hear the phone ringing upstairs. This meant that I often ended up answering the telephone for the other half a dozen summer 'stay-behinds' scattered across the block, but I didn't mind: at least it gave me the chance to break out of what sometimes felt like a monastic vow of silence. When her call at last got through, I'd only speak to her for two or maybe three minutes — weekend calls to the UK, as my mother never stopped reminding me, being charged at the ruinous rate of 80p a minute. She'd start by telling me what my sister Mariela had been doing that week with her friends, then mention something about the weather (*Hace una caló aquí increíble, Brian!*), then talk a little about my cousins and my aunt … before finally rounding things up in the usual way:

'But why don't you just come back for a few days to see me and your sister, *Briallito*? *De verdá que no lo entiendo.*'

'I'm too busy at work, Mum. I've told you before. There are a lot of people who are on leave at the moment and it's difficult for me to take any time off.'

'Well, it's just not fair, *Briallito. Eso es tó lo que te digo.* Me and your sister are really missing you over here, *Briallito.*'

Briallito. I always hated being called that. It was what the other kids at Laguna had called me while I was growing up. Brian, but with a belittling Hispanicized suffix, the *-ito* presumably referring either to my smallness of size or the insignificance of my personality. Also, I don't think my mother missed me as much as she made out — but that's another story. The main thing is that she felt obliged to say what mothers are supposed to say and I, for my part, was compelled to respond in kind. Finally, towards the middle of September, with only ten days left before the beginning of the new term, I gave in: I handed in my notice at the library and, strolling down to the Fly-u-Right travel agency on Sidney Street, booked a return flight from Gatwick to Gibraltar with British Airways. The plan was to leave on Sunday and come back five days later on Friday. With a bit of luck this would give me enough time to assure my mother and my sister that I hadn't entirely forgotten about them and also to locate Portas and ask him what the hell had happened.

20.

I got to Gibraltar at seven o'clock that Sunday. It was very warm and tangles of low stratus cloud concealed most of the Rock. The sun could be seen through a rent in the clouds, a yellow smudge reminiscent of an iodine-stained wound. The chime of the runway traffic barrier echoed harshly in the near distance. Pulling out my passport from my jacket pocket, I entered the terminal building and joined the short queue leading to the immigration counter.

'You've come to Gibraltar on holiday, sir?'

'*Soy de Gibraltar.*'

'Ah, *vale. Pasa, pisha, pasa.*'

The sun seemed even hotter by the time I came out of the other side of the building. A dense throng had gathered outside the terminal's narrow exit, making it hard to manoeuvre my luggage trolley. If that wasn't annoying enough, the passengers in front of me kept stopping to hug or kiss their friends and relatives, forgetting there were others behind them trying to come out too. I looked to my left and then to my right, but couldn't find my mother. *Great,* I thought as I fended off the probing advances of a taxi driver. *I'm stuck here with my trolley and no money to catch a taxi!* Then I felt a soft tap on my shoulder. Bringing the trolley to a halt, I turned around and saw my mother and sister, both looking very tanned, in front of a hoarding advertising Royal Crown cigarettes. '*Hola, Briallito,*' my mother said with the nervous smile of someone who hasn't seen you for a long time. 'Hello, Brian,' my little sister muttered a fraction of a second later, blowing out a bubblegum bubble.

The journey back to Laguna Estate took only ten minutes in my mother's old Fiat. Throughout this time Mariela talked nonstop about her new Girl Guide group and a swimming gala she was attending on Thursday at the Nuffield Pool, the usually MOD-only swimming pool. *Pinchitos* were being served at the end of the gala, she said, and the group's leader had told her they had booked a magician for the evening. As she leaned over at one point to pick up a magazine from the seat pocket in front of me, I noticed with some discomfort the outline of two fledgeling breasts under her T-shirt. When we reached the flat a short while later, my mother asked me to close my eyes and stand to one side. I did as I was told, wondering what all this was leading to. She then took me by the hand and guided me into the living room. 'Okay,' she said, coming to a stop. 'You can look now.' Opening my eyes, I saw that the dining table had been laid out with bread buns, olives, chorizo slices, *jamón*, sausage rolls, miniature pork pies and other types of Anglo-Spanish finger food. Hanging from one end of the sideboard to the other was a handwritten sign; it was pink and yellow in colour and said 'Welcome Home Dear Brian!'

'Well, what do you think?'

'It's very nice.'

'Your sister made the sign herself, *Briallito*, and I prepared the food earlier this morning. We thought it'd be a nice surprise for you.'

'Yes,' I said, trying to inject some enthusiasm into my voice, 'it's a very nice surprise.'

'Why don't you sit down at the table and have something to eat? You must be starving after such a long journey.'

I didn't really feel like eating anything, but I thought it would be churlish to go straight to my room, so I sat down and poured myself half a glass of Coke. Then I started nibbling at a vol-au-vent. My sister began blathering again about her swimming gala, telling me about the events she'd be competing in (the 25m backstroke and the 100m individual medley) and how hard she had trained for them. At length I got up and said that I needed to lie down for a while. 'Are you sure you don't want anything else to eat?' my mother asked. 'You've hardly eaten anything at all.' 'I'm sure, Mum,' I replied, faking a yawn. 'I'm just a bit tired, that's all. I didn't sleep well last night thinking about today's flight. A lie-down will do me good.' 'Okay, then, *Briallito,*' my mother answered with a weary smile. 'Go and get some rest, then, *Briallito.*'

Early next morning, I left the flat and went for a walk. It was clear and sunny, the previous day's Levantery greyness having been blown away by the westerly wind. Coffee-drinkers and people-watchers lined the terraces of the Main Street cafés, either reading the *Gibraltar Chronicle* or observing the world go by. Unshaven PWD workers swept the streets in various states of lethargy. I was tempted to sit down somewhere and have a *café con leche,* but I resisted the urge and carried on striding determinedly up Main Street. Soon it was a quarter to ten and I was standing before my destination, the head office of Portas and Sons. Situated at the southern end of Irish Town, it was a typical patrician building insofar as you needed to take your eyes off its shabby entrance and look upwards to realise its intrinsic Victorian grandeur. Many buildings in Gibraltar are like that. Disfigured by tacky plastic fascia panels, vulgarised by shockingly bright signage, there is something about them that makes you think about laundrettes or car dealerships or maybe even fast-food outlets — until you look up and find yourself dazzled by an assembly of pediments, cornices and other original nineteenth-century features.

All right, Brian, I thought. *Time to get to the bottom of this little mystery.*

With a pounding heart, I entered the building and walked down a narrow corridor. Not long afterwards, I reached a cramped lobby split in two by a wall-to-wall counter. Panelled with sheets of light-coloured Formica, this counter was topped by a board of imitation granite that had clearly seen better days. Three small metal clocks hung from a side wall, showing what time it was in New York, London and Tokyo. A rubbery odour, similar to that given off by new carpets, floated in the air, although it was mixed with something organic and slightly rancid — like the smell of sawdust or wood shavings. Two yards behind the counter stood a partition made out of frosted glass which rose to within a foot of the ceiling, but was separated from the walls on each side by a good three feet. The interplay of light and shadow streaming through the glass suggested that there was a large office behind the screen and, if you listened carefully, you could hear the sound of working typewriters and even the whirr of a revolving ceiling fan. Fixed to one of the few wooden bits of the partition, there was a portrait of an old man with a grizzly Tolstoyan beard — evidently some famous Portas from the past. Under the ever-watchful gaze of this long-dead patriarch sat an elegantly dressed young woman with a polka-dotted neck scarf and a lizard brooch pinned on her blouse. She was speaking in English to someone on the phone. From her accent as well as her mannerisms, I assumed that she was British — and only came to realise my mistake when, just before putting the receiver down, she used the phrase '*Venga, ya nos veremos.*' Feeling a touch self-conscious about my own Gibraltarian accent, I approached the counter and asked her if I could please speak to Henry Portas.

'Which Henry Portas are you after?' the Anglo-Gibraltarian secretary asked with a smile. 'Henry Portas Junior? Henry Portas Senior? Or old Mr Portas?'

'Henry Portas Junior, I guess.'

'Henry Portas Junior,' the receptionist replied, shaking her head, 'isn't technically based in this building, although he is still part of the firm and is always coming in and out of the office. I don't think he's in at the moment, though. If you want to leave a message with me, I'll make certain he gets it.'

I scribbled down my mother's phone number together with a suitable message and then left the building. For the next few days I either stayed at home or made sure that my mother was in the apartment when I wasn't there, not wanting to miss Portas's phone call. Sadly, though, the days went by without any news from him. By Wednesday morning I had already called Portas and Sons on three occasions, only to be told each time by their secretary that Portas already knew about my note and would be contacting me soon. 'But are you sure that he knows it is me?' I asked at the end of my third call, unable to mask my growing exasperation. 'Brian Manrique? His old mate from Cambridge?' 'Yes, Mr Manrique,' the secretary replied, 'I told him that Mr Manrique from Fitzroy College in Cambridge had phoned and he said he'd call you soon.' The next time I called, at around midday on Thursday, I was informed that Mr Portas Junior had travelled to Algeciras via Tangier and was not expected in Gibraltar for at least three weeks. When I angrily demanded why he hadn't bothered returning my call, the secretary (who obviously was not very adept at lying) cleared her throat and said she thought he had some urgent business to attend to in Spain. Fighting back the urge to make an ironic remark, I thanked her for her time and put the phone down.

21.

By the time I got back to Cambridge, the city was once again heaving with freshers and returning second-, third- and fourth-year students. Since my application to stay another year at the college had been rejected, I was forced to move out of Fitzroy and rent a room in a house on Victoria Road, a long, narrow, characterless residential thoroughfare tucked between the Cambridge Ring Road and Huntingdon Road. The property was cold and draughty and suffered from the inconvenience that many drivers coming into Cambridge via the A14 and Huntingdon Road frequently cut through Victoria Road to reach the eastern suburbs of the city. There was also a shelter for the homeless about four doors away — a large, grey-bricked Victorian house that attracted crowds of down-and-outs first thing in the mornings and last thing in the evenings. Of the four rooms at 12 Victoria Road, mine was the smallest and cheapest — at just £28.70 a month. Sharing the bathroom and kitchen facilities with me were three other students: Khalid, a fourth-year medical student from Lahore; a friendly one-armed Australian geophysicist called Mitch; and an acne-ridden German (I believe she said her name was Heike, but her accent was so strong that I was never totally sure) who was finishing an MPhil in Linguistics while working as a part-time waitress at a city-centre restaurant. Being extremely busy individuals, they were never around much and, apart from the odd occasion when I'd bump into Heike in the kitchen or stumble across Khalid on the way out of the bathroom, I hardly had anything to do with them.

Several weeks passed and we edged closer to 1975. During the Christmas holidays I stayed in Cambridge and lived off the money I had saved while working at the library over the summer. It was a dull and lonely period in my life, but I did not mind. By a strange quirk of fate, my routine was now similar to the one I had followed during my first weeks in Cambridge — with lessons and library time during the day succeeded by lengthy, aimless hikes in the evening. The only difference was that these days I wasn't walking because I wanted to avoid the people I was living with. Now I walked simply because it helped me relax and take my mind off my looming final exams. At times during these long marches, I'd think of my old mate Henry Portas and wonder how he was doing back in the clutches of his dreaded relatives. Had the prodigal son reformed his ways? Had his father forgiven him for not finishing his Law degree? Or was he still boozing and chasing after women and climbing old buildings? Since the beginning of the academic year, I had written two letters to him care of Portas and Sons at Irish Town, Gibraltar, but I had never received any replies. It was tempting to imagine him dangling from some weathered ledge halfway up the facade of Saint Mary the Crowned, the Catholic cathedral, but in my heart of hearts I knew that he'd probably be crouched over a desk in the office behind that squalid glass partition, slowly getting acquainted with the family business he hated so much. If so, he wouldn't have been the first son of a big businessman to go down that particular route. Bourgeois children always go through a period of escapism and rebellion before being dragged back into the fold. It's part and parcel of the upper-middle-class experience. You smoke a couple of joints, date a long-haired hippie for a few months, maybe even talk about marrying somebody from a different race — but in the end you always toe the line and become a carbon copy of your own bourgeois father or mother. That's the template these people follow: rebellion to conservatism by way of parental coercion. The strange thing was not that Portas had succumbed to such compelling pressures, but that we had ever been friends in the first place. The wild bacchanalian parties, the brotherly sessions at the Mitre and the Baron of Beef, the dangerously *hungover* rides in his Citroën cabriolet — it all felt so distant and dead. Even the four or five girls who, thanks to Portas's intercessory efforts, had once come my way now seemed like a mirage, an already fading dream. Had I really bedded those women? Had I brought them back to my room and whispered garbled words of love into their ears? Sometimes it felt as if the person involved in those acts of drunken sensuality had been my doppelgänger and not the solitary, cheerless individual who now roamed the streets of Cambridge. Brian Manrique, the great Gibraltarian seducer? You had to be kidding, surely!

Nevertheless, there was one part of my life which benefitted dramatically from Portas's absence. Freed from the demands of all that constant pubbing and partying, I was able to concentrate on my studies and significantly improve my assignment grades. So pronounced was this improvement, in fact, that Dr Franceschetti, my balding Italian tutor from Turin, drew me to one side one morning in early January and, nodding contentedly, told me that there was a real chance I could get a 2:1 for the final part of my degree instead of the 2:2 he had previously predicted. '*Sì, sì, certamente,* Mr Manrique,' Franceschetti said, rearranging his cravat with his plump fingers. 'I think we have a distinct possibility on our hands here. A very distinct possibility. Your grades, Mr Manrique, were terrible in your first year, average in your second year, terrible again in your third. But this year, *fu — che trasformazione!* You have gone from plodding no-hoper to better-than-average in *un batter d'occhio*. If you continue like this, *chi lo sa*, Mr Manrique, you might just surprise us all and obtain a 2:1 for your final exams!'

Inspired by Franceschetti's words, I cut down on my walks and concentrated even harder on my studies. I even began to skip meals and reduce my hours of sleep, utilising every last minute to brush up on my French and Italian grammar. Breaking with three years of truanting tradition, I started to attend every supervision that came my way and — even more astoundingly — frequently took the lead in classroom discussions. There I was most days at the front of the class, putting my hand up whenever questions were asked and arguing with anyone who contradicted my views. This wasn't just odd behaviour for someone like me; it was completely unprecedented. For as long as I could remember, I had always positioned myself in class as far away as possible from the tutor. I had sat there half-cowed and withdrawn, religiously avoiding eye contact with everybody in the room and only answering questions put directly to me. Part of the reason for this was that I was naturally shy and hated the thought of being the centre of attention. But an even more important reason was that half the time I spoke — at least half the time *I spoke in English* — people had problems understanding my Gibraltarian accent. A bit of a conundrum, this one. Okay, so most students at Cambridge have polished English accents. That much is true. But now and then *you do* come across some isolated Geordie or Scotsman who speaks like he is choking on a plateful of rock cakes. No one has any trouble understanding *them*, do they? Yet, whenever I opened my mouth and spoke in the fairly neutral tones of my Gibraltarian accent, I'd stand a 50-60 per cent chance of hearing the same depressingly familiar words: 'Pardon me?', 'Excuse me?', 'Say again, Mr Manrique?' Pretty demoralising stuff. Quite humiliating, actually. For a while I even thought that the others were taking the mickey, that they enjoyed seeing me blush and stammer as I struggled to strip my accent of all hint of foreignness. *Estos guiris! As xenophobic and malaje as ever!* But as time passed and I came to discover what a carefree, droopy, generally apathetic creature your average English student is, I realised that there was nothing personal about it. It was just a matter of *what they were used to,* that's all. Sure, Scotsmen and Geordies may not be a dominant presence in the Home Counties — but they still appear on the national news and in one or two TV comedy programmes. We Gibraltarians, by contrast, are an unknown quantity, a curious novelty. That's why people in the UK find it so hard to understand our accent: we simply don't cross their radar. If any proof of this was needed, it surely came during that final year at Cambridge when, seduced by Franceschetti's prognostications of academic success, carried along by the momentum of my own growing confidence, I began to regularly contribute verbally to college supervisions. Students who had always looked perplexed whenever I spoke gradually stopped raising their eyebrows. Professors no longer scrunched their faces when I answered their questions. It was not an overnight transformation by any means, but it did prove the important point that, once you get used to its sounds and cadences, Gibraltarian English is *essentially no different to other varieties of spoken English.*

By mid-April all lessons came to an end and we entered the final period of revision leading up to our exams in late May/early June. This is a very stressful time for most students in the UK, but it is even more stressful at Cambridge because, even though the university does not award formal degree classifications, your de facto classification is *always* determined by the grades you obtain in your final year exams. Notch up an average grade of 70.0 per cent across your final year papers and you'll be able to look people in the eye and say you got a 'First' at Cambridge; score 69.9 per cent, on the other hand, and you'll be forever consigned to the ranks of the solid but uninspiring. It doesn't matter whether you achieved spectacularly good grades in your first- and second-year exams; those examinations are important, yes, but only in the sense that you must pass them to progress to the next academic year. On balance, it is probably an unfair system, one of those anachronistic pieces of Cantabrigian whimsy. But it does have *some advantages*. For those who have spent their time at Cambridge loafing and gadding about, there is always the chance of eradicating three or four years of academic underachievement in the space of a couple of weeks.

In the final run-up to the exams, I went *all out* to get that cherished 2:1. Together with a group of twenty or thirty other fellow swots and 'crammers', you'd find me standing outside the library building every morning, waiting for the doors to swing open at nine so that all of us could run inside and claim our respective desks. For the next ten or twelve hours I'd barely leave the reading room. I must have looked a right sight: weary-eyed and unshaven, wearing the same clothes I had worn now for the last few weeks, my unwashed hair scraping against my shoulders in a flurry of dago curls. On the table before me was a prayer card of Saint Jude that my mother had given to me during my visit to Gibraltar the previous September. I didn't really believe that the apostle's intercessions could improve my study skills or keep me from falling asleep, but I reasoned that it did no harm to place him there — all potential aids to success, as far as I was concerned, being legitimate and justifiable. Now and again I'd get up and use the Xerox copier or go and buy a sickeningly strong coffee from the vending machine outside the reading room toilets, but most of the time I'd simply stay by my desk: taking notes, stifling yawns, reading and rereading articles on Voltaire, Maupassant and Lampedusa, chewing my pen, looking at my watch, memorising key historical dates, cursing the embarrassingly loud rumbling in my stomach, shaking my head whenever anyone talked in a loud voice, looking up words whose meaning I wasn't sure of, rubbing my eyes, persuading myself that I was a worthless schmuck who knew *nothing about nothing*, mentally going through some tough French conjugations, belching under my breath, shaking my head, sighing aloud, looking at my watch again….

22.

My final Tripos exams were held between 27 May and 7 June 1975. For the first time in my undergraduate career, I was in a quietly confident mood. Not only had I crammed all sorts of facts and grammatical formulas into my head, but I had also worked hard at improving my areas of weakness. Vocabulary, pronunciation, irregular verb forms, French and Italian politics and culture — I had left no stone unturned. But when those exam hall doors finally swung open on the morning of the twenty-seventh, my brain went into intellectual anaphylactic shock. Biting the end of my pen, feeling the sweat drops slide down my temples, I found myself staring at the examination paper with all the bewilderment of an illiterate peasant regarding a complex algebraic problem. *Start writing, you bastard,* I thought. *Stop biting your pen! DO BLOODY SOMETHING!* Out of sheer panic, I at last stopped chewing my biro and began scribbling down whatever came into my head — but my answers were messy and poorly expressed, filled with contradictions. The same thing happened during the next nine exams. As soon as I sat down at one of those little wooden tables, I wilted. Completely lost my nerve. At the time I couldn't believe that I kept unravelling in this way, but looking back it is clear that I was only doing what came naturally to me. Self-sabotage, after all, had always been one of my specialities. A *Manriquian* forte. You could witness this regrettable frailty of mine when I tried to make friends or date women or do anything else that ordinary blokes are supposed to do instinctively. Every time I had a strong desire for something, I'd end up becoming so tense and nervous that I'd wind up with the opposite of what I wanted. A bit of an unfortunate trait, *en realidad.* And it certainly played its part in ruining what should have been my week of academic triumph. To my utter dismay, I underperformed in each and every one of those crucial exams — my listening comprehensions, my textual translations, my three scheduled papers on art and culture ('Politics and Statecraft in the Nineteenth-Century French novel', 'Rhetorics and Rhetoricians in Enlightenment France' and 'Post-war Reparations: Place, Language and Meaning in Italian neo-realist cinema') and my two language orals. If you're wondering just how badly my nerves affected my exam performance, then consider my Italian oral, in theory one of my strongest subjects. My topic of choice was the work and life of Cesare Pavese, an Italian author whom I had admired since my days in Venice and whose books I knew inside out. With this in mind, you'd have thought I would have had the sense to stick firmly to Pavese and his novels. But did I do that? No, of course not. Not me. Surrendering once again to those damned nerves of mine, I somehow steered the conversation away from Pavese and on to other Italian authors whom I knew almost nothing about, especially on to Curzio Malaparte, a writer whose oeuvre had always baffled me and whom (if that wasn't problematic enough) I had only read in English translation. As a result, I not only lost my thread and started imming and amming like an English tourist asking for directions in Rome, but my Italian grammar and pronunciation went to pieces too. *Una catastrofe totale e assoluta,* for sure.

Anyway, all of this is neither here nor there. All that matters is that, when the results were announced ten days later, I got a 2:2 instead of a 2:1. Old Franceschetti, whom I came across in the foyer of the Faculty of Modern and Medieval Languages shortly after our marks were pinned up on the main noticeboard, told me that I had missed my objective by the slenderest of margins, my average grade for my final year papers being 59.7 per cent instead of the 60 per cent I needed for a 2:1. Listening to him speak these words proved a bitter pill. Even as I stood there shaking the professor's hand, all I could think about were all those sleepless nights and headache tablets and unheated cans of baked beans, wondering why on earth I had put up with all that shit just to end up with a crummy 2:2. It was only when a few days passed, and I remembered that a mere twelve months ago I had been told that I would struggle to even obtain a third-class degree, that I finally began to take some pride in the achievement. Yes, I may have only got a run-of-the-mill 2:2, but, hey, at least I had a degree, which was more than could be said for that posh idiot Portas. Smiling at the thought, I got dressed and set off in the direction of the Baron of Beef with the intention of buying a belated celebratory pint of beer. It was the first time that I had been out in three days, too, so I felt a little woozy on my feet. As I walked down Castle Street, I saw a pair of blue-uniformed traffic wardens pushing a motorbike into a tow-away truck — a fairly common sight in Cambridge. When I reached the entrance to the pub minutes later, the place was jam-packed with celebrating students, many of them in fancy dress. A bouncer stood at the door, arms crossed and chewing gum. Some girl in pyjamas was sleeping on a street bench. The music coming from inside was so loud that I could feel the flagstones quivering under my feet. I toyed with the idea of joining the party, but in the end decided against it and headed to the mini-mart at the bottom of Magdalene Street. There I bought a 75cl bottle of VAT 69 and a pack of King Edward VII Imperials. Once back outdoors, I tucked the packet of cigars into my waistband and unscrewed the bottle top, taking a small sip of whisky. I then belched softly and walked down Northampton Street in the direction of Westminster College and the Backs. Cars were inching their way past me — slowed down, in all probability, by the build-up of traffic at the roundabout between Queen's Road and Northampton Street. Drivers intermittently beeped their horns; some revved their engines while stationary. Fleetingly, I thought about going to the library and taking the whisky with me to some secluded spot in the library tower. But when I got to the mentioned roundabout, I decided that I didn't feel like going anywhere — so I turned around and started heading back towards my room on Victoria Road. Moments later, I remembered that Portas had once said there was a famous art gallery near here. What was its name again? Kettle House? Kettle Meadow? Tightening my grip on the whisky bottle, a tad surprised by the recollection, I walked across the street to search for the place. It did not take me long to find it. Behind a low brick wall, in the centre of what looked like a traditional suburban garden, I spotted a sign saying 'Kettle's Yard — one of Britain's Finest Art Galleries.' I decided to go in. There was only one problem: I had a bottle of whisky in my hand. Undaunted, I uncapped the bottle and brought it to my lips, hoping to finish it off in a few gulps. But the task was too much for me: I couldn't go beyond the halfway mark. Then I had an idea. By the entrance to the gallery there was a large bush. What if I hid the bottle behind this bush? Looking first to one side and then to the other, I approached the shrub and, making sure that no one could see what I was doing, thrust the bottle behind it. That done, I got up and wobbled into the gallery. In the foyer a woman stood cross-armed by a counter. Large hoop earrings, sleeveless cotton dress. Something hippyish about her. From the moment I first walked in, she didn't take her eyes off me, leading me to surmise that either she could smell alcohol on my breath or had seen me thrust the bottle into the bush. Irritated, already feeling quite drunk, I approached her and asked her if there were any Christopher Whites in the gallery.

'Christopher Whites?' she screeched, looking at me with a mixture of wariness and cultural snobbery. 'You mean Christopher Wood, surely?'

'Yes, that's the man: Christopheros Woodos. You got any pictures by Chrissy-lad in the gallery, *la mia vergine inglese dei dolori?*'

She pointed silently at a painting on the other side of the hall. I spun around to look at it, but abruptly changed my mind and sauntered off in the opposite direction. I walked past a few paintings — 'Ulysses and the Sirens', '*Le Cygne Volant*', 'Animals Crossing a Flooded River', 'Death Ship' — wondering if Portas had ever admired them during his Cambridge days. One or two were rather eye-catching, but the majority were stark abstractions which didn't tickle my Latin fancy. After a while I decided that I couldn't be bothered with it all and walked out of the gallery. Then I staggered up to the bush and, to the horror of an old lady passing by, got down on my knees and began to look for the goods. Yep, the bottle was still there. Ready to be enjoyed and savoured back at home, I thought, retrieving it and standing up again.

The sun was already high in the sky when I woke up the next morning. Cars could be heard chuntering along Victoria Road. Birds were twittering and trilling. Our friendly neighbourhood tramps, bless 'em, were once again causing a minor rumpus outside the nearby homeless shelter. As I opened my eyes wider and slowly came back to life, I noticed that the bottle of whisky was lying on its side on the windowsill — empty except for a trickle of liquid. Surprisingly, I didn't have much of a hangover. Just some dryness in the mouth and a smidgen of tension between the eyes. Impressed, I stretched my arms and tumbled out of bed. Then I got dressed and went out with the intention of getting a bite to eat. The streets were full of students enjoying the warming June sun. They all seemed to be carrying something: guitars, crates of beer, portable barbecues, lilos, inflatable beach balls. Mixed with the roadside stench of car fumes, there hung in the air the smell of burning charcoal — probably coming from the dozens of celebratory barbecues taking place on Jesus Green and Midsummer Common. Fighting back a yawn, I shoved my hands into my pockets and started heading down Regent Street towards Hills Road. I was vaguely aware that I was walking in the direction of the train station, but my attention was mainly focused on the world going past me — on the tramps begging for money and the mothers pushing prams, on the laughing school kids and the tottering pensioners, on the wiry postmen and the high-spirited students. They all looked so pale, I thought to myself. So Northern European. It may sound bizarre, but I had never been so conscious of just how pale and drained of colour most people in the UK *actually are*. It was almost a revelation, one of those 'epiphanic moments' which Dr Hartfield-Dubois, my French Literature tutor, often talked about. After a few minutes I did indeed turn left into Station Road, but I was still too preoccupied with the sights and sounds around me to give much thought to what I was doing. Finally, as I reached the end of the road and came before the soot-encrusted front of Cambridge Rail Station, I knew what I wanted to do: I wanted to catch a train and get away from Cambridge. That's what my subconscious had been screaming at me all along. Escape, bugger off, get the hell out of here. Go to London, get a job, start a new life. Leave it all behind: Cambridge, Fitzroy College, Portas, Victoria Road, the Baron of Beef, Franceschetti, my mother, Gibraltar, the whole fucking lot. So appealing was the thought that I even went into the station and bought a train ticket to King's Cross in London. But in the end, I am ashamed to admit, I didn't have the bottle for it. I simply couldn't do it. I had my possessions back at the house to think about, hadn't I? I had to hand in the form saying that I wanted to graduate *in absentia*. I had to close my bank account, return my library books, say goodbye to Franceschetti, claim back my tenancy deposit, take some farewell photographs of the Senate House and Trinity College, et cetera, et cetera. In any case, a voice murmured in my mind, what can you hope to find in London with a French and Italian degree? More house-sharing with strangers? More desultory walks on your own? It's not as if you're ever going to have much fun there left to your own devices, is it? Gutted, I tore the ticket in two and began the long walk back to my room on Victoria Road.

23.

I arrived back in Gibraltar on the twenty-third of June 1975. A day of hazy Mediterranean sunshine, pleasantly warm and windless. The moment my plane landed, I felt the satisfaction that homecoming

Gibraltarians feel when first glimpsing the Rock looming through the low-lying Levanter cloud. But when I exited Customs and Immigration and found my mother leisurely chatting with some acquaintances outside the arrivals hall, all that euphoria evaporated. Maybe, just maybe, this was due to the sheer provinciality of the scene before me. (Where else, I ask you, could you walk out of a supposedly international airport and bump into a gaggle of friends and distant relatives on its doorstep?) Or maybe you can blame the pitiful drabness of that combined arrivals and departures hall, with its greying walls and its rusting weighing scales and its scratched linoleum tiles? Whatever the reason for it, this first mood swing set the pattern for the next few days. At times I felt happy and relaxed, quietly revelling in the knowledge that I had accomplished what I had set out to do four years earlier and come back with a degree. But other times, particularly when I was home with my mum in the evenings listening to her *radionovelas*, I'd wonder if I should have stayed in the UK and looked for a job in London. To keep my spirits up, I'd remind myself that I was a Cambridge University graduate and that there were no more than six or seven of us in the whole of Gibraltar. 'All you need is a job and a bit of structure in your life, Brian,' I'd say, standing in front of the bathroom mirror. 'Then everything will change for the better. *Seguro que sí!*'

But getting a job in Gibraltar was not as easy as I anticipated. Over the following weeks I applied for several posts and was even invited to attend four interviews, but I never got past that tricky final hurdle. The explanations I received from those who turned me down were surprisingly varied: I was too qualified, I was not experienced enough, I didn't have a strong mathematical background, I was too young for such a sedentary position. Yes, I know, I know. Anybody would think that, with a Modern Languages degree from Cambridge University, at a time when few Gibraltarians had college degrees, I'd have fared better than this. But that was Gibraltar in the mid-Seventies: either there were not enough vacancies going around or, during the rare moments when there were, you needed to know someone who knew somebody else to have a sniff of a chance.

By the end of the summer, I was still jobless and living in my mother's flat. I must have written to twenty-five separate companies by then and attended at least eight different interviews. I was also being less picky about jobs. Throughout July I had only applied to the more prestigious companies and organisations — the MOD, the Gibraltar Government, the big local law and accountancy firms. But now that three months had passed, I was applying for *almost anything* advertised in the pages of the *Gibraltar Chronicle:* receptionist in a Main Street dental clinic, part-time retail clerk at the Prince of Wales cinema, junior administrator at a car dealership, assistant warehouse supervisor at Lipton's supermarket. Even my way of dealing with joblessness itself had dramatically changed. During July and most of August I had interspersed my trips to the Manpower office with long walks just like the ones I had gone for in Cambridge. These walks had taken me all over the Rock: Rosia, Scud Hill, Catalan Bay, the Upper Town, Saint Michael's Cave. Because I had been away for so long, moreover, everything around me felt novel and fresh, dressed in vibrant colours. I even began to notice things that I had never previously registered: the poignancy of some of the funerary inscriptions at Trafalgar Cemetery, the magnificence of the view from O'Hara's Battery, the craggy, bone-white immensity of the Rock as seen from Eastern Beach. I'm sure that other returning Gibraltarians have experienced something similar. It's almost as if you need to physically tear yourself away from Gibraltar, to tread the paths of self-imposed exile for some years, to realise what a unique place our Rock is.

The problem with feelings of this sort, of course, is that they never last long. If you carry on walking the same streets again and again, if you continue traipsing down Queensway every morning, for example, and then heading up Rosia Road before turning around at Rosia Parade and walking back to Laguna via Main Street and the Casemates car park, you will soon reach a point where, just like your more settled and untravelled compatriots, you desensitize yourself to your surroundings and once again take things for granted. This is more or less what happened to me at the start of September 1975 — I began to feel sick of walking, got to the stage where I couldn't face another leisurely stroll through Queensway or another aimless shuffle down Line Wall Road. Reading, lying in bed, cleaning my room, watching television, playing Solitaire, even sitting in the kitchen with my mother listening to her *radionovelas* — anything was better, my God, than *going round and round in circles like that!*

Looking back on it now, it was a difficult period, one of those transitional phases where, if you are not careful, your whole life might stall and spiral into freefall. But fortune was about to smile on me. While waiting to be interviewed one morning for a clerical post at the local library, I found out that one of the interviewers was married to the son of my mother's second cousin on her father's side. Actually, I never discovered this 'wondrous coincidence' myself; the lady in question informed me about it. 'You're not by any chance the son of Mary Manrique from Laguna who works from home as a *costurera?*' she asked, pushing aside my CV and squinting in my direction. 'Do you know that my husband's mother is your mother's second cousin?' And that was basically it: I knew that the job was as good as in the bag. Never mind that I had a BA (Hons) degree in Modern Languages from Cambridge University. Or that I had received a special commendation for my spoken Italian from the Ca' Foscari University of Venice. Or that I was an alumnus of Fitzroy College, alma mater to such illustrious worthies as Subhas Chandra Bose, 56th President of the Indian National Congress, or Lee Kuan Yew, first and so far only Prime Minister of the Republic of Singapore. No, none of that mattered. What mattered was that I, Brian Paul Manrique, was the son of Mary Manrique, who in turn was the daughter of Joseph Smith, who in turn was the second cousin of Luisa Delgado, who in turn was the mother of Joseph Di Maria, who in turn was married to Elizabeth Di Maria nee Attard, who in turn, God bless her grizzled head and the system which makes such nepotistic machinations possible, happened to be the most senior interviewer out of the three interviewers sitting in the interview room that day.

As for the post itself, it was uncannily similar to the part-time jobs I had once done at Cambridge University Library. On paper my title was 'Assistant Director and Counter Manager', but in reality my duties rarely stretched beyond shelving, cataloguing and issuing books — a state of affairs largely explained by the fact that the head librarian, a hefty, permanently bow-tied gentleman by the name of Charles Michael Pozo-Jones, was a meddling workaholic who thought that anyone under the age of fifty could not be trusted with any sort of 'responsibility.' The only concession granted to me was that I was left in charge of our French and Italian shelves. As Pozo-Jones explained, this was not something that he would have considered under normal circumstances, but, as my knowledge of French and Italian Literature was 'probably better' than his, it would be 'a shame' not to utilise my expertise in some way. As a result, I was responsible for ordering new French and Italian books and also for ensuring that our Italo-Franco collection never extended beyond its allotted three and a half shelves. As a small act of rebellion, I began to order the most shocking and controversial titles that I knew in both languages. Given that practically no one borrowed books from the foreign literature section, this was never going to be a career-imperilling act of defiance. But it still gave me a thrill of pleasure to think that a library like ours, which until 1973 had owned no copies of James Joyce's *Ulysses* and which even at the time of my induction refused to carry Lawrence's *Lady Chatterley's Lover*, was slowly filling up with books by Bataille, Mirbeau, Silone and other anti-establishment radicals.

Ordering subversive books, though, only accounted for a minuscule fraction of my working day. Most of the time I sat behind a counter near the main entrance, updating the card catalogue and typing letters to book suppliers. Every now and then, too, I'd have to stop what I was doing and issue the odd book. In general, there were three types of library users: pensioners, schoolchildren and geeks. The pensioners, the majority of whom were immaculately permed and perfumed Gibraltarian ladies, would saunter up to the counter and thrust their Catherine Cookson and Barbara Cartland novels at you without saying a word. The schoolchildren, for their part, would always be giggling and nudging each other — for what reason I never found out. The geeks, poor sods, would deposit their books with a guilty face on the counter and then look aside until you'd date-stamp and hand back *The History of British Railways, 1903-1953* or *The Intimate Journals of Paul Gauguin* (or whatever other title they were borrowing). The one quality all three groups shared was that they saw the person behind the counter as an automaton, a robot hardly worth engaging with. The only exception to this rule was a short, chubby, intensely effeminate, partially bald, club-footed chap called Jonathan Cortijo. A forty-five-year-old ex-Welfare Information Officer who had taken early retirement after suffering a nervous breakdown, Cortijo used to come into the library every Friday morning to read the *Times Literary Supplement* and, on the rare occasions when we got a copy delivered, the *New York Review of Books*. At first he paid just as much attention to me as the others, his only form of communication with the issuing counter being a subdued raising of the eyebrows each time he limped in through the library doors. He seemed like a morbidly shy guy, one of those fragile, oversensitive homosexual men who drag their disaffection and loneliness like a trampled bridal train behind them. But then one day, acting probably on a tip-off, he hobbled over to the main desk and, laying his elbows on the counter, in a voice crackling with androgynous excitement, cried out, 'Do you really have a degree from the University of Cambridge?' *Oh why oh why oh why did I have to yield to vanity and confirm that I had indeed studied at that educational institution?* From that moment onwards, not a single Friday morning went by without the club-footed Cortijo stopping at the issuing desk and rabbiting on about how much he admired me for having studied at Cambridge, and how he wished he had studied there instead of at the University of Newcastle, and how 'sad and frustrating' it was to see '*un talentazo como usted*' ('a major talent like yourself') wasting his time behind a library counter. 'You see this gentleman here,' he'd say to whoever was within earshot (usually one of the natty pensioners or one of the giggling schoolboys). 'He's got a degree from Cambridge and they've got him stamping books in this shoddy joke of a library. That's just so typical of this AACR government! So absolutely typical!'

24.

But enough about Jonathan Cortijo and over-scented old bibliophiles. Let's go back to Portas. Chances are you will be wondering whether I saw him since returning home, right? If that's the case, yes, I did see him several times. Living in a small and overcrowded place like Gibraltar, it would have been impossible not to! Our first meeting came before I even started working at the John Mackintosh Hall Library. It happened on a Monday morning, as I was heading back home after yet another futile trip to the offices of *el Manpower*. The sun was beginning to peep out from a bank of low cloud and you could smell the fumes coming from the Puente Mayorga oil refinery across the border. Car drivers were beeping their horns at a Saccone and Speed truck that had stopped just outside the Three Horseshoes to unload some beer kegs. In the greyish-white light of morning, everything stood out in stark relief: pedestrians, delivery vans, the tubular frame of an old woman's shopping cart, the metal buttons on a policeman's uniform. Intent on escaping all this hustle and bustle, I left Main Street and hurried through one of the archways built into the House of Assembly and connecting with John Mackintosh Square. As I reached the far end of the square, I turned right and walked down the steps leading to Irish Town. In doing so, I nearly clattered into a suited man coming in the opposite direction. Unsettled as I have always been by men in suits, I muttered an apology and quickly got out of the way — only to feel a large and powerful hand grip me around the neck. 'My, my, my, if it isn't my old mate Manny from Fitzroy College in Cambridge! How are you doing, old goat? Still living with your mum up at Laguna? Long time no see, *no*?' Yep, it was Henry Portas. Formerly of Trinity College and now of Portas and Sons, Irish Town, Gibraltar. I almost hadn't recognised him at first due to his double-breasted suit and his deeply tanned face. His hair, once so unruly and untamed, was now cut short and combed to the side. His clothes gave off the part-*cinnamony*, part-citrusy odour of some expensive eau de cologne. For about ten minutes he stood there — calmly telling me how well everything was going and how much he was enjoying working for the family firm. He said he was living these days in a house on Devil's Tower Road, but that he also spent a lot of time in Spain. Whether it was because of that pin-striped suit, or whether he had grown older over the last fourteen months, it is hard to say, but Portas seemed more mature and at ease with himself, with none of that spark of fiendish mischief that had characterised him back at Cambridge. Smiling amiably, he asked me for my telephone number and scribbled it into a small, leather-bound notebook which he produced from his inner jacket pocket. He then patted me a little condescendingly on the back and informed me that he had to get going. 'Listen,' he said, already moving away, 'let's get together soon for a few beers, shall we? There's so much that we have to talk about!'

Our second encounter came about two weeks later and was even more fleeting. It was a Tuesday and my mother was out doing some errands. I had already had my job interview at the John Mackintosh Hall and was waiting to hear from my future employers. At around half past twelve, I went out to buy a packet of cigarettes. I could have gone straight to the mini-mart on Sortie Road, but I felt like stretching my legs and heading into town. An easterly wind gusted over the stone ramparts of Line Wall Road, blowing wrappers out of rubbish bins and rattling shop signs. Groups of school kids were making their way home for lunch. A local drunk was slumped on one of the concrete benches behind the Casemates car park, dejectedly surveying the sea of G-registered vehicles before him. A few minutes later, as I left Casemates and entered Main Street, I saw Portas coming out of Galliano's Bank. He was dressed in a dark brown suit and a thin trench coat. A soft woolly cap with a herringbone design — the type known as a 'Baker Boy' — sat atop his head. Once again he stopped and said we had to meet up one day for a couple of beers, but this time he only remained by my side for twenty seconds, claiming that he was running late for an important meeting. 'We really have to get together one evening,' he said, trotting off in the direction of the House of Assembly. 'God, there is so much I have to tell you!'

Our next three encounters conformed to the same pattern: he'd stop, shake my hand, tell me that we'd have to 'get together for a few beers soon one day' and hurriedly march off. Then, on our sixth meeting, a slight but nonetheless significant development: he didn't stop. He didn't even slow down. Quite the opposite: he *appreciably speeded up.* Mouthing a quick 'hello', he shook his head and rolled his eyes and then, just as he came parallel to me, made a gesture with his hand which, judging from the way his index finger pointed forwards and wagged up and down, suggested that he was running late for a meeting or something. *Can't stop to talk,* the wagging finger said. *I'll stop and chat next time. Speak to you then.*

Following this episode, our chance meetings were always awkward affairs. If Portas felt in the mood, he'd lift his eyebrows in a gesture of acknowledgement and then, looking aside, without uttering a word, walk past me. Other times — particularly when he was out with his business acquaintances — he would pretend that he hadn't seen me and stride by as if I wasn't there. Knowing what he was like, none of this surprised me — but I still tried every trick in the book to justify his behaviour. Again and again I told myself that he was a very busy man, that he must have had loads of meetings to attend, that he didn't have time to stop in the street and gab about *el Levante* and other irrelevancies. Deep down I knew I was only kidding myself, but it couldn't have been otherwise: I had to give him the benefit of the doubt.

The final break between us took place on Christmas Eve, when most businesses close early and Gibraltarian workers gather for their annual end-of-year parties. The library had shut at midday that day and all the other staff had gone for their Christmas lunch to the Angry Friar, a small bar not far from the Governor's residence. I had been invited to join them, but had made up some cock and bull about not feeling that great and started heading home. It was a sunny but deceptively cold day, one of those bright December afternoons when it feels pleasant enough in the sun, but disagreeably chilly in the shade. Bands of revellers were already roaming through town, sipping from bottles of cava and singing English carols and Spanish *villancicos*. Policemen lined the busier parts of Main Street, smiling sternly. In my eagerness to get away from it all, I sank my hands into my pockets and walked as fast as I could. I was thinking about the matching pink silk scarves I had got for my mother and sister the previous day from Marks and Spencer. I was a little annoyed that I had paid £8.98 for both scarves and I was wondering — rather ungraciously — if my mother and sister would appreciate how much their presents had cost. As I turned the matter over, I spotted Portas with a group of other toffs outside one of the two Piazza kiosks. He was wearing a cardboard party hat and a string of tinsel around his neck — part of some Christmas do get-up. Not wishing to embarrass him with my presence, I crossed the street and continued walking along. But Portas, the eagle-eyed sod, must have spotted my last-minute evasive manoeuvre. 'Hey, Manny,' he shouted from the other side of the street. 'How's it going, mate?' Moments later, he has left his friends and is standing before me. His cheeks are flushed and his eyes have that glazed, intoxicated look that I remember so well from our Cambridge days. The half-Windsor knot on his tie is loose, revealing an unfastened mother-of-pearl shirt collar button and a few tufts of darkish blond hair sprouting behind it. An unopened bottle of Heineken pokes out of his jacket pocket. Struggling to make himself heard over the drunken carol singers, he tells me that it is great to see me, that he hopes my mother is in good health and that 1976 will bring the best of everything for her. 'By the way,' he yells, nudging me on the shoulder with his knuckles, 'let's see if we can meet for a few beers one day, eh? We really have to do that one evening, you know, Manny. We were really good mates during our time at Cambridge together, *después de todo*, weren't we? Weren't we, Manny?' He then enfolds me in his arms and kisses me on the back of the head. 'Merry Christmas, my friend,' he mutters in a voice thickened with maudlin emotion — and walks off back to his mates.

That transient encounter outside the House of Assembly changed the complexion of that lonely Christmas for me. Without it, I would have probably spent the entire holidays bored out of my head in my mother's apartment — furiously chain-smoking in my room or listening to the radio in the balcony beyond the kitchen. Now, instead, I kept thinking about those thirty or forty seconds in Main Street and replaying them in my head, trying to gauge their significance. Yes, it was true that Portas had been drunk and that I had barely understood his words. But, then again, doesn't alcohol cause people to drop their guard and say what they really feel? If so, then what I had initially taken for Portas's coldness towards me could have been simple defensive embarrassment. Think about it. The guy had abandoned his studies while I, his best mate, had pressed on and obtained a BA (Hons) degree. Clearly, he must have felt awkward about approaching me — so awkward that he had needed to be *totally plastered* before making the first genuinely conciliatory move. That's what happens when people are deeply embarrassed about something, isn't it? They stay away from you. Put up their defences. The good thing, I told myself, was that the ice had finally been broken. From now on, things were bound to get better between us. For sure they would. All right, maybe we would never be inseparable companions like we were in Cambridge, but surely we would be civil with each other and even go for the odd drink together from time to time. That was not outside the realms of possibility, was it?

I soon realised just how badly I had misread the situation. On the second of January, as I was making my way back to the library for my first day of work after the holidays, I saw Portas striding down the unpaved zone opposite the Governor of Gibraltar's palace. He was carrying a long-stemmed brolly fashioned out of a light-hued wood like ash or hickory. A stripy green and white tie lay between the lapels of his suit jacket, its upper half decorated with a crest depicting two towers in a yellow roundel. I wasn't too sure, but I had a feeling that green and white were the colours of Stonyhurst College, Portas's old Catholic public school. However, what struck me most about our meeting was neither Portas's tie nor the extravagant brolly in his hands. What struck me — more than that: *what practically knocked me out cold* — was that, just as we crossed each other by the loam-coloured front of the Governor's Palace, Portas *purposely looked the other way.*

25.

There was no further communication between us after that. No more raising of the eyebrows. No more half-hearted nods. No more promises to meet up for a few beers one day. And yet it was not as if Portas entirely disappeared from my life either. Through the medium of the *Gibraltar Chronicle*, which was delivered to the library every morning, I was able to keep track of news and developments in the Portas family. In March 1976, I learned that old Mr Portas had passed away and that Henry had been promoted to the post of managing director in the ensuing company reshuffle, Henry's father having replaced the deceased as chairman of the board. Eight months later, a long editorial appeared in the *Chronicle* praising the recent restructuring at Portas and Sons. Spread over two pages, and sounding suspiciously like a paid advertisement, the article provided its readers with a description of the company's ultra-modern new premises in Queensway and commended Portas and Sons' dynamic new managing director for his 'visionary and forward-thinking form of leadership.' There was even a quote from Henry Portas Junior himself: 'To be a competitive company we have to be a company that keeps on renewing itself. It is no use looking back and resting on past glories. That's why we have moved away from Irish Town to our new premises here on Queensway. This is our way of saying *yes* to the future and *yes* to growth and expansion.' Meanwhile, photos of Henry appeared regularly in the *Chronicle* — at all times smiling and elegantly suited, usually engaged in some magnanimous act of charity such as handing a cheque for fifty pounds to the manager of the Lincoln Red Imps Under-15 football team or presenting the director of Mount Alvernia with a brand-new orthopaedic bed. Looking at these photographs was always a peculiar experience for me. Crouched behind the library's issuing desk, I'd gaze at the pictures and think about the Henry Portas I once knew, the one who kept pet tarantulas and chain-smoked hastily rolled spliffs, who wore old cricket jumpers and walked fifty miles for the sake of a two-shilling bet, who climbed the 'Wedding Cake' at St John's New Court and then swam four hundred yards down the Cam to elude his pursuers. *Could this suited, perpetually smiling guy in the newspaper really be the same person as that other Henry Portas?*

Then, in January 1977, the paper carried news of a Portas family tragedy: on the twenty-ninth of December, Henry Portas, MBE, CBE, chairman of Portas and Sons and three times past president of the Gibraltar Chamber of Commerce, former adviser and personal friend of the Chief Minister of Gibraltar, had passed away when his car skidded on a patch of poorly surfaced road and plunged down a forty-foot ravine not far from his second home in Opayar, near Ronda in Spain. His beloved wife Julie Anne, who was in the car with him, was taken to the Hospital Universitario Virgen de la Victoria in Málaga with serious head injuries, but sadly expired shortly afterwards. The precise circumstances leading up to the accident were still unclear, but it was understood that the *Guardia Civil* were questioning the owner of a Seat delivery van who was driving along the same stretch of road at the time of the misfortune and who, allegedly, had been under the influence of drink. Arrangements were currently being made to repatriate the bodies of Mr Portas and his wife so that they could be buried in Gibraltarian soil. It was expected that the date and time of their joint burial would be announced soon. Members of the public wishing to express their condolences to the Portas family were requested not to deliver any floral tributes to their offices in Queensway, but to instead make a donation to the Royal National Lifeboat Institution, a charity the late Mr Portas had always been heavily involved with. The paper went on to list all the many wonderful things that Henry Portas had done for the local community (his campaign for the beautification of Main Street, his long association with the Gibraltar Song Festival, his establishment of the Portas Young Musicians' Foundation, his unfailing patronage of the Gibraltar Society for the Mentally Handicapped) before declaring, with a solemnity of expression highly unusual for a Monday morning editorial, that the deceased had belonged to a generation where honesty and reputation were more important than mere pecuniary gain. In the last line of the article, almost as an aside, it was stated that ownership of the company would now pass on to Mr Henry Portas, the twenty-five-year-old son of the late Mr and Mrs Portas, and his eighteen-year-old sister, Miss Sophia Magdalena Portas.

All during that week I felt bad for Portas. I wanted to call him, to speak to him, to tell him that I was sorry about what happened and ask him if there was anything I could do for him. *Pick up the phone and dial his office number,* a voice in my head continually whispered. *Tell him you're sorry about his loss. Leave a message with somebody if he doesn't want to speak to you. Don't avoid doing the right thing because you've had a stupid fall-out.* But I couldn't bring myself to do it. Repeatedly I picked up the phone and rang the first four digits of the Portas and Sons listing in the Gibraltar Telephone Directory, only to put the receiver down before completing the five-digit number. No, I just couldn't do it. Memories of that upsetting January morning in Main Street kept forcing their way into my head, smothering my resolution. Besides, what was the point of saying sorry to the guy? As far as I could remember, he had never liked his parents anyway. His Lordship and Lady *Enterado-de-Mierda* — that's what he always called them. The Baron and Baroness of *El Puto Culo del Mundo Opayar*. Fair enough, people often say a lot of bad things about their relatives while they are alive and then go into paroxysms of grief once they pass away. But I doubted that Portas was one of that kind — if the cynical way he'd cut me out of his life was anything to go by. No, most probably he'd be telling everybody how desolate he felt, but secretly celebrating his mother's and father's demise. I could see him in my mind's eye: sitting on some padded leather armchair, dressed in those ridiculously posh clothes of his, calmly sipping Dom Perignon or Veuve Clicquot or whatever else sneaky Machiavellian bastards drink to celebrate the closure of a good deal. Screw him, I told myself. Why should you call him? Do you think he'd call you or try to contact you, Brian, if your own mother died? Like hell he would!

And so I abandoned the idea of contacting him and slowly put the episode out of mind. Didn't waste any more time dwelling on the matter. Except that … well, I don't think I ever *completely* forgave myself for being so callous towards him. Once or twice a month from this time onwards I'd find myself dreaming about Portas. My dream was always the same: I'd be in a busy street, with lots of unknown folk striding past me. It looked a little like Main Street, but the buildings on each side were tall and crooked, converging inwards to within touching distance of each other. The people filing past showed no traces of emotion and they were all heading in the same direction. A thick layer of fog had settled over the scene, but it didn't smell briny and laden with damp like the sea mists we sometimes get in Gibraltar; it smelled of melted wax and burning incense. I couldn't see Portas around me, but I knew he was there somewhere in the crowd. I also sensed that something terrible awaited the marchers at the end of that street. Something majorly cataclysmic. I couldn't understand at first what this terrible thing was, but then, as one of the marchers stopped by my side and whispered the word '*lujuria*' in my ear, I realised that the world *terminated there* at the end of the street. I know it sounds strange, but that's how it was in the dream: the world ended there and then there was nothing, just an infinity of dark and starless space. Desperately, I made my way from one person to another, trying to find Portas so that I could warn him about the chasm ahead. I screamed his name. I pushed bodies aside. I spat and cursed. I punched the air in frustration. But it was no use: I'd only catch sight of Portas just as he was about to walk off the end of the earth….

26.

Time passed. In the summer of 1977, Portas married the daughter of a local property developer. She was a slim and pretty woman with an aquiline nose and a partiality for dark sash-tied dresses. There was also a childlike gawkiness about her that suggested a sheltered, or at least a rigidly monitored, upbringing. The happy couple tied the knot in Saint George's Cathedral, Southwark, the church most associated with the Gibraltarian expat community in London, and their photograph appeared in the *Gibraltar Chronicle* a few days afterwards — the bride looking resplendent in a traditional wedding dress of glacé silk, the husband proud and square-jawed in top hat and tails. Nine months later, the following notice was published in the *Chronicle's* classified section:

> PORTAS. On March 3, at St Bernard's Hospital, to Isobel, née Peresso, and Henry, God's precious gift of TWINS – MARIA ELENA and HENRY CHARLES STUART. Sincere thanks to Dr Massaro and all the staff on Lady Mackintosh Ward and the Maternity and Obstetrics Unit. *Deo Gratias*.

For two or three months after the announcement there was no news about Portas in the local paper. No pics, no charity donations, no presentation of raffle prizes — nothing of the sort. But once this self-imposed moratorium was over, it was very much business as usual, with hardly a week going by without Portas's photograph appearing in the back pages of the *Chronicle*. Typically, he'd be standing there in a suit and with a big grin on his face. A jumbo cardboard cheque would be passing from his hands to the hands of the President of the Gibraltar Football Association or the Chairman for the Gibraltar Society for the Mentally Handicapped or some other smiling local worthy. What was really strange was that, even though his picture kept appearing in the paper, I seldom saw him anywhere. It was almost as if he no longer lived in Gibraltar, as if he didn't want to mix with the community he was supposed to be doing so much for. I could only assume that he was spending most of his time in the family home in Spain and just came to Gibraltar now and then to oversee his business affairs … and be photographed for the *Chronicle*.

As for me, I continued stamping books and issuing late-return fines at the John Mackintosh Hall Library. I'm not sure what else I can say about those first few years back in Gibraltar. For eighteen months or so I told myself the usual lies that people cling to when trapped in a job they don't like: that I'd soon find a different job, that my time at the library was only a stop-gap, that I'd go back to the UK if I didn't find anything better by the end of next summer. I even wrote down all the horrible things I'd say to Pozo-Jones on the day of my departure and frequently rehearsed them in my head. Sadly, though, the opportunity to call my boss an '*entrometido de mierda*' and a 'self-satisfied fucker' never materialised. Slowly, without realising it, I began to abandon all hope of escape — till in the end I simply stopped believing that I'd ever leave the library. You could call it the usual dead-end job story: you swallow so many daily doses of poison that in due course you can no longer taste the venom.

Then, in June 1978, I embarked on an ill-fated liaison with a woman called Sarah Anne Aguilera. She worked at the canteen on the ground floor of the John Mackintosh Hall, where she served coffee and bacon sandwiches to the centre's patrons, and she was ten years older than me. Angular bony hips. Undyed flecks of grey in her hair. Always carried crumpled balls of tissue stuffed in her skirt pockets. Roughly twice a month she'd come upstairs to the library and borrow one of those Harlequin Romance novels which were so popular in the Seventies and Eighties. She was not beautiful in the ordinary sense of the word, but she had the tiniest hands that I had ever seen — delicate, blue-veined scraps of cartilage and skin which reminded me of those waxen ex-votos found in most Catholic countries. I can't remember how it happened, but one day we got talking at the issuing counter and a couple of evenings later we went on our first date together. The venue for our rendezvous was the Regal Cinema on Reclamation Road; the film we watched *Logan's Run*. Having lived a life of celibacy for a number of years, I found myself gulping down mouthfuls of saliva and grinding my teeth during the entire showing, unable to concentrate on anything except the ectomorphic form of my companion sitting in the dark beside me. *Shall I put my arm around her shoulders, or shall I sit here and play it cool? Shall I take hold of her hand now, or shall I wait until the interval when the lights are switched on?* Over and over again I'd decide what I was going to do, only to lose heart and change my mind at the last moment. Finally, just as I thought that nothing would ever come out of this damned situation, Sarah Anne Aguilera leaned towards me and gently laid her head on my shoulder.

Our relationship was an odd one right from the start. On a typical day, Sarah Anne would wait for me by the John Mackintosh Hall's entrance (the canteen closed at a quarter to six, fifteen minutes before the library) and then we'd walk quietly together to the damp-infested pre-War flat she shared with her mum and two older sisters on City Mill Lane. Sometimes we'd stop for a cake and a coffee at the Piazza Grill — consumed on the outdoor terrace in rigid silence — but most of the time we'd go straight back to hers to watch whatever was on the telly that night: game shows, soap operas, comedies, adverts, football matches, even documentaries if there was *'nada interesante'* on the other TVE channel. At first I didn't mind that she was so quiet and watched so much TV. She did read those Harlequin Romance novels now and again, after all, didn't she? And I also knew that she browsed through the *Gibraltar Chronicle* every morning at work. In any case, there was something rather refreshing about her taciturnity. A ladylike air of modesty. However, as the weeks passed and I got to know more about my new belle, I slowly revised my opinions. Still waters may sometimes run deep, as the saying goes, but in this case they were so still they were practically stagnant. What a bastard, I can hear you exclaim. Looking down at the woman just because he studied at Cambridge. But wait a minute, wait a minute. It's not as if I even wanted intellectual conversation from her, for Christ's sake! All I wanted was normality. Plain, bog-standard normality! You know: mood swings, half-hour trips to the bathroom, a love of gossip, an obsessive interest in shoes and handbags, saying that she wasn't hungry and then duly helping herself to food from my plate. That kind of thing. What I didn't want, what I could never for the life of me have envisaged, was someone whose *sole intellectual input* during our time together was to turn around halfway through a TVE documentary on the Second World War and, lowering her coffee mug, with a perfectly straight face, ask me if I had ever heard about 'this Auschwitz place' before.

By the seventh or eighth week, I couldn't take it any more: I knew that I had to get rid of her. To put it bluntly, Sarah Anne bored me. Bored me *big-time.* She also embarrassed me. Wounded my already delicate sense of self-esteem with her silly remarks and her even sillier face. One afternoon, as we sat together outside the Piazza Grill, I saw Portas walk by in one of his Savile Row suits and I found myself inwardly cringing at the thought that he might have spotted me sitting with her. Actually, was that a sneer on his lips? It seemed like one, didn't it? As I reached for my coffee cup, I looked at Sarah Anne and then I thought about Portas's long-legged, slim-hipped wife with the model looks. Yes, it must have been a sneer. Of that there was no doubt. *The guy had seen my partner and sniggered.* The thought saddened me, but it also stiffened my resolve to dump Sarah Anne before things got even more complicated. The question was how to get rid of her without upsetting her fragile mental equilibrium. From her eldest sister, I knew that Sarah Anne had been really devastated after splitting up with her last boyfriend, a one-eyed insurance clerk from Glacis called Hector. 'Our poor *chiquita's* just so frail, Brian,' the sister once said to me, picking up a digestive biscuit and dunking it in her tea with a menacing look. 'Had to spend nine months on Trazodone after that business with that nasty *tuerto* Hector. Absolutely torn to shreds she was, *la pobrecita mía.*'

For weeks and weeks I bided my time, hoping to find the right place and moment to do the needful. What I did not know, alas, was that, just at the same time that I was plotting my great escape, my poor *chiquita* had grown just as disenchanted with me and was hatching a similar disentangling manoeuvre. In fact, the wily lass beat me to it! Putting down a half-eaten *mantecado* on her plate one afternoon at the

Piazza Grill, she leaned across our table and, in a surprisingly calm voice, said, 'Look, I know you're a really nice guy and all that, Brian, but I don't think things between us are working, are they? Please don't take it the wrong way, but I just find being with you a little boring. Maybe it's better if we call it a day once and for all, *no crees?'*

What a funny old world it is, isn't it? I had spent weeks plotting how to get rid of Sarah Anne, only to be dumped in the end by the victim of my intended 'dumping.' Yet that is not all that was strange about my first foray into the world of adult relationships. Even more weirdly, I found myself wishing that we had never split up. Can you believe that? *I actually regretted that I was no longer with Sarah Anne Aguilera!* Had I dumped her myself, I am sure I would have effortlessly forgotten her and her *monosyllabicity*. Goodbye, *chiquita mía,* I'd have thought. Hope you enjoy watching your silly TVE programmes without this mug around. But because she dumped me first, because in doing so she caught me unawares, I could not get the lady out of my head. On going to bed at night, I'd constantly think about her and our afternoons together at the Piazza Grill, mentally recreating how she used to sit there staring at the bar snacks menu or eating her *mantecados* without spilling any crumbs. I'd remember all her positive qualities: her honesty, her gentle spirit, her impeccable moral compass. Similarly, when arriving at the John Mackintosh Hall in the mornings, I'd slink past the downstairs canteen, trying to catch a glimpse of my 'former beloved' behind the serving counter, wondering how I could have ever looked down on someone who, almost in every way you could think of, was a much better and more decent person than me. Unsurprisingly, I felt confused and a touch disorientated, unable to understand what was going on in my head. However, all that was nothing compared to what was about to happen next. As Shakespeare writes in *Hamlet,* 'When sorrows come, they come not single spies/ But in battalions.' Or as they say a little more gruffly, but no less insightfully, in the bars and backstreets of present-day Gibraltar: *Cuando llueve no solamente llueve, sino que cae a cántaros.*

27.

It all started with my kid sister Mariela. The last time we encountered her, remember, was in September 1974, just before the start of my fourth and final year at university. I had returned home for a few days and my mother had picked me up at the airport. On the drive back to Laguna, Mariela had sat beside me and rattled on about a swimming gala she was attending at the Nuffield Pool — a fidgety, pigtailed thirteen-year-old who just wouldn't shut up. Now, four years later, Mariela was seventeen and doing her A-levels at the Gibraltar Girls' Comprehensive School. Slim and athletic, tolerant by inclination and slow to take offence, she was one of those blessedly uncomplicated kids who are loved by everybody in class and always end up being inducted into positions of responsibility. Her track record for the last few years spoke for itself: head girl at Saint Anne's Middle School, Girl Guide leader at fourteen, captain of the Gibraltar Girls' Comprehensive Debating Society at the age of fifteen. Needless to say, my mother loved Mariela. Adored her with a real passion. What's more, she was convinced that the kid would follow in my footsteps and gain admission to either Oxford or Cambridge and do something '*muy importante*' there like Law or Medicine.

This, then, was how things stood at the beginning of October 1978. Mariela was going to go to Oxford or Cambridge. And she was to become a doctor. A neurosurgeon, perhaps. Or maybe an oncologist. Somebody important, at any rate. Worthy of respect. Of course, there was a lot of wishful thinking in all this. Just because I had gone to Cambridge didn't necessarily mean that my sister was going to do the same. In fact, if you sat down to think about it, *it was a veritable miracle* that one of us had done so well. First and foremost, there was our social background — dragged down as it was by my mother's *costurera* duties on one side and my late father's militant trade unionism on the other. Then there was our upbringing, which was hardly spectacular either. Yes, our mother always made sure that we had pens and protractors and everything else that we needed for our lessons. That much I admit. But did she sit and read with us like middle-class parents do with their children? Did she scrimp and save so that she could send us to private lessons? Did she ask us from time to time how our studies were going? No, of course not. Education, as far as my mother was concerned, was a mechanism you wound up once and left to run on its own accord, rather like one of those self-winding Swiss watches that were so popular in the late Sixties.

Anyway, I know that all this is a bit of a digression, but it is one that will shed light on what happened next. Early one afternoon — it couldn't have been more than a week or two after Sarah Anne and I split up — Mariela came back to the flat and said she had something very important to tell us. 'Actually, I've got *two* very important things to tell you,' she said, swallowing hard. The first thing was that she now had a boyfriend. Thomas Michael Campbell was his name. A twenty-two-year-old private serving in the Royal Anglians, the resident British regiment. The second thing … well, it's not that difficult to guess: she was pregnant. Three months gone already. 'You can just about see the bump if you look carefully,' Mariela said, patting her stomach over her white school blouse. 'I've already told my form tutor Miss Cerisola that I'll be leaving Westside at the end of the month.'

There are revelations that upset us, and revelations that pin us down, spit in our face and then rent the fabric of our measly terrestrial existence. For my mother this was one of the latter. Though all she did was stand there and nod like one of those novelty dogs that people put in the back of cars, I knew that her entire world had been turned upside down. *Turned upside down and inside out,* to borrow the words of the famous Diana Ross song. And I also knew, from the feverish glimmer in her eye, that she hated this Campbell kid with every fibre in her being. She hated everything about him: that he was English and not Gibraltarian, that he was a soldier in the British Army, that he was older than Mariela, that he wasn't Catholic, that he had the same name as a can of soup. But what she hated above all else, what she could never forgive him for, was that the horny little bastard had singlehandedly destroyed her dream of seeing her *Marielita* strutting around one day in the white gown of a highly paid hospital consultant.

'*Anda, niña,*' I said, trying to lighten the atmosphere, 'you sure kept that one quiet, didn't you?… Don't you think, Ma?'

But Mary Manrique didn't respond. Instead she shook her head, looked at the floor, shuffled out of the living room and, locking herself in the toilet, started howling *like a mortally wounded animal.*

28.

My mother barely left her room in the next few days. Pots and pans were soon lying heaped and unwashed in the kitchen sink. Towels and clothes accumulated on the bathroom floor. It was only when Mariela went out to see her boyfriend that Mary would emerge, careworn and heavy-lidded, into the half-light of the living room. Slowly, without looking me in the eye, she'd sit down by the statue of Jesus she kept on the sideboard and start complaining about *la gran vergüenza* that had befallen our family. She'd moan about all sorts of unrelated things: how this kid Campbell had ruined her *niñita's* reputation, how she wished she had stopped Mariela from going out so much, how her own life — *mi puerca, puñetera vida,* as she called it — was no longer worth living. To make her feel better, I ventured that perhaps, who knows, Mariela might have not got into Cambridge anyway. This, alas, only made things worse. 'But what are you saying, *Briallito?*' she snapped. '*La niña* would have gone to Cambridge *or ese sitio* Oxford for sure. Everybody knows that, *por Dios!*'

I didn't press the matter any further, but the more I thought of it, the more I doubted that Mariela would have made it to Cambridge. It's not that her grades at school were mediocre (in fact, they were consistently above-average); it's just that she was too popular and well-liked to be an exceptional student. Most classrooms have a kid like that. They are so good-looking, so good at sport, so good at making friends, so good at bloody everything they do, that they don't feel the need to devote themselves wholeheartedly to their studies. Why should they, really? What's the point of studying if you can achieve everything you want *simply by being who you are?* Viewed in this light, Mariela was my very antithesis. She had friends by the dozen; I had none. She was good looking; I was physically unremarkable. Clearly, out of the two of us I had drawn the short straw. But being such an outsider was not a completely bad thing either. We outsiders seek refuge in our studies, we are driven by the need to continually prove ourselves. To the casual eye it might seem as if we are always alone, but do not be fooled: there is always a demon trudging by our side, an invisible devil who prods us past the barriers of class, ethnicity and upbringing. Obsession, fixation, hysteria, enduring resentment, the desire to work harder and longer than anyone else — these are the weapons we bring to the classroom and the exam hall. Mariela, fortunately, was never part of this cursed breed. Mariela was an *insider*, she was a being of light, she was the sun around which others revolved. That is why I knew she would have never made it to Cambridge: she was too good, too simple, too pure. Like her friends at school used to say: *esa Mariela es una 'buenacha' de verdá.*

My mother never stopped believing that Thomas Michael Campbell wrecked her daughter's academic career, but she couldn't keep Mariela at bay for long. I think it had something to do with the bump that was getting bigger and bigger on Mariela's belly with each passing week. As a man I am not exactly qualified to talk about these things, but I suppose that it is relatively easy to hate your daughter when she is standing there looking as scrawny as ever, but somewhat harder when it becomes visually obvious that your own grandchild, *your own flesh and blood*, is growing inside her. Anyway, whatever the cause, mother and daughter soon patched things up. More than that: they became practically inseparable. Not a day would now go by without Mary buying some knick-knack for Mariela's unborn kid; not an hour would pass without her speculating what this half-English, half-Gibraltarian grandchild of hers would look like. 'What do you think, *Briallito?*' she'd say. 'Do you think he or she will have *ojos oscuros* like your sister has, or *ojos claros* like this Campbell boy?' Yes, no doubt about it: the old girl was excited, genuinely keyed up. What kiddy clothes she'd buy, where she'd take baby for his or her walks, what names would match the surname Campbell (Camilo, Nuno or Charles if a boy; Manuela, Rosario or Karina if a girl), where we'd celebrate *el bautizo*: she had it all sussed out, all carefully planned. But then came the bombshell that smashed everything to smithereens: we heard that the Royal Anglians were being deployed to Cyprus at the start of the new year.

'But is it wise to follow him to Cyprus in your condition, Mariela?' my mother asked, pausing from her sewing duties in the living room. 'Can't he just give up his job and find *algo aquí en Gibraltar?*'

'He can't do that, Ma,' my sister gently but firmly replied. 'He's under contract with the army until August 1982. In any case, he wants to stay in the army until he finishes his electrical engineering training. Says he will be able to get a much better civilian job once he gets his qualifications. I think he's got a point, too.'

Mary nodded and smiled at these words. But I knew that she was terribly pained. I could see it in her eyes — an unspoken but deep-seated anguish. That same afternoon I told Mariela how concerned I was about our mother, but there was nothing, of course, that the poor girl could do. She merely smiled sadly and said she'd try to talk to Mary in the evening. And, to be fair to our Mariela, she did her best to cheer up our mum: promising that she'd write regularly, that she'd phone every week, that she'd visit us every summer and every Christmas, that she'd send loads of pictures of her child when he or she was born. To all this Mary responded by smiling at Mariela and tenderly stroking her daughter's long brown hair. 'You're a sweetie,' she said, choking back a tear of emotion. 'A real sweetie-pie. Do you know that, *niñita mía?*'

And so, on the third of January 1979, Mariela caught a military flight to Limassol with Thomas Michael Campbell. Mary and I watched them leave from the upstairs terrace of the airport terminal, frantically waving at her as she boarded her RAF transport plane. Then we went to fetch our car, which my mother — uncharacteristically for her — had left parked on double yellow lines outside the terminal building. For the next few days my mother talked incessantly about Mariela — wondering if she liked the food in Cyprus, asking me what language they spoke there, hoping that she was getting along with the other Army girlfriends and wives. There was still a little bitterness in her voice, but it was nowhere near as pronounced as I had anticipated. One day she even said that perhaps it was a good thing that Mariela had got together with an Englishman, since her child would technically be English and therefore stand a better chance of getting a good job in the long run. '*Tu sabes* what these things are like, *Briallito. Contra más inglés*, *más* opportunities *tiene uno.*' Listening to these words gave me some hope, made me feel that she was at last accepting things for what they were. Regrettably, it was only a mirage. On the fifth of March 1979 — just a week before Mariela's due date — my mother lay down in bed and never got up again. *Massive myocardial infarction*, Dr Jayawardena, a locum at Saint Bernard's Hospital, told me later that night. *Would have died in seconds, Mr Manrique. Not a bad way to go, if I may say so.* Even after the news was relayed to me, I could not stop pacing up and down the corridor outside the bereavement suite, so bizarre and unreal did it all seem. It was almost as if my brain knew that Mary was dead, but my heart and body refused to accept the idea, as if a part of me still clung to the hope that any minute now I'd be called into the suite by a nurse and I'd see my mother in there, propped up groggily against her pillow and with breathing tubes attached to her nose. So I just carried on walking up and down the corridor — with my hands behind my back and my eyes fixed on the floor, counting the cracks on the rubber tiles, blocking out all unpleasant thoughts … until in the end, just after one in the morning, a hospital porter came along and said I needed to vacate the corridor because he had to shut down that part of the hospital for the night and he could not do it while I was still there. If I needed a place to go to, he said, there was always the waiting room outside the maternity ward on the other side of the hospital. Some of the seats there, he said, were comfortable enough to sleep on.

29.

At first sight there was no connection between Mariela's departure and my mother's demise. An interval of two months separated one event from the other, and, if that wasn't enough, my mother had seemed really happy and relaxed in the run-up to her death. But in my heart of hearts I knew that the doctors at Saint Bernard's had got it wrong. It was no blood clot in a coronary artery that killed Mary Manrique; it was that her daughter had robbed her first of one dream and then of the other. The enormous shock, the shattered hopes, the sense of abandonment and betrayal: that was what had killed her. Did this mean that Mariela was responsible for my mother's death? No, I don't think so. Though I initially hated my sister for the turmoil she had put Mary through, the poor girl had just stood by her man and acted in the best interests of her unborn child. You couldn't really blame her for that. In fact, as the days passed and my brain went through the usual post-funeral mental somersaults, I completely exonerated Mariela and blamed myself for what had happened. Why hadn't I taken better care of Mary during the last two months? Why hadn't I tried to cheer her up? Why had I thought she was slowly getting over Mariela's departure (when all along she was sinking into a morass of darkness and despair)? No, Brian, don't kid yourself about all this, I thought. Stop passing the buck. If anybody is to blame for the death of Mary Manrique, it is not the eighteen-year-old girl who faithfully followed her husband-to-be to a foreign country, but the grown-up son who was so self-absorbed that he failed to spot the signs of impending tragedy.

So once again I found myself in the same old position — pissed off with life and wishing that I could turn the clock back and do things differently. What made the situation even worse was the realisation that I had always been so indifferent to my mother in the past, so uncaring. Subconsciously, I had assumed that she would always be there — bumbling around the apartment with her duster or sitting on the deckchair in the balcony sewing and listening to her *radionovelas*. Never for a moment had I thought there'd come a day when the place would be without her. Number 18 Boyd House without Mary Manrique? Nah, that couldn't be right. The old girl will still be pottering around the flat well into her nineties. For sure she will. And yet now, just three and a half years after my return from Cambridge, Mary Manrique was gone, taken away from this earthly life at the cruelly young age of fifty-six. Why didn't I tell her that I loved her when I had a chance? That I admired her for having undergone so many hardships for my sake? Had it really been so difficult? Couldn't I have spared just a few minutes to let her know about my feelings? *Thank you, Mum, for always being there for me,* was all I needed to say. *You may irritate the shit out of me with your radionovelas and your Spanish television programmes, but I still love you more than anyone else in the world. I always have and I always will!* The worst part of it all was coming back to the empty flat after work. Every room in that apartment was impregnated with different associations for me; every last corner imbued with pain-inducing memories. Here the woollen throw used to protect my mother's second-hand leather sofa; there the Hitachi radio she had bought in December but had not taken out of its box yet because, Mary being Mary, she wanted to 'save it' for a new *radionovela* starting in May. To make things easier, I began to get rid of the old furniture and redecorate the flat in my own style. For once I was ruthless — painting the walls in bright colours and placing my mother's jewellery and other personal possessions in cardboard boxes well out of sight. Above all, I wanted to 'deconsecrate' the place, to purge it of old resonances and associations. But even so, the memories carried on assaulting me. They came in the guise of resurfacing objects — a silver thimble found one day behind the living room sideboard, the Ventolin inhalers turning up at the back of drawers and cupboards, a handwritten shopping list lying in a tatty handbag. Strangely, whenever I was reminded of my mother in this way, I also thought about my long-gone father. I thought about the bits and pieces I had once associated with him: his Bic pens, his Tom Thumb cigars, his union membership card, his white linen handkerchiefs, his tubs of Vicks ointment. Had my mother also come across these items after his death? Had she suffered a similar sense of loss whenever they occasionally resurfaced? Most probably, I told myself. You know what it is like with these things: you try your best to forget about the dead, but the dead *keep reaching out and reminding you not to forsake them.*

The weeks passed and nothing changed. I carried out my duties at the library with even less interest than usual and then wearily returned home in the evenings, still having to hold my breath for a few agonising seconds before I opened the door and walked into what I still regarded as Mary Manrique's domain. By this stage the flat had been stripped of all my mother's possessions except for her numerous Sacred Heart statues which, more out of superstition than filial devotion, I could not bring myself to get rid of. You'd encounter these former emblems of her faith in every room. Statues just a couple of inches taller than Action Men. Statues that came all the way up to your waist. Statues with chipped toes and fingers. Statues that had toppled over and cracked into different pieces (and which Mary had subsequently put back together with a mixture of Polyfilla, glue and Airfix model paint). For over four months, despite the uneasiness I felt being surrounded by so many figures, I had kept all the statues where my mother had left them. In some ways, it was like being under surveillance. Roll over in bed to switch on the bedside lamp, say, and, what do you know, Jesus Christ would be there parting his cloak and pointing at his eviscerated heart. Walk into the toilet to do your business and who's staring down at you from the windowsill if not good old JC again, this time standing there with a doleful expression and his ripped-out heart resting on his palm. It was spiritual harassment, that's what it was. And I was getting sick and tired of it. One day, after a particularly stressful afternoon at work during which Pozo-Jones had scolded me for ordering two globe-shaped bookends, I decided to take remedial action. Going around the flat, I gathered all the statues together and then took them one by one into the balcony, where I lined them up in rows. There they remained for a week or two, an orchard of different-sized, multi-coloured figures occupying the entire balcony floor. However, even in this out-of-the-way location, the damn things continued preying on my mind. So one morning I walked to the Cathedral of Saint Mary the Crowned with one of the smaller pieces and asked the resident priest if he wanted a collection of twelve different statues of the Sacred Heart of Jesus. The cleric, an old fellow with a goatee and hairy nostrils, said they had more Jesus statues in the cathedral cellar than they knew what to do with, but thanked me for the offer anyway. Slightly disappointed, I turned around and walked along the central aisle of the church with the statue tucked under my arm. Before leaving the building, though, I decided to sit down for a breather on one of the back pews. Here I remained for about ten minutes, gazing at a couple of *beatas* praying on their knees and with their eyes closed. The midday sun was filtering through the stained-glass window behind me, imprinting hazy patches of yellow and pink on the marble floor tiles. Candles flickered hypnotically in front of a life-size statue of the Virgin Mary. As I sat there with the small figurine at my side, I started to relax and forget about the problems associated with the world outside. Maybe it had something to do with the heady smell of incense. Maybe it was the sight of all those carnations and roses laid around the main altar. Maybe it was the fact that it was so quiet in there and the hustle and bustle of Main Street only reached you as a far-off whisper. Frankly, I don't know what triggered it. All I know is that, seated there on my own, nothing mattered except the actuality of the present moment. My mother's death, my sister in Cyprus, my troubles at the library, all those statues I couldn't get rid of — none of it counted any more, none of it had the power to haunt me. Resting there with my unwanted Christ, I had found my own private and protected space.

30.

The last time I regularly attended church was in 1964 or 1965, before Mary, Mariela and I moved to Laguna Estate. We used to live back then in *el Patio Carrera*, a long, shadowy alleyway just off Engineer Lane. Every Sunday morning my mother would take my little sister and me to Saint Mary the Crowned, the three of us attired in newly washed and ironed clothes. Like most young kids forced to attend church, I found the services long and tedious and kept looking at my watch to gauge how much longer I needed to be there. At a certain point, though, I was offered a part-time job sorting and delivering newspapers for Sacarello's the newsagent on a Sunday morning. The working hours were from seven to midday, which meant that if I accepted the job I could no longer go to the ten o'clock service that my mother liked to attend. At first Mary was against the idea, saying that no son of hers would imperil his immortal soul for tuppence-ha'penny an hour. But when my father (who by this stage, bless him, only had a few months left to live) said that getting a part-time job would teach me the value of hard graft and that, in any case, I could always attend one of the Saturday evening services on my own, she grudgingly relented. 'Okay, then, *Briallito*. Take that job if you must. *Pero* don't forget to keep your promise: you have to attend Mass on your own every Saturday evening.' For the first couple of weeks, I did her bidding and went to the Cathedral of Saint Mary the Crowned every Saturday afternoon, fervently praying that none of my classmates at Saint Anne's would spot me walking into the building dressed in the ridiculous shirt and tie get-up that my mother compelled me to wear. Then one day, as I was about to submit myself to yet another round of liturgical torture, I saw a group of them seated on the wrought-iron benches opposite the cathedral's entrance. '*Qué pasa, Miliki?*' one of the kids shouted. 'Going to church to see little baby Jesus, are we now, *compá?*'

I knew my tormentor well: his name was Almagro and he was one of the nastiest bullies in my class. Large of head but small of brain, he was one of those sadistic bastards who pounce on the slightest scrap of vulnerability and then store it for future reference, cruelly regurgitating every last detail about your weakness when you least expected it. Entering the cathedral now, evidently, wouldn't be a good idea. No, not just that: it would be the kind of thing hurled against me once back in the classroom. Clearly, I had to come up with some sort of get-out plan — and I had to do so fast. To this end I continued walking past the building's entrance and then shouted the first words coming into my head:

'Sorry to disappoint you, Derek. But I'm only on my way to my cousin's at Humphrey's. See you on Monday, guys.'

After this incident, I never went to church again. What I did instead was to wander around the centre of town just long enough to make my mother believe that I had attended the Saturday evening service. My route tended to be the same each week. Up Main Street and past the Humphrey's tower blocks on Red Sands Road, then back down into town via Rosia Road, Line Wall Road and Cooperage Lane. A stroll of forty-five minutes, maybe fifty if I stopped to buy a packet of Treets at the sweet shop near John Mackintosh Square. Sometimes, if it was raining or a strong Levanter was blowing, I'd cut out the 'Humphrey's loop' and turn back at the Trafalgar Cemetery, thereby reducing my spell away from home by ten or twelve minutes. Each time this happened, I could feel my mother's eyes probing me back at our Carrera's Passage flat, studying my countenance for signs of trickery or deception. But I always had all bases covered. 'It was Father Carter officiating tonight. Nice and quick as always,' I'd say, smiling ever so sweetly. Or: 'Funny, what happened this evening. There was a power cut halfway through the Creed and Father Bruzon had no option but to dismiss us with a quick blessing.'

Visiting the cathedral all those years later, however, was a very different experience. Where before there had been embarrassment and uncertainty, now there was only equanimity and tranquillity. Whereas in the past I had associated churches with old women and decrepitude, now they stood for stillness and the smell of incense and flowers. Yet it would be a mistake to assume that I went there for traditional religious reasons. For a start, I never prayed or dialogued with God in my head. And I never attended Mass either. Actually, I avoided it like the plague. If, by some remote chance, I got my times mixed up and walked into the building just as a service was beginning, I'd march straight out and spend the next half an hour meandering up and down Main Street, waiting for the Mass to finish and the cathedral to disgorge its *feligreses*. The only service which I didn't particularly mind, thinking about it now, was the recitation of the rosary. There was something soothing about all that chanting, oddly comforting.

Anyway, the weeks passed and I continued going to Saint Mary's. As a rule, I'd visit the building on the way to work in the morning and again on the way back home in the early afternoon — times when the church was guaranteed to be empty. With the help of these visits and the passing of time, I finally started coming to terms with my mother's death, slowly consigning the event and its memory to a past that no longer had the power to oppress me. What's more, the flat lost many of its painful associations. In fact, so complete was the transformation that I even began to remove some of the Sacred Heart statues from the balcony and place them back where they had originally stood. Meanwhile, back at the library, things were just as they had always been. Pozo-Jones kept pontificating and finding it hard to delegate; Cortijo didn't stop harping on about my Cambridge degree; and the punters carried on borrowing their Catherine Cookson and Barbara Cartland novels. Granted, now and again I'd go through moments when I was conscious that I was leading an extremely boring life and that my youth was slowly haemorrhaging away. But thankfully these episodes didn't last very long. Besides, boredom meant no nasty surprises. Boredom meant no upheavals. Boredom meant knowing what was in store tomorrow morning and the day after tomorrow. And that, when all was said and done, was just how Brian Manrique liked it.

31.

And so the years passed. 1979 became 1980, which in turn became 1981, which in turn became 1982. What can I tell you about those years that you won't be able to imagine for yourself? I carried on going to church twice a day and I continued stamping books at the library and I also began to grow a fair share of grey hairs on my head. Suffice to say, there were precious few highlights during this time. At least twice a year the rumour would spread through the library that Pozo-Jones was about to retire on medical grounds and that I would be promoted to the post of director in his absence. But by the end of 1981 I had heard this rumour so many times that I no longer paid any attention to it. Subconsciously, in any case, I already knew what would happen: Pozo-Jones would stay there until the age of seventy or seventy-five and I'd carry on ordering what I thought were subversive French and Italian books without realising that they had long since become established literary classics. Apart from that — what else? Well, every Christmas I'd receive a card from my sister containing a picture of herself and her little boy. The postmark on the envelope always showed a different place: Akrotiri,

Aldershot, Hiddenhausen in Germany. Inside there'd be twelve or fourteen lines letting me know how she and her family were doing. There'd also be a five-pound note so that I could buy a bunch of white carnations to take down to North Front Cemetery and place on our mother's grave. A truly beautiful gesture, sis. Very poetic and thoughtful. Anyway, what else can I tell you about those twilight years when nothing seemed to matter any more? Surely, there must be something else? Surely, there must! Oh, yes, *there is* one more thing — in October 1981 my ex-girlfriend Sarah Anne Aguilera married a policeman called Michael Rogelio. News of the event was brought up to the library by Mrs Amelia Ferrara, one of the John Mackintosh Hall cleaners. Wheezingly, resting both arms on the issuing counter, she declared that Sarah Anne had looked quite stunning in her bridal dress on the day of the ceremony and that her husband too had scrubbed up really well. This was confirmed days later when Mr and Mrs Rogelio's photo appeared on the classifieds page of the *Gibraltar Chronicle* — she with a surprisingly low décolletage, he smiling and thrusting out his chest like a *machote* policeman. A year or two earlier, this grainy black-and-white photograph might have triggered a series of 'what ifs' in my head. But the truth is that I rarely thought about women any more. Just as I had given up hope a long time ago of obtaining a job away from the library, so too I had abandoned hope of ever finding a wife or a girlfriend. Occasionally, yes, I'd think back to that first year at Cambridge and the half a dozen conquests I somehow managed to make. But every time I did so it was with a feeling of puzzlement, rather like the ninety-year-old ex-mountaineer who, looking back on the memorable day when he climbed the Matterhorn some sixty-five years earlier, scratches his grizzled chin and thinks, 'did I really do something like that?'

So this, more or less, was how things stood for me at the start of 1982. I was twenty-nine years old and I lived alone in a government flat with twelve different sized statues of the Sacred Heart of Jesus and I hadn't been with a woman for about three and a half years. Taking all this into account, you would have never thought that my life was about to undergo one of those dramatic, mind-jolting turns that only occur in books and films, would you? Yet this is exactly what happened after the Christmas holidays, on the second of January 1982 to be precise. To all appearances, it was just like any other day. I had spent the afternoon listening to Pozo-Jones's complaints about the increasing number of children's books being vandalised and then made my way to the cathedral, where I had sat near the votive candle stand for around fifteen minutes. By the time I got back home to Boyd House, it was close to seven. Though it was already quite dark, the lights still hadn't been turned on in the stairwell. A stiff easterly breeze blew through the unglazed concrete fenestrations set into the side of the building, bringing with it the smell of the sea and the unmistakable sound of a Hercules transport plane screeching to a halt about two-thirds of a mile away on the airport runway. On entering the flat, I switched on the vestibule light and hung my coat on the peg attached to the back of the front door. I yawned aloud, scratched my neck, then kicked off my shoes. Driven not so much by hunger but by a desire to stem the gurgling in my stomach, I put a frozen meal in the oven and settled on the sofa with a library book — *Les Caves du Vatican* by André Gide. I had reached the part in the novel where the protagonist, Lafcadio Wluiki, finds himself alone on a night train from Rome to Naples with the naïve and God-fearing Amédée Fleurissoire. Lafcadio is a violent man, a thug subject to irrational impulses. Succumbing to one of these moments of madness, he gets up from his seat and says to Amédée, 'Sir, your presence offends me; I fear I am going to have to kill you.' He then grabs the bumbling provincial by the neck and tries to push him out of the train. It was precisely at this point, just as Lafcadio was about to murder Amédée, that I heard someone knocking on my front door. Three sets of three short raps. Brusque, bristling with impatience. Bloody Jehovah Witnesses, I thought, shaking my head. Always turning up at the most inopportune times. Annoyed, I laid the book on the sofa's armrest and marched to the door, already thinking how to get rid of the pesky irritants. But when I unfastened the latch and swung the door towards me, I almost had to rub my eyes to make sure I wasn't hallucinating:

'My God … Henry. What are you doing here? Are you okay, man? You look dreadful.'

32.

It was a lie: he looked *worse than dreadful.* Rivulets of sweat were trickling down his forehead, forming a constellation of drops in the shallow depression above his eyebrows. His thick blond hair was messy and uncombed. His gaze, normally so alert and piercing, was now distant and unfocused, his tired eyelids hanging like scraps of ancient parchment over two shrunken eyes. Splattered across his suit jacket was a dark crimson substance which I at first took for blood, but which, judging from its stickiness and the way it hadn't fully coagulated yet, I soon realised was no more than hot chilli sauce. He was also swaying unsteadily on his feet, as if he were about to collapse at any second. Before he had a chance to explain what was going on, I put a steadying arm around his shoulders and helped him through my front door. As we staggered our way down the corridor, he kept mumbling the word 'sorry' over and over again. He repeated the word so many times, and in such a robotic tone, that it felt as if he was saying 'flannel' or 'jelly' or 'belfry' or something else that made no sense. Still holding him up by the shoulders, ignoring the smell of alcohol on his breath, I turned towards him and asked him what he was sorry for.

'For everything, old boy,' he replied, sounding surprisingly lucid for a moment. 'For turning up at your flat in this drunken state. For not even warning you that I was coming. For having forgotten you during all these years. For being such a false and faithless friend.'

I led him to the sofa in the living room and sat him down. Then I helped him take off his jacket and, making sure that the sauce-stained bits were facing up, laid the garment on the coffee table. The thing reeked not just of kebab meat and chilli sauce, but also of sweat and strong alcohol. Fighting off a wave of disgust, I crouched by his side and asked him what had happened.

'I'll tell you in a minute, old chap,' he croaked in an oddly high-pitched voice, 'but first of all do me a favour and get me a drink, please. Preferably a whisky, if you have some.'

'Are you sure, Henry? I mean, look at the state you're in. Do you think it's wise to carry on drinking alcohol when you're in this sort of state?'

'Listen, Brian, my dear old friend,' he slurred with one eye more open than the other, 'I know your intentions are good, but I can assure you that one more whisky won't make the slightest bit of difference to the state I'm in. I'm already fully pickled, *amigacho,* as high as a kite. So, please, old boy, don't make me beg you. Just bring us a drink of whatever you have. Whisky. Rum. Gin. Cognac. Brandy. It doesn't matter what it is as long as it's strong. As soon as I have a drink in my hands, I'll explain the circumstances that have brought me here.'

Fortunately, I had a bottle of Bell's whisky in the cupboard under the kitchen sink. I had won it two years earlier at work's annual Christmas raffle, but, having been a teetotaller for some time now, had never touched a drop of the stuff. Reluctantly, I went into the kitchen and fished it out of the cupboard, using my shirt sleeve to wipe off a thin film of dust that had accumulated around its base. Then I walked back into the living room with the whisky and a coffee mug. Slowly, exercising more care than was necessary, I uncapped the bottle and poured him a drink.

'You've got quite a collection of these things,' Portas said, pointing at some of the 'Sacred Hearts' on the sideboard.

'Yes, they belonged to my mother.'

'Never took you for the religious type, old boy.'

'I'm not,' I said, sitting down beside him and offering him the mug. 'It was my mother who was religious. I inherited the statues when she died.'

He took the mug with an appreciative smile and brought it to his lips. Incredibly, the moment he imbibed some of the golden liquid, his eyes widened and he pulled himself up on the sofa, one leg crossed over the other and with his chin held up, as if he were already feeling better. I again asked him what had happened.

'It's all gone,' he said, looking me in the eye.

'What do you mean — it's all gone? What's all gone?'

'Everything,' he said, finishing his whisky in one gulp. 'Portas and Sons. My house in Opayar. My house on Devil's Tower Road. My cars. My boats. My wife's jewellery. My horses. My late father's collection of luxury watches. Even Isobel and the children. Everything's gone,' he repeated, shaking his head.

'But how can that be?' I asked, pouring another drink for him and taking an impulsive swig from the bottle myself. 'I thought you guys were raking it in. All those articles in the *Chronicle* about how well your company is doing and all the money you keep donating to charity, and so on.'

'We *were* doing well, Brian — I mean, really, really well — but now it's all gone. Everything's gone. Kaput. Fucked up. Gone to the dogs.'

'I don't follow you, Henry. How can all this have happened?'

'I took risks, Brian,' he replied, staring at the red mug between his hands, ' — that's how it happened. I made really bad investments. You know what I'm really like under all this,' he said, removing a hand from the mug and tugging at his trouser pleats. 'I'm a gambler, a compulsive risk-taker. Jerks like me shouldn't be trusted with their children's post office savings account, let alone with a company with a twelve-million-pound annual turnover.'

'But I thought you had settled down,' I said, placing the bottle on the coffee table. 'Mr Henry Portas, president of the local Lions Club and patron of the Gibraltar Society for the Mentally Handicapped. Member of the Most Excellent Order of the British Empire and personal friend to His Excellency the Governor. Married to a Sophia Loren lookalike and father to two little cherubs. A serious, sober *pater familias*. Are you telling me all that was just an elaborate sham?'

'No. Not entirely. At least in the beginning it wasn't. For the first few years, Brian, I tried to buckle down. I really did. That's why I cut you out of my life all those years ago. You reminded me of a past I wanted to leave behind, see. Plus you wouldn't have fitted well in the circles I was now moving in.... I know, I know: I was a damn fool, wasn't I? You were the only friend who ever knew what I was really like, the only one who saw me as Henry Portas the person instead of Henry Portas the heir to Portas and Sons. And I let you down. I treated you like utter shit. That's so typical of the miserable jerk that I am.... Anyway, that's beside the point now,' he said, tossing off his whisky. 'The point is that I've fucked up, Brian. I've fucked up really badly. And now I'm big-time in the shit.'

He took the bottle from the coffee table and refilled his mug. Then he coughed softly and began telling me how he had landed in so much 'shit.' It was a real gambler's story, packed with all the expected elements. Cocky youth. Domineering father. Family of quarrelling, ever-scheming eccentrics. Piles and piles of hard cash. Due to a quirk of fate, the father suddenly disappears from the scene and the youth finds himself heading the family's vast business empire. For the first year and a half he enjoys the thrill of the ride — lording it up over his new charges, taking great pleasure in overturning the policies laid down by his predecessors. Then he begins to feel bored. Cannot be bothered with it all. One day, driven by a combination of ennui and rising frustration, he starts secretly dabbling in the stock market. At first he only makes small, risk-free investments, never laying out more than a thousand pounds at a time. Gradually, though, his profits increase and he becomes bolder. Sinks more and more of his own capital into the market. Then, without warning, he sustains a massive loss. Sees nearly 30 per cent of his fortune wiped out overnight. Inevitably, his wife and business partners find out and create a big hullabaloo. Crestfallen and ashamed, the gambler promises to reform himself. Vows that he will never play the market again. Over the next couple of months he visits the top psychiatrist in the Costa del Sol and joins the Marbella branch of Gamblers Anonymous; he even attends the local Catholic *cursillo* in Opayar, where, red-faced and stammering, continually gazing at his clasped hands, he tells a group of mainly working-class Andalusian men about his 'addictive and compulsive nature' while tactfully refraining from mentioning what he is addicted to. Despite these pre-emptive measures, the serpent never leaves him alone. Almost every day it whispers to him, reminding him of past thrills, tempting him with new opportunities. For nearly two years he keeps the old viper at bay by reciting the words of a prayer taught to him by one of his wife's *cursillo* friends: 'Begone, angel of Satan. I stand between Jesus and Mary. Go back to Hell whence you came, for you have no power here.' Finally, one night in May 1980, after his wife discovers that he is having an affair with one of his secretaries and threatens to divorce him, he succumbs to temptation and starts gambling again. His first act is to buy seventeen thousand pounds of shares in an emerging ICT company and then sell them for three times the price when the company unexpectedly declares record end-of-year profits a few weeks later. Ecstasy grips him, a wild, delirious joy. Before long, he loses all self-control and is once again wheeling and dealing like in the old days. The only difference is that this time he is conducting his business through trusted foreign intermediaries and using secret offshore bank accounts. *This time,* he thinks, *no one is going to find out what I'm up to. This time it's me and the market and nobody else!* For a while everything goes well: he is making so much money that he is having to open new bank accounts all over the world. Jersey, Belize, Bermuda, the Cayman Islands. At the close of each big deal, he tells himself that he will soon stop, that he will shortly pull out of it all and concentrate on running Portas and Sons. But he never does anything of the sort. Instead he raises the stakes higher and higher, borrowing money to fund his increasingly speculative ventures, using his assets to secure bigger loans. 'I just couldn't stop myself,' he admitted to me, sitting in my living room with the bottle of Bell's now tucked between his thighs. 'It was just like in the old days when I used to go around climbing old buildings. The higher and more difficult the building, the more I wanted … no, the more *I had* to climb it. It was just like that with the stock market, Brian. The more difficult and risky the venture, the more I was compelled to take it on.'

'And in the end you fell flat on your face, right?' I said, continuing with the climbing analogy.

'Precisely. I had raised about thirty million dollars to invest in a small Californian plastics and composites company which my instinct told me was about to go big. I was convinced of it. I could feel it in my blood. This was going to be the motherlode, Brian, the big bastard deal that would take my fortune soaring above the fifty-million-dollar mark and allow me to finally walk away from it all knowing that I had mixed it up with the big boys, that I had climbed the stock market equivalent of Mount Everest. But instead what happens? The company's CEO is exposed as a maverick fraudster who lied through his teeth to his credulous investors and is thrown into jail. Overnight, Brian, I'm left with thirty million dollars of shares that no one's going to touch with a barge pole. I'm fucking destroyed, man. Shredded to the bone. In fact, having borrowed more money than I was worth, I am eight million pounds *in the red*. That's how bad it is, my friend — I am what is technically known as *utterly shafted.'*

'So what does it all mean?'

'What does it all mean? All hell's broken loose. That's what it means. The Portas board of directors have found out. The banks have sent out their threatening letters. The house in Opayar is on the point of being repossessed. And a few days ago my wife took the kids with her to her parents', saying I'd never see them again.'

'That must have been tough.'

'Tough, Brian, but predictable. My wife's a bitch. Always has been. A manipulative, grasping, overbearing bitch who only married me for the money and who pretends to be a devout Catholic, but is just a holier-than-thou cow who loves it when misfortunes befall others. And it's not like she and the kids will be badly off either. Because of all the insurance policies she forced me to take out in her name, she'll still have quite a few pennies rolling in. Do you know what she once said when I told her about you and how much I missed your company? She said, "You're off your head, Henry. Wanting to run back to all your crummy little mates. Do you think your father would have consorted with cruddy low-lifes like that?" That's what she called you, man — a cruddy low-life! Incredibly ironic, don't you think? A poisonous *culebra* like her calling you that? But anyway, all that's beside the point. I can't blame her for the way I ditched you,' he said, gazing grimly at the mug between his hands. 'That's entirely my fault.'

'What about the kids?'

'The kids? They're just miniature carbon copies of her. I don't know how Isobel's done it, but she's managed to pass on to them all her worse traits: her stubbornness, her bad temper, her manipulativeness.

The boy is a right sod, he is. Only a few weeks ago, he threw a tantrum because I came back home with a teddy bear for him instead of some giant panda that he had seen earlier during the week at Teuma's toy shop. You should have seen him bawling his eyes out…. I suppose it's partly my fault for never having given the kids the time and attention they deserve, what with running after women and my obsession with the stock market. Yes, on second thoughts,' he added gloomily, 'I am a lot to blame for them being like that.'

Listening to Portas ramble on in this way made me realise how badly I had misjudged him. For the last four or five years I had thought that things couldn't have been going better for my old friend Henry Portas. I had thought — erroneously, but understandably — that he was what ordinary people see as a natural winner, a man who seemingly had it all in life. Cars, money, property, influence, a beautiful wife and doting kids, the adulation of a grateful populace — it was almost like someone had waved a magic wand over him and given him everything that the rest of us mere mortals can only dream about. Yet through it all he had been fighting a titanic battle with his personal demons and locked in an acrimonious and loveless marriage. Just goes to show, doesn't it? You can read about a man's life every day in the papers and still not know a damn thing about him….

'Bet you never thought that was how things stood with me, did you?' Henry said all of a sudden, as if reading my thoughts. 'Mr Henry Portas, such an upstanding pillar of the community, the great patron of all those Gibraltarian charities … in reality no more than a wild-eyed gambler with a toxic bitch of a wife and a pair of spoiled brats in tow?… I suppose my bankruptcy is the fitting climax to it all, the predestined ending that was always waiting to happen…. And yet … despite all that … well, I can't help feeling that I've fucked up big time, that I've betrayed my family name. All those generations of bewhiskered and monocled Portas patriarchs — striving, struggling, slogging their guts out to build up the company…. And then along comes this fuckwit Henry Portas and sabotages it all in a moment of idiocy. Something almost obscene about that, don't you think, old boy? Depraved…. Then there is my kid sister Sophia, who owns half of Portas and Sons but just lets me run the company for both of us. She still doesn't know anything about what's happened, you know. Can't bring myself to tell her. She's so frail, so delicate. Spends all her time cooped up in Opayar because she suffers from crippling attacks of agoraphobia when she leaves the house. Goes terribly dizzy and gets bad nosebleeds…. Weird, isn't it? I turn out to be a compulsive risk-taker, whereas poor old Soph's unable to cope with the slightest change to her everyday routine. Doesn't say much about the way our parents brought us up, does it?'

'Well, parenting's never been the most predictable of arts, has it?' I said — and immediately regretted coming up with such a banal comment.

He reached for the bottle between his thighs and poured himself another drink. His hands were shaking again and beads of sweat had reappeared on his forehead; his lower lip looked paler than ever and bore the faint imprint of his own teeth marks. From the glaze that fell across his eyes, I could sense that he was whipping himself up for some final ground-shaking disclosure, that he was struggling to get it all out. Touching him on the arm, I asked him if everything was okay.

'It's my sister back in Opayar,' he admitted, raising the mug to his lips. 'I'm just so worried about her. Can't imagine her taking all this well. In fact, I fear all this will destroy her.'

'Still, you have to tell her at some point. You can't keep her in the dark forever.'

'I don't know, Brian,' Portas said. 'I don't think I can go through with it.'

'Maybe it's better if you tell her over the phone, then. At least that way you won't have to deliver the news face-to-face.'

'Are you kidding me, Manny?' Portas shot back angrily. 'I've told you she's a very sensitive kid. God knows what she's capable of doing to herself if she finds out over the phone!'

'Then just go back to Spain and tell her,' I suggested, a hint of coolness creeping into my voice. 'You have to bite the bullet at some point, Henry.'

'That's the thing, Brian,' he said in a softer tone, placing the bottle on the floor. 'I don't think I can bring myself to face her. The kid idolises me. Thinks I've put my wild days behind me and turned into some kind of upright humanitarian capitalist. Can you believe that? The silly cow has got it into her head that I'm the benevolent, ethically minded business guru and community leader that she frequently reads about in the *Gibraltar Chronicle*. I can't just turn up in Opayar and tell her that everything she believes in is a lie, that I'm the biggest fuck-up in Gibraltarian mercantile history, that the house we Portases have lived in for almost seventy years is about to be taken away from us. It will break her heart into a thousand pieces and probably be the end of me as well.'

'Can't you get someone to go and tell her, then?'

'Someone?' he said, growing angry again. 'What do you mean — *someone?*'

'I don't know — your wife maybe. Or one of your old company employees.'

'Wouldn't trust any of those scumbags,' he said, dismissing the suggestion with a shake of the head. 'God knows what they'd tell her and what ideas they'd knock into her brain.'

I got up and walked over to the living room window. 'I'm a bit confused, Henry,' I said, gazing at the crumbling limestone cliffs behind Laguna Estate. 'What would you like them to tell her? That you tried your best against impossible odds? That what happened was just a piece of bad luck? Is that what you want her to hear,' I asked, turning around, ' — that none of this mess is your fault?'

'You don't understand, Brian. I don't want any of those poisonous turds to be the ones who deliver the news, that's all. You don't know what they're like. They'll stick the blade in, and then turn it around a few times for their own delectation.' He brought out a small brown envelope from his trouser pocket. 'Actually, I've already written a letter to her explaining what has happened.'

'What's in the letter?' I asked, still standing before him.

'Nothing much — just the usual stuff. That I know that she, of all people, doesn't deserve this. That it is killing me to think I have heaped so much misfortune on the one person who also had to go through what I went through as a kid. That I would gladly jump from a bridge if I knew that by doing so I could somehow spare her the torment and distress which my recklessness has created for her.'

'So why haven't you posted it yet?'

'I can't,' he said, lowering his gaze. 'I'm scared of what she'll do when she receives it.'

'What do you mean?'

'She's too volatile. Too highly strung. Too spontaneous. She could end up jumping off a balcony or slitting her wrists or something equally drastic.'

'So what are you going to do, then?'

He dropped the letter onto his lap and looked up sombrely. 'I need to find someone whom I really trust and who will take the letter to her and make sure she doesn't do anything stupid once she's read it.'

'And how do you propose to do that?' I asked, feigning ignorance but already suspecting what he had in mind.

'You already know the answer to that question, my friend.'

'Oh, come on, Henry,' I burst out. 'You can't expect me to do your dirty work.'

'I'm not asking you to do my dirty work, Brian,' he said anxiously. 'I'm just asking you to take this letter to my sister and make sure she doesn't do anything stupid after she's read it. All you have to do is stay with her for an hour or so. If she doesn't react badly during that first hour, then I'm sure she will be fine afterwards. I know what she's like. It's only during that first hour that there's a danger she might do something stupid.'

I shook my head and sighed under my breath.

'I know it's a big favour to ask, Manny, old chap, but I can't think of any other way to do it, I swear.'

I sighed again, this time a little louder.

'Look, Brian, I know I've treated you abominably in the past and that you'd be more than justified if you sent me straight to hell. But I also know you're a good guy and that you'd never let a friend down. That's why I'm asking you, from the bottom of my heart, to set aside any reservations you may have about me and help me out. Think about the good times we once had. Think about all those afternoons we spent drinking together at the Green Man or driving around in my old Citroën. I know that I've acted like a right oaf since then, but you were like a brother to me back in those days and I know, here, in my heart, that you also felt the same about me. So, please, my friend, I'm begging you: help me out if you can. Do it for the sake of our old friendship if nothing else. After you've taken the letter to Sophia, I'll never bother you again if that is what you wish. Just help me out this one time. Just this once, please. I beg you, please.'

He looked down at the floor and then turned to face the other side of the room. As he did so, I saw something that back in my Cambridge days would have knocked me out cold: there were tears gathering in his eyes. They hadn't started to stream down his cheeks yet, but they were there all right. Mixed emotions swept through me during those moments. Part of me felt sorry for the guy, part of me felt terribly shocked, but — worst of all — I'm ashamed to admit — part of me *enjoyed* seeing the great Henry Portas, the ex-judoka and fearless stegophilist, the champion sprinter and Don Juan, reduced to such a crumbling wreck. *There,* a voice even whispered venomously in my head. *This is what you get for betraying friends!*

'How would I get there if I decide to go?' I said, not because I wanted to deliver the letter, but because I hated how much I was enjoying seeing him suffer. 'I haven't been to Spain since the frontier closed in 1969.'

'You're willing to take the letter for me, then?' he murmured, an almost childlike look of relief on his face.

'Possibly,' I said.

'It'd have to be by ferry, I'm afraid. My two boats were impounded three days ago.'

'Ferry?'

'Yes, I've been told it's a largely hassle-free trip. You basically catch the *Mons Calpe* at eight o'clock in the morning and it gets into Tangier at around a quarter past eleven. There you switch on to the *Ibn Batouta*, which leaves at twelve and gets into Algeciras about three-thirty. Then you just hop into a taxi and you should get to Opayar around five-thirty, six. Which means that if you catch the eight o'clock service tomorrow morning, you could be with my sister in just under twenty-four hours from now.'

'You expect me to go tomorrow morning?' I said, not quite believing what I was hearing.

'Yes, I know — it's very short notice. But it's vital you get to her before she hears about what has happened from somebody else. At the moment there's only Sophia and Matilda, one of the maids, in the house. I spoke to Matilda earlier today and she said that Sophia still doesn't know anything. It's imperative you get there as soon as possible. It's only a matter of days now before the press gets wind of my bankruptcy and the story is splattered all over the local papers. When that happens, one of her Gibraltarian friends is bound to call her and tell her about it. That's why it is so important that you go tomorrow.' He dug his hand into his trouser pocket and brought out a business card and a tightly rolled wad of notes. 'There's about three hundred pounds in pesetas and sterling in here,' he said, extending the wad towards me along with the envelope and the card. 'That should easily cover your costs and leave you with a few quid for anything you might want to buy for yourself. My Queensway office number is written on the card, together with the address of our property in Opayar. I'll call both Sophia and the maid later on tonight and tell them to expect you tomorrow. As soon as Sophia reads the letter, please phone me and let me know how she's taken the news. I'll be in my office waiting to receive your call. Please don't delay in phoning, Brian. I'll be anxious to hear from you.'

'Wait a minute, wait a minute,' I said, refusing to accept the money, the card and the envelope. 'You said the taxi will get to Opayar at around six in the evening. What am I supposed to do with myself up in the mountains after I visit your sister? I can't just turn around and head back home, can I?'

'Catch another taxi and head back to Algeciras,' he said in the manner of someone brushing off a triviality. 'Tell the taxi driver to take you to the Hotel Reina Cristina. It's just beside the port area and it's nice and clean and quite majestic in a quirky, old-fashioned way. Stay there overnight and then in the morning catch the nine-thirty ferry to Tangier. Then catch the five-thirty ferry back to Gibraltar. You'll be back home around ten o'clock at night.'

'What about tickets for the ferry? Will I be able to buy them before boarding?'

'Yes, yes, don't worry about that,' he said, handing over his bits and pieces. 'I have already checked and you can purchase tickets for all four legs of the journey from the travel agent at the pier tomorrow. Just concentrate on calling me after you have spoken to my sister, please. Like I said, I have calculated you will get to our place in Opayar between five-thirty and six in the evening. I will stay in my office from five o'clock onwards to make sure I receive your call. Please, don't forget to make it, Brian. We have plenty of phones in the house,' he said, picking up the bottle of Bell's from the floor. 'Just ask Matilda to direct you to one of them. If you don't call, I'll assume that something bad has happened. You won't forget to call, will you?'

'Don't worry, Henry,' I replied, pocketing the card and the money. 'I won't forget.'

'You promise?'

'Yes, I promise.'

He uttered a sigh of relief and passed me the whisky bottle. 'I knew you wouldn't leave me high and dry,' he said. 'I knew I could count on you.'

I smiled uncomfortably and put the bottle back on the coffee table.

'Anyway,' he said, rising from the sofa and picking up his jacket, 'I think I've spoken enough for one night. I'll leave now and let you get ready for your trip.'

He walked slowly across the living room and into the corridor leading to the front door. I watched him with a mixture of pity and disgust, then gazed down at the envelope still in my hand. Portas's sweaty fingerprints could be seen on its face — nebulous marks that had spread across the coarse manila paper like the patterns in a Rorschach inkblot test. Suddenly a thought entered my head:

'Henry?'

Portas turned around with a weary smile. 'Yes?'

'Can I ask you a question before you go?'

'Sure, buddy. Fire away.'

'It's something that's been on my mind for a few years now,' I said, moving closer to him.

'Go on, then. I'm all ears.'

I tucked the envelope into my shirt pocket and cleared my throat. 'Why did you leave Cambridge just before your finals? You were studying so hard and everything seemed to be going well. Why did you go and chuck it all away like that?'

'It was *precisely because things were going well* that I left.'

'I don't follow you.'

'Well, it's like this,' he said, leaning against the corridor wall. 'You know that I never wanted to be a lawyer, don't you? I saw it as conforming, bowing down to the system, following in the footsteps of my father, et cetera, et cetera. Anyway, during my first two years at Cambridge I was never really worried about the prospect of becoming a lawyer because I genuinely thought I would never pass my degree. It was all a big joke, wasn't it, a never-ending piss-take. The drinking. The partying. The women. The long drives in the Citroën. I mean, come on, you'd have got better odds on Henry Portas joining the priesthood than on him completing his Cambridge Law degree. But that May in 1974 — for the first time ever — well, it suddenly dawned on me that there was a real chance that I might just pull it off. So I panicked, didn't I? I got really scared. I thought, "Fuck it. If I carry on studying like this, there's a good chance I might end up getting a BA in Law and becoming just like my father." So I upped sticks and ran off.'

'But that doesn't make sense. You say you left Cambridge because you didn't want to end up like your father — and yet you went straight back to Gibraltar to work for his firm.'

'But I *didn't* go to Gibraltar, did I?'

'You didn't?'

'No, I flew to Amsterdam instead.'

'Amsterdam?'

'Yes, I thought you knew,' Portas frowned.

'Not me, mate,' I replied, shaking my head. 'You never told me anything about Amsterdam.'

'No, on reflection, I suppose I never told you,' he said a little apologetically.

'Anyway, why did you go to Amsterdam?'

'I'm not sure.... I suppose I must have heard from someone that Amsterdam was the ideal place to go when you wanted to escape your problems.'

'And what did you do there?'

'Not much,' he answered. 'I got drunk, I took drugs, I visited a few brothels. What guys normally do when they go to Amsterdam, I guess.'

'And did all that help?'

'Well, I found it all very flat and artificial and a tremendous bore, but I suppose it did help me forget about Cambridge and my parents and everything else I wanted to forget about. So in a sense, yes, you could say that the trip wasn't so bad.'

'How long were you there?'

'I don't know — six or seven days, maybe?'

'And after that you simply returned home to Gibraltar?'

'Yes, something like that. Except that before I left Amsterdam … well, something happened that shook me up and put things into perspective for me.'

I looked at him questioningly.

'It was around two o'clock in the morning,' he continued. 'I had come out of a bar called the Red Kite and was walking down the *oudezijds voorburgwal,* the main street in the red-light district, on my way back to the hotel. Suddenly two men came up to me and asked me to hand over my watch and wallet. They both had knives in their hands and I had a feeling I had seen them before. In a flash I realised they must have been at the bar and followed me out.'

'That must have been a scary experience,' I said, not knowing what else to come up with.

'Actually, there was something rather comical about it all, Brian. The first guy was not really a guy at all, but a South American transsexual with a white shawl. The other fella was a Dutch guy with a small pointy ginger beard. He reminded me a bit of the Van

Gogh you see in some of the famous self-portraits. Except he was much thinner and scrawnier than the old *Fou Roux*. More *rodenty*, if you know what I mean.'

'Okay — so what happened?'

'Well, my first thought was to hand them my wallet and my Patek Philippe and get it all over and done with. But then I thought, "What the hell. Why should I give what's rightfully mine to these two low-life comedians." So I shouted at them to fuck off. Told them to clear off before I fucking thrashed the pair of them.'

'And did they go away?'

'No, they came towards me with their knives and we had a bit of a tussle.'

'Jesus, Henry! Did you get hurt?'

'Well, I managed to fight them off and they both ran off into the night, but in the scuffle the he-she somehow nicked me with her blade on the shoulder. It was only a minor wound, but there was a lot of blood everywhere. It was dripping all over the place and settling in between the cracks in the pavement. As I stood there watching the mess, it suddenly occurred to me that those two scumbags were not really that dissimilar to the members of my own family. Their mode of operation was essentially the same. They wanted something really badly … and they just reached out and tried to take it. That's what my father had been doing for years now. And his father before him. And his own father in turn before him. An interlinked chain of cut-throat racketeers stretching all the way back to when the company was first founded in the 1850s. Not that I blamed them for being like this. All human beings are like that to some extent or the other. Grasping. Materialistic. Intensely possessive. In fact, as I stood there trying to stem the flow of blood, I experienced something of a revelation. What could be described as a moment of lucidity. I realised that what we term history is just a big lie. A huge phantasmagorical illusion. At school and at university we get taught that the real heroes of history are the artists and the poets and the scientists and everybody else who contributed to the spread of what we commonly know as civilisation. But history is not really about these things, is it? All that's just retrospectively applied gloss, baubles and tinsel that we add much later to make things look pretty. Real history is about envy and coercion, it is about exploitation and intimidation, it is about theft and expropriation, rape and plunder, pillage and mass oppression. *It is about those who take things from others, and those who have things taken from them.* Look at our own Rock. First, it belonged to the Phoenicians, then to the Carthaginians, then to the Romans, then to the Visigoths, then to the Spanish, then to the Moors, then to the Spanish again, then finally to the British. What does that tell you about history? Not much, I suppose, except that he who is strongest sweeps the board and lays down the law. That's what it's all about, Manny, at the end of the day: power, domination, subjugation, the need to feel superior to those around you. That's the way it's been and the way it will always be. You can call it Dog-eat-Dog, Social Darwinism, Malthusianism, whatever. The history of humanity is the history of those who eat and those who end up being eaten.'

It was an extraordinarily impassioned diatribe, but what was even more extraordinary was the way that Portas now stood slumped against the corridor wall, his forehead bathed in a film of humidity, his eyes glittering with feral malevolence. Wincing, I asked him what happened after the mugging.

'Nothing,' he replied through gritted teeth. 'I just packed my bags the next morning and made my way back home.'

'So you went back after you realised your family were no better than those two would-be muggers?'

'Yes.'

'But *why?*'

'Cowardice, maybe? Laziness? Selfishness? Plain self-interest? A fear of remaining in Amsterdam on my own? The dread of getting mugged again one night by two better and more proficient muggers? What do you want me to say, Brian? It is one thing to realise the nature of the beast, quite another to have the moral courage to stand up to it.'

'So you sold out? Is that what you're telling me? You just gave up on everything you believed in?'

'Yes, I suppose that's what I did.'

'And you don't regret it?'

'No. Not really. What alternatives did I have? Staying in Amsterdam and becoming a drug pusher? Returning to the UK and bumming around without purpose? Sometimes it is easier to give in and accept the inevitable than to carry on fighting a lost cause on your own.'

'And what about your father?' I asked. 'What did he say when he found out you had dropped out of Cambridge?'

'Nothing,' Portas replied quietly. 'He said nothing. I think he was a bit disappointed deep down, but he never showed it in front of me. He just created a job for me within the firm and let me get on with it.... So there you go: that's the story of what happened to me while I was in Amsterdam. Hardly a medieval morality play, eh?'

'Yes, you could say that.'

'Anyway, I've bored you enough, Brian,' Portas said, already heading towards the door. 'Better push off and let you get some rest. You won't forget to call me once you hand the letter over, will you?'

'Don't worry,' I said, edging past him and sliding back the latch for him. 'I won't.'

He then shuffled out into the landing and started walking down the stairs. I listened to the fading echo of his steps for a moment or two, then closed the door and went back to the living room, where I polished off what was left of the whisky.

33.

At ten to eight the next morning, I boarded the *SS Mons Calpe* with a small suitcase of clothes and over two hundred pounds in pesetas stashed in my trouser pockets. It was humid and overcast, one of those unusually warm winter days when almost the entire Rock is sheathed in a low-lying Levanter cloud. Oil tankers anchored offshore intermittently sounded their foghorns. Seagulls crawled along the adjacent stone pier. As I climbed the gangway leading into the ferry, I thought about my boss at the library and how he'd react to my taking time off work without his permission. *Bloody irresponsible kid,* he'd probably whine. *Head up in the clouds, like most people of his generation.* For all that, I felt cheerful and tolerably optimistic. For the first time in nearly seven years, I was leaving Gibraltar. For the first time in a long, long time, I was breaking the repetitive, changeless routine that saw me walk every weekday from Laguna to the John Mackintosh Hall and back, with nothing more interesting along the way than the odd stop at the cathedral and the even odder visit to Lipton's supermarket. The thought excited me, energised me. Relishing the feeling, I strode through the ship's entrance and went straight to the bar. I ordered a bottle of Heineken and took it with me to a table on the other side of the passenger deck. The ship was only half full at present, but quickly filling up with expat Moroccan workers travelling back to their homeland. One or two were dressed in Western clothes, but the majority wore the coarse twilled hooded djellaba that is standard daywear in most parts of the Mahgreb. There was something calm and dignified about those guys. An air of Islamic unflappability. Scattered among them were a handful of European backpackers — young Germans and Scandinavians with compasses hanging around their necks and rucksacks and sleeping bags strapped to their backs. Two of the Teutons were seated at the table directly opposite mine. A bearded guy with a red bandana and a woman with pigtails. Easy-going, hippie types. Lots of amulets, bangles and beads. A map covered in yellow Post-it notes spread across the table before them. Ditching my usual reserve, I leaned forward and asked the couple where they were heading.

'We're on our way down to Nouakchott in Mauritania,' the bearded man answered in that peculiarly lilting tone that Scandinavians have when speaking in English. 'We've signed up to do some charity work with Africa Contact. How about you?'

'Oh, I'm just on a short business trip — nothing exciting.'

'*Tanger?*' the Swede asked, pronouncing the word in a way that made it sound like 'Tongue-out.'

'No, no, I'm changing ferries at Tangier and then heading back up to Algeciras in Spain. I've got some business to attend to in the mountains near Ronda.'

'Cool.'

He smiled at me and I smiled back at them, but I could tell they were not impressed by my destination or the nature of my journey. I then leaned back and, stretching my legs under the table, thought about Portas and the muddle he had got himself into. I thought of all those articles in the *Chronicle* praising his firm, of all those photos showing him smiling and handing out cheques to different charities. I also tried to remember the only time I had met his sister, back during my student days. She had been sitting in the back of his Citroën, hadn't she? A moody little git who chewed gum with her mouth open and whose hands and forearms were covered in blue biro marks. At the time she never struck me as the type to succumb to nervous disorders, but if I had learned anything from my friendship with her brother it was never to judge a Portas on first appearances alone. Another thing that puzzled me was the level of concern which Portas had shown the previous night for his sister. Call me cynical, but back in 1972 or 1973 (or whenever it was) those two had been as badly matched as a Rock ape and a Jack Russell Terrier. Had the passing of the years, I wondered, softened his attitude to his sister? Had he become more protective towards her now that he was a father himself? Or was Portas simply feeling guilty for having squandered Sophia's birthright? As I grappled with these and other similar thoughts, I looked out of the window behind me and received a pleasant surprise: we were already within sight of the Moroccan coastline.

Changing ferries at Tangier was a relatively unproblematic affair. The inbound travellers were funnelled into one of the arrival halls, while the transiting passengers were herded along the landing pier and straight into the *Ibn Batouta,* the ferry taking us back across the straits to Algeciras. The interior of the ship was larger and more modern than that of the *Mons Calpe.* A series of rounded oblong windows lined the perimeter of the main deck, giving an elevated view of the berthing pier below. Since the vessel was already quite full, I assumed that the bulk of the passengers must have boarded earlier and been waiting for us to come aboard. Manoeuvring my way through the masses, I found an empty table near a window and plonked myself down with my suitcase. For the next three and a half hours I divided my time between *Les Caves du Vatican* and mentally fuming at the sheer ridiculousness of the journey. Where else in the world would you have to catch two ferries and hop over to another continent just to travel to a country which, if the post-Francoist authorities hadn't been so hell-bent on garrotting Gibraltar, could be reached by foot in a matter of minutes? That something like this was happening in 1982 was *an absolute bloody disgrace.* Finally, at around twenty past three, as I was on the point of dozing off, we cruised past Punta Carnero and began the final push towards the port of Algeciras. Yawning, I sat up straight and stretched my arms above my head. Ever since we had left the Rock, the sun had been accompanying every step of our journey and it was still there above us, as fierce and unseasonable as ever. Through the window I had a clear view of Gibraltar on the other side of the bay, rising out of the sea like some oversized ichthyosaur and looking as Levanter-ridden as it had done in the morning. Strange, I thought. To think it's so bright here and yet so gloomy over there! No wonder the British held on to Gibraltar after ditching Minorca in the early nineteenth century, I told myself. The Levanter cloud often makes the place look just as dismal as London on a foggy morning!

I had no problems clearing Spanish customs and immigration, although the *guardia civil* who stamped my passport sarcastically remarked how great it was to see a Spanish surname on a British travel document. He was a jowly chap with a thick moustache and a black leather *tricornio*. A *Virgen del Pilar* medal rested against the base of his neck, half-obscured by a tuft of crinkly chest hairs. I noted the plain epaulettes on his shoulders and hurried past his post. Once out of the terminal, I brought out my packet of Rothmans and lit a fag. I took a few slow puffs, letting the smoke swirl down into my lungs, then prematurely discarded the cigarette and stubbed it out with my heel. I hadn't been to Spain for nearly fifteen years and scarcely remembered anything about the place, but I instantly recognised the *smell*. That Andalusian odour of *lejía* and *zotal*. Of oldness smothered by disinfectant. It is a melancholy smell. A *sarcophagal* smell. The smell of a nation struggling to emerge from the catacomb of its morbidly religious past. Preoccupied with these fancy thoughts, I strolled over to a nearby taxi stand and asked a taxi driver how much it would cost to get to Opayar. The man in the car, a tawny fellow with tinted glasses and the half-smoked remains of a fat cigar between his lips, scrutinised me for some seconds before coming up with the figure of nine hundred pesetas (about four pounds) — *más lo que usted me deje como propina.* I said that this was okay and climbed into the back of the vehicle. Its interior smelled of sweat and corroded leather, reminding me a little of the smell in the passenger deck of the *Mons Calpe.* A rosary was wrapped around the stem of the rear-view mirror, its shiny black beads contrasting strikingly with the dirt-caked windscreen. The triangular vent window on the driver's side was missing and had been replaced by a sheet of compressed wood. As I made myself comfortable, I noticed the taxi driver observing me via the rear-view mirror. 'You're from Gibraltar, *verdad?*' he asked wheezingly in Spanish seconds later. 'Yes,' I replied, 'how can you tell?' 'It's your accent,' the man muttered with his cigar still clamped between his teeth. 'It's a bit funny. *Un poco curioso.*' He didn't say anything else after that, but I could sense that he resented that I was a Gibraltarian. He reminded me of the Spanish exchange students I had met now and again during my time at Cambridge. Ultra-chic Madrid *pijos*, mainly. Funded by the Bank of Mummy and Daddy back in Salamanca or Alonso Martínez or some other posh metropolitan district. The moment they discovered you were from Gibraltar, they'd look at you as a renegade Spaniard, an odious desecrator of the national honour. Blinded by their government's anti-Gibraltarian propaganda, they'd shake their heads and tell you that you couldn't possibly be a Gibraltarian because Gibraltarians didn't really exist — there being nobody on that pestiferous scrap of rock, as everybody well knows, apart from a sprinkling of *soldados guiris,* a handful of renegade Andalusian smugglers and one or two *malditos monos*....

Easing warily back into my seat, I folded my arms and looked through the window. I could smell the diesel fumes coming from the taxi's engine, a rancid metallic odour that forced me to close my mouth and breathe through my nose. Even though it was only ten past four, there was hardly anybody out in the streets, with just a few solitary figures looming into view now and again. An overweight woman dragging a canvas shopping trolley. A one-legged man sitting on a bench. Two urchins kicking a deflated football. Something else that surprised me, too, was just how dirty and dilapidated everything appeared. Broken pavements, rusted street signs, unfinished buildings, potholed roads, bus stops disfigured by graffiti — you could see the signs of wear and deterioration wherever you turned your gaze. Brought up, like most Gibraltarians, on tales of Spanish laziness and unreliability, I had half-expected something like this all along, but I had never imagined that things could be *this bad.* After all, whenever you walked over to the Four Corners on the Gibraltarian side of the border and looked beyond the barbed wire-topped fence, their roads and buildings seemed *relatively okay.*

Before long, my thoughts returned to Portas and his visit to my Laguna flat the previous evening. In particular, I remembered the frightening sense of pleasure I had experienced when he broke down before me. What had possessed me during those moments? I wondered, winding down the passenger window. Was I really as vindictive and mean-spirited as that? Had I hated Portas *that much?* While I deliberated the matter, I noticed the imposing shape of the Levanter-shrouded Rock across the cold blue waters of the Bay of Gibraltar. There it stood, no more than five or six miles away — a limestone behemoth that looked nothing like the arid flax-coloured land around us. As I beheld its universally recognised form, the taxi driver coughed in an attempt to grab my attention.

'So you think they're finally going to open *la verja* like everybody keeps saying?'

'I don't know,' I replied.

'Well, I hope they do,' he said, fixing his eyes on mine by means of the rear-view mirror. 'I really hope so. *De verdad que sí.*'

'And why's that?' I asked uneasily.

'Because once it's open, it won't take long before *la Roca* will finally be returned to us once and for all.'

'I doubt very much that will happen.'

'Why not? You're all Spanish there more or less, aren't you?'

I looked at him via the rear-view mirror and saw that his diminutive Andalusian eyes had contracted even further and were now surrounded by a tangle of cross-hatched wrinkles. I sensed that *el cabrón* was really enjoying himself.

'Well, actually, you are wrong,' I responded with surprising firmness. 'We are not Spanish. We are Gibraltarians. And we don't want anything to do with Spain. All you guys have done is harass us and try to make life difficult for us. In Franco's time you disrupted our telecommunications and cut the supply of oxygen to our hospitals and made it an offence for Spaniards to export any goods to Gibraltar, before finally closing the frontier gates in a despicable attempt to economically garrotte us. Now you talk about opening the border, but at the same time you say you want to do so in a way that will stop Gibraltar from benefitting economically from the situation. Do you really think that Gibraltarians will forget all this bullshit and come running to you with open arms? I somehow doubt it very much. So yes, you can open the border if you want. You can allow cars and pedestrians and even donkeys to pass through. *Le diré algo*: we will never have anything to do with Spain unless the Spanish Government drops its animosity and starts treating us fairly.'

'*Vale, vale,*' the taxi driver said, focusing back on the road. 'No need to bite my head off, *jefe*. I was only saying what I hear every day out *en la calle*, that's all.'

I looked down and tried to calm my breathing. I was angry and extremely agitated. I wanted to carry on telling the taxi driver about the innumerable acts of hostility that we Gibraltarians have suffered at the hands of the Spanish. I wanted to tell him about every single little thing: the insults we occasionally get when we travel to Spain, the calumnies about us in the Spanish press, the excessive checking of our documentation at ports and airports by the *Guardia*

Civil, the vetoing of our applications to the IOC and other sporting bodies. But as I gazed at the back of his head and at the rosary swinging pendulously from the rear-view mirror beside him, I decided that there was no point. He wouldn't understand. He'd just block it all out. If there is one thing, after all, that characterises the Gibraltar dispute, it is the extreme bias of all those concerned. This bias acts like a dense mental fog, bounding our rationality and stopping us from understanding the positions and aspirations of the other participants in this unholy ménage à trois. The Spaniards suffer from this mental fog. So do the Gibraltarians. Even the British, usually so diplomatic and even-handed, cannot free themselves from this sense of entrenchment. As I reflected on these ideas, I thought about Portas and the estrangement that had arisen between us. Were we a bit like Gibraltar and Spain, I wondered — stubbornly keeping our distance from each other over the years? Or was our relationship more like the one between Britain and Gibraltar? That of a master who has grown tired of his subservient underling? I could not be certain one way or the other. The only thing I was sure of, the only point that lay beyond dispute, was that I still resented Portas for cutting me out of his life. Actually, if I'm going to be honest, even back during our Cambridge days I had always resented him a bit. I had resented his money and his effortless charm, his posh accent and his chiselled good looks, his flashy motor and his big house in Trumpington, his innate ability at sports and his annoyingly confident way with women, the fact that everything that cost me, Brian Manrique, so much effort and energy just came so goddamned easy and natural to him. Yes, yes, that was what I had resented the most: the fact that everything came so bloody natural to him. Could anyone really blame me for taking a little pleasure in seeing such a God-like being cut down to size?

34.

The taxi arrived at Opayar at around five-thirty. It wasn't dark yet, but the sun was already sinking towards the horizon. The last fifteen miles of the journey had taken us up the Sierra del Hacho, the semi-mountainous region beginning after the 'white village' of Castellar, and had seen us negotiate one hairpin bend after the other. Going past Taraguilla, I started to get a strong feeling of déjà vu. I couldn't understand what was happening at first, but then I remembered that when I was a kid, well before Franco closed the border, my parents and I would sometimes drive along this route on our way to *la Almoraima*, an area of woodland popular among Gibraltarian picnickers and campers. The memory startled me and made me focus harder on my immediate surroundings. The two main differences between the natural landscape here and back at Gibraltar, as far as I could see, were the enormous amount of space on the one hand and on the other the thickness and quantity of the scrub — which in Gibraltar grew in isolated knotty clumps out of bone-white limestone rock, but which here sprang everywhere out of a dark, reddish-brown soil. Another difference was the tremendous variety of avian wildlife. Just on the short stretch between Taraguilla and Castellar, I had seen a peregrine falcon and two ospreys, as well as the hundreds of storks nesting on top of the electricity pylons lining the road. Not being funny or anything, but in Gibraltar all you ever see are *gaviotas* and *gorriones.*

Opayar itself was a small collection of whitewashed houses clustered around a primitive stone fountain, the whole ensemble clinging precariously to a narrow escarpment bulging out of the mountain behind it. The only non-residential buildings in the vicinity were a tiny church that looked like it had been boarded up for years and a bar called *El Boquete*, the latter's entrance shielded by a screen of old-fashioned beaded curtains. Stray dogs dozed on the steps of the fountain; a cat lay curled up under a Seat *furgoneta.* The smell of *lejía* could once again be detected in the air, but it was nearly drowned out by a resinous odour which, I imagined, was coming from some nearby field. Meanwhile, the driver pulled up beside the fountain and, hooking his brawny arm around the passenger seat's headrest, turned to face me.

'*Bueno,*' he said, his Andalusian features made even darker by a thin film of perspiration, '*aquí estamos.* This is Opayar. Where do you want me to drop you off, *jefe?*'

'I'm not sure,' I replied, bringing out the card which Portas had given to me with his house's address. 'All I have is this: Finca White Haven, El Camino del Alcornocal, Opayar, Provincia de Málaga.'

'*Finca Guay qué?*' the driver half-yelled, snatching the card from my hands.

The man looked at the card for a few seconds and then shook his head, visibly irritated. I was about to tell him that he could drop me off here in the centre of the village and that I'd make my own way to the finca when he suddenly opened the door and lumbered out of the vehicle. 'I'll be back *en un momento*,' he grunted, pulling up his unbelted trousers and moving away.

From the back seat I saw him cross the square and enter the bar. I am not sure how long he remained in that establishment, but it seemed like five or ten minutes or possibly even longer. When he finally came out, he was shaking his head and clenching his fists. He was also spitting furiously — as if a fish bone had lodged itself in his throat.

'Bloody *paletos*,' he said, clambering back into the cab moments later.

'Did you find out where we need to go?'

'*Putos analfabetos patanes!*'

'So you haven't found out, then?'

'*La madre que los parió a todos!*'

'Excuse me, *señor*. I'm talking to you.'

'Yes, yes, *me cago en la leche*, I have found out where this place is, okay?!' the taxi driver at last answered me with a half-apologetic, half-menacing look. 'I'm just annoyed at these fucking country bumpkins, that's all. I went in there and they were all staring at me like I had come from another *puto planeta*. Thank God that I am a born and bred *Algecireño* and not some *puto de mierda cabrero* from up here in the sticks!'

It turned out that the Portas finca lay another two miles away, at the end of a narrow dirt track that began just behind an abandoned brick factory on the outskirts of the village. It took us about ten minutes of slow driving to get there (if I could use the term 'driving' to describe the uncomfortable combination of lurching and bouncing our poor Seat 131 was being subjected to). My *Algecireñan* taxi driver, needless to say, was not impressed with it all. Terrible blasphemies continually escaped his lips, and he shook his head so much, and so vigorously, that flecks of nervous sweat kept shooting off in different directions from the tip of his nose. *Apoplectic* — that's the word that most sprang to mind seeing him hunched over the steering wheel. *Demented*, perhaps, running a close second. At last, though, the path came to an end before a high brick wall and a set of wrought-iron gates. Here I got out of the vehicle and paid the driver, giving him an extra five hundred pesetas for the inconvenience of driving down the dirt track. Charming fellow that he was, he pocketed the money without a word of thanks and began to perform a jerky three-point turn, desperate to get the hell out of there. I watched him in silence for some moments, then sighed with a half-smile and turned around. The gates were tall and tipped with sharp iron finials which reminded me of the spade symbol in a deck of cards; their metal bars glistened as if freshly painted. Beyond them I could see a long gravel drive flanked by a series of towering fir trees. This drive was at least fifteen yards wide and one hundred or one hundred and twenty yards long. However, the most remarkable thing about the view before me was neither the sinister black gates nor the monumental drive nor even the two lines of rustling fir trees; it was simply the fact that there, at the end of it all, a hundred yards from where the taxi had left me and a mere couple of miles from the centre of Opayar, stood a house so typically and so characteristically Edwardian, so absolutely and so cringingly English in design, that for a moment I thought I had to be hallucinating. It felt like I was beholding a homesick Englishman's desiderata, a piece of England that had been uprooted and lovingly transplanted into the sun-cracked Andalusian soil. Deep bay windows, exposed roof rafters, wide eaves with triangular brackets, even one of those goddamned neo-Tudor red-brick turrets — every single Arts and Crafts feature you could think of was visible at the end of that drive. 'So this is Portas's place in the country,' I thought, inwardly bristling at the notion that one family could own so much when all the villagers just down the road led a semi-medieval existence. Shaking my head, succumbing to a fierce bout of class hatred, I put down my suitcase and pressed the button on the intercom attached to the right gatepost.

35.

'*Dígame?*' a youthful female voice crackled out of the intercom speaker.

'Sophia Portas?'

'*Hablando.*'

'Hi, my name's Manrique,' I replied in my poshest English accent. 'Brian Manrique. I'm a friend of your brother Henry. He said you would be expecting me.'

The intercom made a clicking sound and the gates opened. I picked up my suitcase and entered the property. Within seconds I was striding along the same forbidding driveway that I had seen from the other side of the gates. Dust clouds wafted from the ground with every step I took, dirtying the bottom of my trousers. Loose gravel crunched under my shoes.

Somehow it felt darker and quieter here than out on the road. Colder. I soon realised that this was because the fir trees lining the drive were so tall and so closely planted that very little sunlight filtered past their heavy foliage. In fact, the light dripping through had a bluish quality to it which gave you the impression you were moving *underwater.* Instinctively, I reached into my jacket and felt for the letter which I had to deliver. Yes, it was still there. Sealed and waiting to be handed over, I told myself. Ready to demolish the foundations of this ridiculously elitist Portas empire once and for all. Satisfied, I let go of the letter and continued shuffling towards the house. Eventually, after a minute or so, the drive opened out into a large quadrangular space, in the middle of which stood an ornamental stone fountain. Triton or some other classical god rose out of its circular porphyry base, an enormous conch shell clasped between his bronze hands. I paused for a second, ran my fingers through my hair. From up close, the house looked even more eccentric and out of place, a spectacularly outsized folly set in the middle of the Andalusian mountains. The moulded lintel above the door was embossed with a heraldic crest: two trees with a lion squatting under the tree on the right. Around the crest could be seen a Latin proverb in the pseudo-Medieval script so beloved by Pugin and other English neo-Gothic artists. *Virtus omnia ostia aperit.* Something like 'Virtue unblocks all doors.' Typical sanctimonious bourgeois crap, I thought. As I wondered what I was supposed to do next, the main door opened and out stepped a ponytailed young woman in a blue cardigan and a white cotton dress.

'Hello,' the girl said, coming towards me with an outstretched hand. 'I'm Sophia Portas.'

'Pleased to meet you, Miss Portas,' I replied, taking the girl's hand timidly into my own. 'Although we have met before, of course. In Cambridge, I mean. When you came to stay with your brother for one night.... Not that you'll remember, anyway.... I mean, it was such a long time ago, wasn't it? You couldn't have been more than thirteen or maybe fourteen.... Anyway, it's nice to meet you now all the same.'

I looked down, irritated by my lack of composure.

'Come,' Sophia Portas said, gesturing towards the open door with a hint of a smile. 'You must be tired after such a long journey.'

I followed her through the door and into a large and shadowy lobby. Its oak-panelled walls were adorned with an assortment of antlers and stuffed stag heads, most of them accompanied by little brass plaques detailing when and by whom each animal had been shot. At the far end of the room there was a grand wooden staircase, its newel caps carved in the form of canine heads. The hunting theme extended to the ceiling, which was painted over with nymphs and spear-wielding huntsmen and at least one poor chap being devoured by his own hounds. Meanwhile, Sophia Portas had crossed to the other side of the lobby and opened a door that lay concealed in the wooden panelling. Glancing behind her, she beckoned me forward. Astonishingly, the chamber on the other side was bright and airy and free of hunting souvenirs. Potted cycads flanked a single load-bearing pillar, an arrangement which struck me as oddly phallic. Three sets of French windows, all flung open, overlooked an extensive terraced garden. The furnishings in the room were soft and feminine and included a lot of velvet cushions and hanging drapery. On the walls were framed paintings of flowers — gauche, childlike blobs of paint whose predominantly red and yellow tonality reminded me (most bizarrely) of the flame-topped hearts on my Sacred Heart figures back in Gibraltar. From the ceiling hung an old-fashioned cast-iron fan, a solid piece of Victoriana that had evidently withstood the test of time.

'Would you care for some tea, Mr Manrique?' Sophia Portas asked, sitting down on a wicker armchair.

I said that some tea would be nice and took the chair opposite her. Sophia then picked up a small brass bell from a three-legged side table and rang it twice. Less than a minute later, a ponderous, black-dressed woman entered the room and stood attentively beside the door. She had thick, bushy eyebrows and a faint layer of down on her upper lip. A network of squiggly varicose veins bulged through the translucent black nylon socks covering her plump calves. A Spanish duenna *de arriba a abajo.* I assumed this was Matilda, the maid Portas recently told me about. While Portas's sister was busy giving the woman her instructions, I was able to look at Sophia properly for the first time. She was still the spitting image of her brother, although the sexless scrawniness of the pre-pubescent had now given way to the rounder, softer, fleshier forms of an adult woman. Her large green eyes were bright and fiery — almost too bright for someone who was supposed to be a sensitive agoraphobic recluse. A small, liver-coloured mole could be seen about half an inch to the left of her mouth, adding a touch of carnality to her lipstick-less lips. Clearly, she was a very beautiful woman — and yet I didn't feel particularly attracted to her. I wondered whether this was because she looked so much like her brother, or because I was so worried about the task that lay ahead of me. Probably the latter, I thought.

'I hope you didn't find it too difficult to reach White Haven,' Sophia said, turning towards me once the maid had gone. 'It can be a bit tricky coming here for the first time.'

'It wasn't too bad. We got some decent directions at the village bar,' I said, blushing for no apparent reason.

'Ah, so you met some of our *Opayaranos*. Delightful set of people, aren't they?'

'I didn't actually go into the bar myself. The taxi driver did.'

'Oh,' she said, 'that's a pity. A real pity.' And then, looking at me with a wry smile that reminded me of her brother: 'Henry said you'd be coming by ferry. I hope your journey was tolerably comfortable.'

'It was okay,' was all I mumbled out. 'Nothing too inconvenient, really.'

'Do you often go to Madrid on business?'

'Madrid?'

'Yes, I thought you were going there on business. At least that's what my brother told me over the phone.'

'Ah yes, Madrid,' I replied nervously, wondering why on earth Portas had told her such a story. 'Yes, I go there sometimes…. Sorry, Miss Portas — I'm just a little tired after such a long taxi ride.'

'I'm sure you are. It's not the easiest of trips getting up here from Algeciras. That document case of my brother's which you are collecting must be very important to justify such a detour in your journey.'

I smiled and nodded hastily in an attempt to conceal my surprise. So I was supposed to be collecting a document case now, was I? Why oh why had that blithering idiot Portas not let me know about this? Was he intent on making this whole experience as uncomfortable as possible for me?

'You look terribly pale, Mr Manrique,' Sophia said, her features twisting into a frown of concern. 'I think a bit of fresh air might do you good. Would you like to go out into the back garden with me after we have our tea? You can leave your suitcase here while we're out.'

I said that going out into the garden would be very nice and looked down at my fidgeting hands. Moments later, Matilda arrived with the tea. She transferred the contents of her tray to the coffee table in front of us, and was told she could retire to her quarters for the evening. 'Yes, Miss Portas,' the maid responded huskily. 'I'll just finish up in the kitchen and go. If you need anything, you know where to find me.' Once Matilda left the room, Sophia asked me if it was true that I had studied French and Italian at Cambridge as her brother had told her. Reddening slightly, I replied that it was true and once again focused on my hands. She then said that she liked to read French and German novels whenever she got a chance. 'Really?' I blurted out, looking up with genuine surprise. 'What sort of French books do you read?' 'Oh,' she replied with a self-deprecatory gesture, 'all sorts.' At this point she began to list some of the French authors that she had been reading lately. I heard the names Rodenbach and Guyotat mentioned among other less famous names, but I wasn't really paying that much attention to what she was saying. Instead I thought about the letter in my jacket pocket. I wondered if the time had come for me to produce it. If I should just pull it out and lay it on the coffee table. I also couldn't stop thinking about what her brother had told me about Sophia's frail and psychologically unstable nature. Was the kid *as bad as all that?* I thought, sipping my tea. She certainly didn't seem unbalanced from where I currently sat. Quite the opposite. She seemed calm and confident, the type of young woman who could cope with whatever life threw at her. Nevertheless, if I knew anything about these bloody Portases, it was that what you saw and what you got were rarely in concord with each other. Therefore, there was a real chance that Henry could be right and that his sister was as delicate and fragile as he claimed. If so, what would happen once she read the letter? Would she faint? Would she break into tears? Would she start screaming? The possibilities frightened me, made me wonder why on earth I had accepted such an emotionally onerous task. In an effort to regain some self-control, I told myself that the best thing to do would be to whip out the letter without any further delay and wordlessly hand it over. Get it over and done with once and for all. But, coward that I was, I couldn't summon up the nerve to do it. Again and again I kept delaying the moment, telling myself that it would be better to wait a bit longer — until we finished our tea, perhaps, or until we were on our way out into the garden, or, even better, until we were actually in the garden itself. In truth, I worried so much about how to proceed that before I knew it the tea and biscuits were consumed and I was already following Sophia out into the back garden, wondering what would happen when the poor girl discovered that she had lost her entire fortune.

It was, as I expected, starting to get dark outside. The sun had nearly sunk behind the surrounding mountains and a dim light had settled over the neatly arranged topiary and flower beds. A soft breeze carried hints of jasmine and rosemary and dry sierra soil. As we strolled across a closely mown lawn, Sophia kept stopping and rearranging the black velvet hair band holding her ponytail in place. She did this calmly and gently, with what seemed like a degree of self-consciousness. Suddenly she turned towards me and said, 'Do you know, my brother has always spoken very highly of you?'

'Has he?' I replied, a little taken aback.

'Yes,' she said, slowing down. 'He once said you were the only person he ever trusted. That you were like a brother to him.'

For the briefest of moments I was tempted to say 'that's why he's had nothing to do with me for the last six years', but instead I merely smiled and carried on walking along the path.

'It must be good to have a friend like that,' Sophia Portas resumed. 'I don't think I could say the same about any of my acquaintances, unfortunately.'

'I suppose it must be very lonely living up here, away from it all,' I said.

'Not really, Mr Manrique. I have many friends who come to see me. It's just that I've never been particularly close to any of them, the way you and my brother are close to each other.'

I smiled uneasily and continued walking by her side. I wanted to say something that would knock her brother off the pedestal she had created for him and in this way prepare her psychologically for the news of their bankruptcy, but I wasn't sure how to begin. In my frustration I blurted out the first thing that came into my head:

'Have you and Henry always been very close, Miss Portas?'

'What do you mean?'

'It's just that you didn't appear to be especially close when you came to Cambridge all those years ago.'

Sophia Portas shook her head with an amused smile. 'Oh, you know what young men are like, Mr Manrique. There's more chance of them howling at the moon than showing any affection for their sister in front of their friends.'

'So you've always been close?'

'Yes, I would say so.... Don't you have any brothers or sisters of your own?'

'I have a younger sister in Germany, but I hardly have any contact with her.'

She allowed a silent 'oh' to form on her lips and then slowly turned her head away. We walked together for a few seconds in silence, the path becoming progressively wider and grander. Up ahead I could see an ornamental metal bridge stretching across a pond of giant water-lilies. We crossed this bridge and then cut through a plain grass lawn which bore the rubbed-off white chalk markings of a former tennis court. Further ahead, I noticed a swimming pool — a gleaming chrome and marble affair that wouldn't have looked amiss in a Hollywood film, though presently it was empty of water and partly covered by a large blue tarpaulin. Past the pool, there was another lawn, only this lawn was neatly laid out with flower beds. Not typical Andalusian flowers like jasmines and carnations, but non-native imports that I couldn't recognise. Once the flower beds ended, there was an area of stone paving and, beyond that, a viewing platform sealed off by a stone balustrade. From this platform you could see most of the Genal Valley, a sprawling patchwork of vineyards, rivers, hills, granite cliffs, chestnut plantations, parcels of arid scrubland and row after row of stumpy olive trees.

'That's some view,' I said, resting my hands on top of the balustrade.

'Yes, I suppose it is. Most of what you see belongs to our estate, although there's one or two little private *cotos de caza* here and there. You see that forest of thick, dark green trees behind that bluish hill in the distance? That's *El Parque Natural de los Alcornocales.* British officers from Gibraltar used to go hunting there until the 1930s. You must have heard of the Royal Calpe Hunt?'

'Yes, I have. That was the name for the old military fox hunt led by the Governor of Gibraltar, wasn't it?'

'Correct. My family were always very involved with the Royal Calpe Hunt, you know. Even before my great-grandfather Henry Richard Portas built this house in 1912. My great-great-grandfather William Henry Portas was actually the first and only Gibraltarian Master of the Hunt. The only non-British Master of the Hunt apart from the Spanish nobleman Pablo Larios. You could say that hunting runs in the veins of the Portas family. What about you, Mr Manrique?' she asked, turning towards me with a scarcely concealed smile of amusement. 'Are you a hunting man?'

'I'm afraid not.'

She turned around again and looked out over the valley, her face illuminated by the crepuscular indigo light radiating from behind the distant hills.

'I think it must have been so weird for the local villagers, don't you think, Mr Manrique — having a group of toffee-nosed, scarlet-uniformed British officers and their Gibraltarian underlings turn up every few weeks with their beagles and their horses and their hunting horns?'

'I suppose so, Miss Portas.'

'All those foreigners coming here and lording it up over them. Riding through their fields and damaging their crops.'

I thought about making a sarcastic remark about her and her brother's high-walled Anglo-Gibraltarian enclave here in quintessentially Spanish Opayar, but in the end I decided against it.

'Sometimes I wonder if we are seen as a similar anomaly by the local villagers,' Sophia said softly.

'You mean you and your brother?'

'I mean, look at us,' she continued in the same barely audible tone. 'We are rich and we are Gibraltarian and we live in this ridiculously English house in the middle of one of the poorest parts of Spain. Our *capataces* and our *sirvientes* always smile and act politely when they are standing there in front of us, yes, but deep down who knows how they feel? Maybe they resent us as much as those nineteenth-century villagers resented the officers of the Royal Calpe Hunt…. What do you think, Mr Manrique? Do you think they secretly thirst for our blood while they cook for us and polish our silver?'

'I think most Spaniards see *anything to do* with Gibraltar as an aberration and a blot on their honour, Miss Portas,' I said. 'However, if you're paying their wages and treating them well, I'm sure no one's going to think badly about you. Politics is one thing; earning one's livelihood entirely another.'

Sophia smiled, evidently pleased by my response. 'Tell me, Mr Manrique,' she said, her thin dark eyebrows coming together. 'What do you think about the Spanish?'

'What do I think about the Spanish?' I repeated, momentarily caught off-guard.

'Yes. What's your opinion on them? Do you think they are kind, perhaps? Friendly? Brave? Cruel? Proud? Caught up in quixotic delusions? Easily influenced by their own government's propaganda? Excessively nationalistic? Tell me, I'd be very interested to know your opinion.'

'And why's that?' I enquired with a smile.

Sophia crossed her arms and tilted her head slightly to one side. 'I always like to hear what our

Gibraltarian visitors think about Spain and the Spanish. You could say it's like a hobby of mine.'

'Because it amuses you?'

'No, because it helps me to understand a political situation which, geographically isolated in this place as I am, I sometimes feel very detached from.'

'Well, in that case let me tell you what I think. I have no problem with ordinary Spaniards,' I said, letting go of the stone balustrade and looking directly at her. 'I think the majority of them are simple, down-to-earth, brave, hardy, decent people who have had to put up with a lot of bad governance over the years.'

'But?'

'But I don't like how, once you mention the word "Gibraltar" to your average Spaniard, he instantly puffs his chest out and starts talking to you as if you had personally cuckolded him in a former life. It's almost like a switch is flicked on inside him, like he had just consumed a mind-altering cocktail. You know the recipe for this powerfully hallucinogenic beverage, don't you, Miss Portas? A pinch of self-delusion, six heaped teaspoonfuls of national propaganda, a great big lump of *españolismo* and a few measly shavings of *amor propio*. Put them all in a cocktail shaker, give it all a bit of a judder … and there you have it: a big glass of pure 100 per cent *Gibraltar Español*. The finest and most potent mental intoxicant currently available on the Iberian Peninsula. Guaranteed to make you forget about your son's homosexuality or your wife's affairs or your neighbour's surliness or whatever else you want to forget about in six quick amnesia-proof syllables.'

'You should be a writer, Mr Manrique,' Sophia said with a grin. 'Has anyone ever told you that?'

'The problem mainly resides with the Spanish media,' I continued in a calmer tone. 'They print such terrible lies about us that it is hard for the average Spaniard to look upon Gibraltar as anything other than a carbuncle attached to Spain's backside.'

'You sound a bit like my brother when you say that, Mr Manrique,' Sophia said, smiling very sweetly.

'Do I?'

'Yes. Except he's not that fussed about whether the Rock belongs to Spain or Britain or even to Morocco. He just doesn't like the way Gibraltar is portrayed in the Spanish media because he says it's damaging to our wider business interests. That's what my brother's like, as I'm sure you already know. Family and commerce above everything else, Mr Manrique. Anyway,' she said, moving away from the stone balustrade, 'let's cross over the bridge now and head to the other end of the garden before it gets totally dark. If you think this view's impressive, wait till you see what the view's like on the other side.'

She turned around and started walking away from the viewing platform. I watched her for a second, my eye drawn to the silky black plait resting on her shoulders. I was very vexed and agitated, seriously stressed by all this talk about Gibraltar and Spain. I decided that I couldn't delay the matter any longer. I *had* to hand over the letter to her before my emotions got the better of me. I just needed to find the correct moment, that's all. Nervously, I thought about the ornamental bridge. Because it was so narrow, we'd have to slow down there and walk side by side. Okay, I told myself. That's settled. At the bridge, I will bring out the letter and give it to her. It is as simple as that. I will retrieve the letter, hand it to her and let her see just what an ass her brother is. However, when we reached the bridge something really awkward happened. As I turned to reach into my jacket pocket, I somehow misjudged the distance between us and my elbow accidentally brushed against her left breast. Mortified, I jumped to one side and prepared to splutter out a hasty apology. Before I could find the right words, though, it occurred to me that she had not pulled away like I had done. The thought unsettled me, caused my heart to break into palpitations. Reluctantly, I let go of the letter and brought an empty hand out of my pocket.

'It's rather hot for a winter evening, isn't it, Mr Manrique? I think we'll have an early spring this year, don't you think?'

I looked at her for a moment or two, quietly holding my breath. Was I hearing right? Had she really come up with such a suggestive remark? Or had she only commented about a simple meteorological phenomenon and I had got the wrong end of the stick? Deeply confused, I thought about the breast I had accidentally brushed against. It had felt weighty and firm, agonisingly sensual. The recollection perturbed me, haunted me like it could only haunt someone who had been celibate for so long. At the same time, I could feel my mouth filling up with nervous saliva. It was so bad, this build-up of saliva, that I had to keep swallowing to make it go away. Soon we reached the other end of the garden. Hoping to camouflage my anxiety, I made some vapid comment about the view. For the next few minutes I talked about all manner of things. Mountain villages, ferry crossings, Moroccan customs officials, Spanish taxi drivers, the lack of private gardens in Gibraltar. I spoke quickly and without making much sense, my only intention being to kill the beast that lurked like a mud-smeared rodent inside me. But the tactic wasn't working. Even as the words poured out of my mouth, I kept thinking about how good it would feel to touch her, how marvellous it would be to enfold her in my arms. Greatly distressed, I told myself that a girl like her would never be interested in a nobody like me, that I was merely indulging in wishful thinking. But it was no use: desire had spread like an infection in my poor febrile brain.

'Shall we go back into the house, Mr Manrique? It's too dark now to properly appreciate the view. Plus I mustn't forget to give you the document case before you go. Matilda left it for you in the second-floor lobby.'

I nodded and followed her in the direction of the house. As we went around one of the last bends in the path, I thought about Portas and how bad it was for me to be lusting after his sister at a time like this. 'This is wrong,' I thought, astounded at my own fickleness. 'Everything about this is wrong.' But even though I knew all this, I could not stop myself. Desire had immobilised my conscience, it had blurred the line between instinct and personal scruples…. And then it happened. Just outside the house's back entrance, I stopped to let her walk ahead of me and she, coincidentally, did the same. For a few seconds we stood there, smiling uncertainly at each other. Then, with a sense of purpose that shocked me, I reached forward and took her in my arms. At first she pushed me violently away — making me think I had just committed the biggest mistake of my life — but then she drew me back towards her and kissed me with just as much violence as she had previously used to repel me. After that, everything becomes fuzzy and a little surreal — so much so that I can only remember what happened next as a series of isolated, dreamlike images: stroking Portas's sister's hair, tasting the blood seeping out of a cut on my lip, half-walking, half-staggering up a set of stairs, entering a room with purple walls and curtainless windows, pushing Sophia against an oaken dresser. Meanwhile, a thousand thoughts hurtled through my head. That much I am sure about. I remember, for example, thinking that all this had to be part of a plot hatched between Portas and his sister, that Sophia couldn't possibly be surrendering herself to me without some kind of ulterior motive. I remember briefly thinking about the letter, about how important it was that I handed it over. I remember inwardly telling myself, 'Oh, well. You can always hand it over a bit later. It's not as if an hour or two will make any difference, is it?' I remember struggling to keep calm when, after a maddening period of frustration, I finally burrowed my fingers under her bra and I cupped my hands around her naked breasts. But more than anything else, I remember thinking about Portas and wondering what he'd have said had he seen me there, kissing his precious little sister's neck, breathing obscenities into her ear, lying together with her on her bed. *Look at me, you goddamned fool. You thought I wasn't good enough to keep your company and yet here I am about to fuck your sister. How does that make you feel, you stuck-up turd? Do you feel betrayed? Do you feel let down? Ha ha ha, ha ha ha. Always thought you were so much better than me, didn't you? Always thought you and your precious family were so superior to the rest of us. Well, what do you know, look at us now: you lying there like some penniless drunk in the gutter while I, Brian Manrique, the eternal nobody, the churchgoing flunky, mount your precious sister and then, just to finish the job, tell her that her brother has frittered away the family fortune. Ha ha ha ha ha. Is the boot on the other foot now, or what?*

Embarrassing, I know. Humiliating. Horribly degrading. To think that with every thrust of my loins I kept visualising Portas's face, taking a savage delight in the knowledge that I was fucking his sister. But in my defence I was half-crazed with the scent of sex and revenge. Not just that: I was finally laying to rest my own personal demons, finally extinguishing the pain that came from so many years of drudgery and emotional self-neglect. With every beastly grunt and thrust, I was letting go of old inhibitions, atoning for the spiritual and sexual numbness which I had subjected my body to for so long. In the meantime, Sophia carried on holding me and covering me with greedy kisses. So intense was her passion that she trembled again and again, throwing her head back, making soft moaning sounds one moment and then fierce guttural noises the next. Transiently, I remembered the modest girl in the white dress who had sat so demurely in the lounge amid her Meissen cups and teapot. Could this really be the same person? If so, what could have precipitated such a Jekyll and Hyde transformation? Was her sexual predatoriness a symptom of the psychological frailty Portas had spoken about? Or was this just her way of getting back at a brother whom she professed to love but subconsciously resented? I was not sure. I was beginning to lose the ability to see things in their true context. *What I can tell you without hesitation* is that during those moments her body was like a fountain to me and that I could not stop myself drinking from it. That — and that I have never felt *so alive* in a woman's arms: torn, as I was, between the urge to defile and the wish to venerate, between the need to punish her for her brother's sins and the simultaneous longing to hold her and caress her and thank her for the precious gift she was bestowing on me.

And then … it was all over. With a final, monstrous, blood-dizzying burst of energy, our voices rose in unison one last time and then faded away amid a series of gasps and shudders. Then there was silence — absolute, terrible, devastating in its unexpected suddenness. It was the kind of silence where all you can hear is the pounding of your heart, where all you can feel is the gushing of blood in your ears. Lethargically, with my eyes half closed and one arm still wrapped around Sophia's body, I turned to one side and looked at the small open window beyond the dresser and the bedside table. For the first time that evening I noticed that it was draped with a thin muslin curtain, now fluttering timidly in the breeze. Again, I found myself wondering whether all this was part of a dream, whether I had mentally conjured up the whole weird episode and was due to wake any moment now. I also thought about the letter still in my jacket pocket. Portas had been so specific in his instructions: 'hand it over to her and then call me straight away.' Part of me felt that I should get up and do as he had requested. That I shouldn't waste another second. But another part of me — the part that was deriving so much pleasure from lying together with his sister — felt deeply opposed to the idea. Why should I rouse myself from this pleasant state of lethargy just to hand over his bloody letter? I can always hand it over when I get up in a couple of hours, can't I? Besides, it's not as if I owe the guy any sort of allegiance after the way he has treated me over the years, is it? Think about Venice, Brian. Remember the way that Portas and Lady Victoria mocked your lowly upbringing. Think about all those times the no-good bastard saw you in Main Street and looked aside. No, Brian, leave the letter where it is for now. Let the wretch stew in his own juices for a bit longer.

Having decided this, I turned again towards Sophia and closed my eyes. In a short while an irresistible languor began spreading through my limbs, slowing down my thoughts and gradually nudging me into insentience. In this semi-conscious state I heard Sophia ask me if I wanted to stay the night and found myself mumbling that I wouldn't mind. Before long, I drifted off to sleep and started having a strange dream. In the dream I was back in Gibraltar, in the pebbled cove known as Sandy Bay. Gigantic waves crashed upon the shoreline, filling the air with columns of hissing sea spray. Flashes of lightning electrified the evening sky. As I watched the scene unfold in all its terrible majesty, I became aware that Portas was standing beside me. He was wearing a T-shirt decorated with a picture of a Ferris wheel — or perhaps a snake biting its own tail. What looked like a woman's scarf was wrapped around his left hand. Tentatively, with a sense of apprehension, I moved towards him and asked him what he was doing there on the beach. 'I'm waiting for the steamboat to Memphis!' he shouted back, unwinding the scarf around his hand to reveal a heavily tattooed palm. 'And so are you, my tuppenny Judas!' He continued shouting meaningless shit like this for some moments, with his palms held open and his blond curls fluttering in the wind. All during this time I wanted to turn around and scurry away, to get the hell out of that desolate beach. And yet I could not move; my limbs were heavy; my feet were rooted to the spot. With a cry of anguish, I sank down on my knees and futilely punched the compressed damp sand. I punched and punched the sand until I could feel the skin on my knuckles tearing and peeling away. Then I looked up and saw that Portas was now wearing a stovepipe hat and a long black cape. A thin magician's wand had materialised between the fingers of his right hand. 'Hello, sir!' he said, winking at me in the manner of a circus promoter. 'Fancy a quick hop on our little Miss Dollymop?'

At that moment I woke up from the dream with a sudden start. For several seconds I remained curled up in the foetal position, my knees tucked against my chest. My heart was beating violently and my body was drenched in a cold sweat; I could feel the hairs on my arms standing on end. Judging by the amount of light in the room, it must have been about five in the morning. In the corner of the bedroom the muslin curtain was still fluttering gently, stirred by the same noiseless wind. I gazed at it for some seconds, deriving a strange comfort from its swaying motion. Then, as I emerged from my sleep-induced lethargy, I turned on my side and realised that Sophia was no longer there. Again, I was filled with doubts, with lingering uncertainties. Had I really slept with Sophia Portas, or had I dreamt up the whole crazy episode? As I pondered the question in my head, I thought I heard the sound of sobbing coming from somewhere. Rattled, I got out of bed dressed only in my underpants and walked towards the bedroom door. Out in the hallway I had no doubts — the sound was that of a woman sobbing and it was coming from the lounge on the ground floor. By now almost shaking with dread, I began to descend the staircase that I had climbed in such a lustful frenzy just hours earlier. I was aware of a musty smell — the sort emitted by decades-old wainscoting and worn carpeting. When I got to the living room door, I hesitated for a moment, then turned the doorknob slowly and walked inside. Airlessness. Heavy shadows. Slivers of grey light filtering through the drawn curtains. Whoever was sobbing was only yards away, but it was so dark that I couldn't make out where the sound was coming from. Then, as my eyes became attuned to the darkness, I noticed something that nearly made me jump out of my skin: Sophia and the maid were huddled together on the living room settee, both clad in their dressing gowns. Sophia lay limp and lifeless in her maid's embrace, drained of all energy and will. Matilda smoothed her mistress's hair with her stubby fingers, all the while staring hostilely in my direction.

'It's the master,' Matilda said, raising her voice over the sobbing girl. 'He hanged himself a few hours ago in his Gibraltar office. I think you should leave now, sir. The main gate's already open.'

I nodded and picked up my suitcase from where I had left it the previous evening. I wanted to tell Portas's sister that I was sorry that her brother had killed himself, but I couldn't summon up the nerve and, in any case, I don't think that Sophia was in a position to register anything that I could have said to her. As I left the room, I felt like a somnambulist or a method actor unable to shake out of a demanding role. I felt *like I was trapped in somebody else's skin.* At the door I turned around half-heartedly with the intention of performing some last valedictory act — asking them if they needed anything, perhaps, or telling them where to contact me if they required any help — but the indomitable Matilda cut me short:

'Please, sir. It's better if you go now. *Please.*'

I nodded again and slipped out of the room. Closing the door, I exhaled with relief and began walking up the stairs, the sound of sobbing already receding into a distant whisper behind me. It was still dark, although the shadows were not as dense as before and I could now pick out the hunting trophies on the lobby walls — chunky, sinister forms that reminded me of medieval gargoyles. Arriving at the first floor, I went into Sophia's bedroom and started getting dressed. I felt calm and collected, but there was something unnatural about my lack of emotion, psychologically suspect. It was almost as if my brain knew that something terrible had happened, but my body was desperately trying to keep the situation under control by pumping out a mix of numbing chemicals and hormones. As I put my left leg into my trousers, I had a vision of Henry dangling from the light fitting in his office, but I quickly pushed the image out of my mind, telling myself there'd be time to worry about all that later. The important thing right now is to get out of here, I reflected, surprised at how composed I felt. That is all that matters right now. With this thought in my head, I finished getting dressed and went downstairs again. The light was much brighter now and it was easier to see where one was going. The hunting trophies no longer looked like gargoyles because you could perceive the whites of their eyes. For a moment or two I stood in the entrance hallway, listening to the sound of Sophia crying and Matilda consoling her. I could even hear the words that the Spanish woman was saying: '*No llores más, mi chiquita. Que el Señor es justo y es pecado contrariar su voluntad.*' Then I opened the main door and stealthily left the building.

It wasn't particularly bright outside, but coming from the near-darkness of the lobby I still had to lower my gaze and shield my eyes. In the quiet of the morning, you could hear birds chirping and gurgling fountain noises, the whirr of a tractor engine somewhere in the distance. Tightening my grip on my suitcase handle, I bit into my lower lip and started moving away from the house. My eyes were still stinging and my mouth had a rough, sandpapery feel to it, as if I had spent the whole night drinking. Twice I stopped and coughed, trying to dislodge the phlegmy crust at the back of my throat. Repeatedly I told myself that I wouldn't turn around to look at the house, that I would exit through the gates and carry on walking as normal down the dirt track towards the centre of Opayar. But when I got to the end of the drive, the urge was too strong: *I had to spin around.* Not that I saw anything strange there at the end of that private road. Just a large and imposing mansion. A bit unusual because of its wide eaves and its red-brick turret, but nothing too out of the ordinary. Shaking my head, I turned around. Then, smiling with a mixture of sadness and relief, I slipped through the half-open gates and began the two-mile trek to the centre of Opayar.

It was only when I was sitting in the taxi on the way back to Algeciras that I remembered I still had the letter that Sophia's brother had entrusted to me two days ago. It was still lying there in my jacket pocket, as sealed and unopened as when Portas had pressed it tearfully into my hand. As the taxi clanked and juddered around yet another hairpin bend, I took it out and wondered whether to open it or not. But in the end I decided not to. There was no point. I more or less knew what it would say and, besides, I was not going to betray Sophia's brother in death as well. So I tore the envelope into little bits and pushed them through the small gap at the top of the passenger window, watching them scatter like confetti in the wind. As the last of the scraps blew away, it occurred to me that Henry might have still been alive had I handed the letter over to Sophia and phoned him immediately afterwards as I was supposed to. After all, he had been very insistent that I should call him as soon as I could. Maybe, knowing how impulsive he was, he had interpreted my silence as a sign that Sophia had taken the news badly. Maybe he had lost his nerve after all those hours sitting fruitlessly by the phone. Maybe he had hanged himself out of sheer frustration….

I finally got back to Gibraltar about ten o'clock in the evening. A few days later, a long obituary on Portas appeared in the *Gibraltar Chronicle.* Its anonymous author talked about Portas's generosity of spirit and his sense of financial acumen, adding, just like good obituarists do, that Gibraltar would never be the same without him. No mention, however, was made of his suicide or his gambling or the fact that his company would soon be going into administration. As for poor Sophia Portas, she simply vanished into thin air, retreating to whatever solitary, penumbral world Fate had appointed for her. All that remained of our night together was the rancid taste of betrayal and deceit. Because, even though I spent most of the taxi ride from Opayar to Algeciras trying to disconnect from the whole affair, even though I told myself that Henry had been psychologically unstable and would probably have killed himself whether I had phoned him or not, *I knew I had betrayed Portas.* I had betrayed him by not handing over the letter. I had betrayed him by sleeping with his mentally unbalanced sister. And worst of all I had betrayed him by never bothering to call him when I knew that he was in such desperate straits. This knowledge didn't exactly crush me with guilt, but it left me feeling irritable and unsettled — so much so that, just seven or eight weeks after coming back from Opayar, I ended up rowing with Pozo-Jones at the library and handing in my resignation. Soon afterwards, I got a job at the Gibraltar Casino, which was taking in new personnel to cope with the influx of punters coming through the recently opened border. My duties were to look at CCTV footage of the card tables and to liaise via radio with our team of doormen. Though I was very busy in the evenings, I had almost nothing to do in the afternoons and it was during those idle hours that I penned most of this memoir. I wrote it partly because I was bored out of my wits, and partly to purge the combination of remorse, shock and anger still fermenting within me after Portas's bankruptcy and suicide. For a long, long time it remained at the bottom of a box of ledgers and logbooks, but a few weeks ago I brought it out and reread the whole thing, adding to it these final explicatory lines. Will I ever publish the manuscript? I don't know. Occasionally, as I sit here in my CCTV cubicle monitoring people around the roulette wheel or the baccarat table, Portas slides into my thoughts and tells me that stories are meant to be read and not just written. Perhaps he is right, but Gibraltar is a small and unforgiving place and an intimate memoir like mine — even though it deals with events that happened many years ago — will surely upset a lot of people. Also, it's not as if I come out of this sordid little tale covered in glory, is it? Anyway, I'm not going to worry too much about this now. *Que será será,* as the saying goes.

--The End--

Further Reading

Sarah M. Abas, 'M. G. Sanchez: an Interview,' *ES Review* 39, 2018, pp. 319-330.

Esterino Adami, 'La Rocca di Babele: narrazioni e trasformazioni linguistiche in M. G. Sanchez,' *Ritorno a Babele: prove di globalizzazione* (Turin: Neos Terrenia, 2013), pp. 71-81.

Esterino Adami, 'An Interview with Gibraltarian author M. G. Sanchez followed by a review of *The Escape Artist*,' *Il Tolomeo* 13, 2013, pp. 29-36.

Esterino Adami, 'Recensione di *Jonathan Gallardo*,' *Il Tolomeo* 18, 2016, pp. 233-35.

Esterino Adami, 'Recensione di *Solitude House*,' *Il Tolomeo* 17, 2015, pp. 185-187.

Esterino Adami, 'A Passage to Gibraltar: Alterity and Representation in M. G. Sanchez,' *Postcolonial Passages: incursions and excursions across the literatures and cultures in English* (Cambridge: Cambridge Scholars Publishing, 2018), pp. 204–214.

Esterino Adami, 'Writing the Rock: An e-interview with Mark G. Sanchez and Giordano Durante,' *AISCLI Newsletter* 16, 2020, pp. 4-6.

Christine Berberich, 'Review of *Gooseman*,' *Wasafiri* 111, 2022, pp. 116–118.

Isabel Alonso Breto, 'Review of *Border Control and other Autobiographical Pieces*,' *Complutense Journal of English Studies* 28, 2020, pp. 229-231.

Isabel Alonso Breto, 'Somewhere between the Colonial and the Postcolonial: An Interview with Gibraltarian Author M. G. Sanchez,' *Ariel: A Review of International English Literature* 52:3, 2021, pp. 249-261.

Miriam Fernández Santiago, 'Review of *Gooseman*,' *Journal of Mediterranean Studies* 31:1, 2021, pp. 127–128.

Rebecca Gabay, 'M. G. Sanchez's *Bombay Journal*: Redressing the Past from the Colonial Present,' *Kervan International Journal of Afro-Asiatic Studies* 22, 2018, pp. 291-294.

Amanda Gerke, 'Discursive Boundaries: Code-Switching as Representative of Gibraltarian Identity Construction in M. G. Sanchez's *Rock Black*,' *Miscelánea* 57, 2018, pp. 35-57.

Ina Habermann, 'British-European Entanglements: M. G. Sanchez's *The Escape Artist* and the Case of Gibraltar,' *Journal for Literary and Intermedial Crossings* 2, 2018, pp. b1-20.

Ina Habermann, 'Gibraltarian Hauntologies: Spectres of Colonialism in the Fiction of M. G. Sanchez,' *Open Library of Humanities* 6:1, 2020, p. 19.

Ina Habermann, 'Something rotten in the state of Gibraltar: M. G. Sanchez's Autobiographical Explorations of borderlands,' *Mediterranean Studies* 30:2, 2022, pp. 163-176.

Ana Maria Manzanas Calvo, 'The Line and the Limit of Britishness: The Construction of Gibraltarian Identity in M. G. Sanchez's Writing,' *ES Review* 38, 2017, pp. 27-45.

Alastair Niven, 'Celebrating an Abundance, 1984–2019: Thirty-five Literary Highlights from Aotearoa to Zimbabwe,' *Wasafiri* 34, 2019, pp. 133-138.

Robert Patrick Newcomb, 'Review of *Border Control and Other Autobiographical Pieces*,' *International Journal of Iberian Studies* 33:1, 2020, pp. 107-108.

Robert Patrick Newcomb, 'Review of *Gooseman*,' *Hispania*, 104:4, 2021, pp. 750-751.

Elena Seoane, 'Telling the true Gibraltarian Story: an interview with Gibraltarian writer M. G. Sanchez,' *Alicante Journal of English Studies* 29, 2016, pp. 251-258

John A. Stotesbury, 'Mediterranean Gothic: M. G. Sanchez's Gibraltar Fiction in its Context,' *British and American Studies* 21, 2016, pp. 156-172.

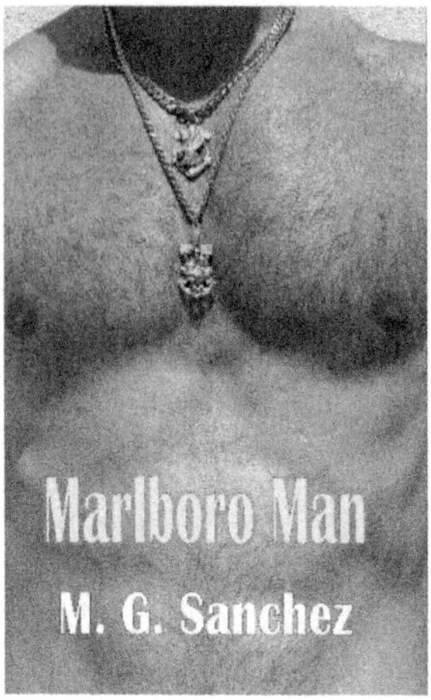

Marlboro Man

Alex Pereira – former 'Winston-boy' and *gayumbero* – left Gibraltar in 1998 to escape his unsavoury criminal past. Twenty-one years later, he is back on the Rock – strapped for cash and stranded in an Uppertown bedsit, with no company save for his fading memories. With *Marlboro Man,* M. G. Sanchez revisits the Gibraltar of the late eighties and early nineties, bringing back to life a chaotic era marked by social unrest and large-scale smuggling.

The Fetishist

Nathan Holgado, admin assistant at Fernandez Funeral Services, loves all things British and military related. He is also obsessed with his Victorian English ancestor, his great-great-great-grandfather Private Edwin Baxter of the 15th Regiment of Foot. Looking at Google Street View one afternoon, Holgado discovers that the house in Yorkshire where Edwin was born is still standing. Filled with patriotic pride, he starts making plans to travel to the UK and visit Baxter's birthplace….

Gooseman

'If there is a date when my story begins, it is 13 September 1981. That day was not only my first day at school; it was the first time that I realised I was not like the others.' So begins *Gooseman*, M. G. Sanchez's new darkly comic novel. Its protagonist is Johann Guzman, a cynical but quick-witted young Gibraltarian loner. Shunned by his schoolmates and bullied by his father, Guzman dreams about leaving the small-town atmosphere of his native Gibraltar and starting a new life in the UK. But when he finally overcomes his demons and cuts the umbilical cord tying him to the British Overseas Territory, things don't quite go according to plan....

Crossed Lines

Crossed Lines, M. G. Sanchez's new volume of stories, focuses on three different, but equally troubled male characters. Jake Wallburger, stuck in a dead-end job delivering frozen fish to shops and supermarkets along the North Norfolk coastline. Graeme Kirkbride, holed up in a bedsit in the outskirts of Tokyo trying to forget about his past. And, finally, Paco Colomán Trujillo, a Spanish crossfrontier worker who pretends to love Gibraltar and its people, but secretly hankers for the day when the Spanish flag will fly from the top of the Rock….

Border Control

Border Control and other Autobiographical Pieces focuses on topics as diverse as childhood bullying, border traffic queues, travelling through Spain, being pickpocketed in China, and life in post-Brexit referendum Britain — all of them filtered through the eye of one of Gibraltar's top authors.

Past: A Memoir

In July 2013, just as a full-blown diplomatic row was erupting between Britain and Spain over the Rock of Gibraltar, Joseph Sanchez collapsed and died while cycling in Taraguilla, a Spanish village twenty miles north of the border. In this honest and sensitively written memoir Gibraltarian author M. G. Sanchez relates the hardships his family endured while trying to repatriate his father's remains during one of the most acrimonious phases in recent Gibraltarian history. Part-family memoir, part-act of remembrance, *Past: A Memoir* mixes personal reminiscences with political and historical commentary in a shifting, multi-layered narrative which explores – and vigorously upholds – what it means to be Gibraltarian.

The Prostitutes of Serruya's Lane

'Smugglers and swindlers, pimps and prostitutes, grog-sellers and generals, soldiers, sailors and ship chandlers, all lived cheek by jowl ... within Victorian Gibraltar.' So wrote the British historian Ernle Bradford in his 1971 study *Gibraltar: the History of a Fortress*. Nearly forty years later, Gibraltarian scholar and writer Dr. M. G. Sanchez uncovers part of this lost world in *The Prostitutes of Serruya's Lane and other Hidden Histories* (2007), a groundbreaking new book of essays on smuggling, prostitution, racism and other little-known aspects of Gibraltar's Victorian history. If you want to know what life in a nineteenth-century British military fortress was really like, then make sure to pick up this book. You will never view the Rock again in the same light....

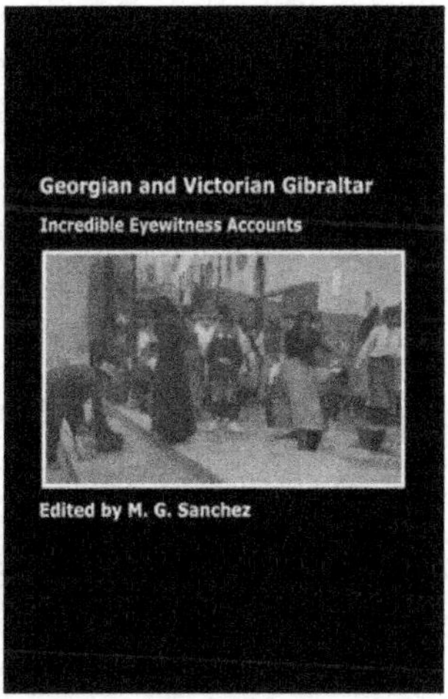

Georgian and Victorian Gibraltar

Drunken sailors, dandified English officers, hard-bitten Gibraltarian boatmen, polyglot Jewish rabbis, winsome Moroccan traders, moustachioed Spanish smugglers, cigar-smoking American adventurers, irascible Catholic priests, hoity-toity British military Governors — these and other emblematically colonial figures are to be found in *Georgian and Victorian Gibraltar: Incredible Eyewitness Accounts* (2012), a large collection of curious and surprising writings about eighteenth- and nineteenth-century Gibraltar compiled by M. G. Sanchez and published by Rock Scorpion Books.

Writing the Rock of Gibraltar

Byron described it as 'the dirtiest and most detestable spot in existence'; Coleridge complained that the onset of the Levanter Cloud made him ill with 'a sense of suffocation' that caused his tongue 'to go furry white and his pulse quick and low'; the Scottish writer John Galt thought that the same was 'oppressive to the functions of life, and to an invalid denying all exercise'; Thackeray was entranced by the mixture of 'swarthy Moors, dark Spanish smugglers in tufted hats, and fuddled seamen from men-of-war' sauntering through Gibraltar's Main Street; Benjamin Disraeli thought that the Rock was 'a wonderful place, with a population infinitely diversified'. These and other comments about Gibraltar are to be found in *Writing the Rock of Gibraltar: an Anthology of Literary Texts, 1720-1890* (2006), a new volume compiled by M. G. Sanchez.

Printed in Dunstable, United Kingdom

63818961R00147